THE HALF-LIFE EMPIRE

BOOK 2

THE HALF-LIFE EMPIRE

BOOK ☢ 2

SHAMI STOVALL

Podium

Podium

RECAP OF EVENTS

The year was 2024 when three clans of aliens arrived on Earth—the Teth, the Vay, and the Frest.

Dr. Benjamin Yamasaki, one of the first designated human ambassadors, learned Tethlite, the language of the Teth, and befriended them on behalf of the United States of America. The Teth, an amenable clan with a strict social hierarchy and the most advanced technology out of the three alien groups, wanted to build a human-Teth nation.

Thus, the Teth shared their scientific knowledge (*alien technology*, or A-tech for short). A-tech improved life on Earth, from fission batteries to hyperloop tunnels—some humans even injected themselves with tiny blood-cell-sized robots known as *nanites* that kept them youthful and healthy.

Most importantly, humanity developed a weather control satellite system to manipulate the climate of Earth.

The Vay, hostile and uncooperative, were determined to cleanse the Earth and make it suitable only for their kind. The Vay slaughtered the Frest and then conquered most of Asia.

The Vay weren't as technologically advanced as the Teth, but they did reproduce far faster, and they quickly swarmed locations. The Vay then set their sights on Africa, and the rest of the world readied itself for war.

With the help of Dr. Benjamin Yamasaki, the Teth managed to reach an agreement with the Vay. They would divide the world, there would be no conflict, and they would develop starships to send more of their kind deeper into the far reaches of space.

But humanity—and the Teth—were betrayed.

Someone from within passed information to the Vay. They gave the Vay blueprints for A-tech *firestorm fission bombs*, and the warmongers in the Vay used their newfound power to cleanse the planet in nuclear fire.

And as part of the grand betrayal, the weather control satellites were tampered with, rendering them useless.

The year when radiation soaked into the land and fallout blotted out the sky was 2035.

The world entered a period known as "the Forever Winter." It didn't literally last forever, but the cloud cover over the planet remained so thick, temperatures across the globe plummeted. A terrible chill killed most life and left the world desolate in many places.

Those with nanites, who managed to survive the worst of the fallout, were known as "Winter Survivors." These special few became the last of humanity who knew how to operate A-tech.

Those born during the Forever Winter—and long after—began to build a new life among the wreckage of civilization. Most were unaware of the world's previous glories, and the A-tech that scattered the landscape was more of a hazard than a boon.

Dr. Benjamin Yamasaki, a Winter Survivor, passed his vast knowledge down to his children, and his children's children.

But then he was killed.

Kita Yamasaki, a granddaughter to the great doctor, used her knowledge of the Teth and their technology to discover that the weather satellites were set to ignite Earth's atmosphere a good fifty years after the bombs were dropped—a fail-safe to make sure everyone and everything was wiped off the face of the planet.

However, since few would ever believe her claim, she traveled across the wastelands with only a handful of allies, to a place known as the *Meteorological Plexus*—a control center for the satellites. Kita would turn them off and save the last of Earth.

Along the way, she was hunted by a woman in a power-armor suit, captured by alien-worshipping cultists known as *Iron-Blooded*, and nearly poisoned by radiation. But Kita never faltered.

She was aided by the junk hunter, Bishop, the mute girl, Chelsy, and the ex-Iron-Blooded soldier, Dallas. Even the woman hunting Kita across the wasteland eventually became an ally. They were a ragtag group of survivors with a goal that no one would believe.

Upon reaching her destination, Kita was confronted by a group of Teth who wanted Earth's atmosphere ruined. One of their unmanned research ships would return to the planet if the satellites started their destruction, and thus, the Teth would have a way to return home.

However, Kita destroyed their means to reach the ship, and then stole some of their eggs, before fleeing from their facility. In the resulting chaos, Dallas gave his life to help the escape.

Knowing the Teth would fix the satellites now that they couldn't escape Earth, Kita decided she would start her own civilization—one with a true human and alien alliance. But first she would need to collect more A-tech.

Which is where the story left off . . .

THE HALF-LIFE EMPIRE

BOOK 2

CHAPTER ONE

I had been maimed, poisoned by radiation, tortured, and maimed, but today was probably the third-most-painful day I had ever experienced.

In order to infiltrate an old-world weapons manufacturing facility, I had to go through a tunnel that was basically covered in rusty nails and chunks of rocks shaped like broken seashells.

If the arms factory had been abandoned, I could've gone through the front door, but I wasn't lucky. The entire building had been taken over by the Iron-Blooded, a group of quacks who worshipped aliens. They got their "clever" name from the nanites in their bloodstream. Those tiny machines made the Iron-Blooded deadlier than standard individuals, and able to interact with most A-tech that others couldn't handle.

Unfortunately for me, the Iron-Blooded gave up their sanity along with their allegiance to humanity. They would gun down anyone who got close to their facilities.

Additionally, if they discovered who I was, and how much I had fucked with their operations in the past, they would likely torture me for years for the sheer fun of it all.

So, I couldn't get caught.

Which led to me crawling through a partially collapsed tunnel under the arms factory. I crept my way along the concrete pathway, acutely aware of the smell and grimacing from the agony. This had once been a sewage drain, I would've bet my life on it. A portion of the factory above had collapsed, blocking most drainage pathways, but at least a few still remained.

Every cut and scrape from the jagged objects across the bottom of the tunnel burned.

"Damn," Bishop muttered, his gruff voice echoing throughout the cramped space.

He was my only companion on this dangerous trek, but I wondered if he'd be able to make it.

Bishop had to squeeze himself through the rubble, his breath rough. He sucked in air as he slid through narrow cracks. Unfortunately, he was larger than me—I stood at five feet six inches, and Bishop was about a foot over that. The man was also muscular, probably from his tough life as a junk hunter out in the wasteland.

"Do you see this?" he asked between huffs of breath. He pulled himself toward me, dragging his shoulder along the ground. A nail cut his shirt and skin, drawing a line of crimson. "It's like crawling on Legos."

"What're *Legos*?" I whispered.

He chuckled and shook his head. "Never mind. Things from the old world. Painful to step on."

"Ah." Legos were probably military traps, then. I had never heard of them.

Bishop carried a little flashlight on the collar of his shirt. It wobbled around with his awkward movements, only partially shining down the tunnel.

I was ahead of him, my own flashlight held in my hand. If Bishop couldn't fit through the tunnel, he was supposed to wait for me to return. He hated being left behind, though.

"We're almost there," I said, keeping my voice low. "Keep it down."

"Kita." Bishop dragged his shoulder over the debris, the sharp bits of concrete and rocks stabbing him in multiple places. Most people would've cried out, but Bishop wasn't like most people.

He started chuckling.

"Do you see this shit?" Bishop crawled up to my legs and motioned to the many cuts and bruises along his shoulder. He laughed as he added, "All this doesn't fall here by accident. I'm willin' to wager someone has a camera on us—this is their most insidious trap. Their crowning achievement in torture technology."

"I seriously doubt anyone is watching us."

Cameras running twenty-four seven required electricity—or at least a stable power source—and all of that was in short supply.

Bishop smacked the side of my calf. He smiled at me, his eyes alight with mischief, his dark hair slicked back with sweat from the long haul through the tunnel. "You're sayin' we're alone? In a dark and cramped location? All hot and sweaty?"

My face heated. I wanted to reply with a witty retort, but my nerves got the better of me. I awkwardly stuttered something incomprehensible, my chest aflutter. I crawled forward, silently cursing myself for being socially inept.

"What's the hurry?" Bishop scooted along the tunnel after me. I had cleared a small pathway with my body—pushing aside some of the nails, rocks, and screws—but Bishop was just so much larger, it didn't matter.

"We can't joke around," I managed to say, my throat tight. I placed my elbow on the ground and flinched. The jagged rubble poked me through my jean jacket. "We only have a limited time to get in and out, remember?"

"Tsk," Bishop said with a click of his tongue. "We've got several hours before those patrol cars get back. Plenty of time."

"Still. I don't think we should waste a single second."

"I dunno. Us—alone—on a dangerous mission? Seems like first-date material, if you ask me."

Again, my social anxiety got the better of me. For years, I had lived alone in a bunker in the middle of nowhere. Whenever Bishop flirted with me, I grew silent and red. Obviously, this wasn't a date.

No.

We were on an important mission.

This wasn't just *any* weapons manufacturing facility—this was a location where they once produced exoskeleton power armor. That was before the bombs, though. Long before the world fell.

Thankfully, the JUDGE-X0 exoskeleton power suits could last hundreds of years in a warehouse and still operate once activated. If I could get my hands on one, it would make gathering material for our new city an easy task.

But first we had to get one.

This was the one time of day when the arms factory had the least amount of Iron-Blooded patrolling the halls. The lunatics often went out to harvest the desolate cities or capture wandering individuals and drag them back to their hideout. While the majority of them were away, I suspected Bishop and I could swipe a single power-armor suit and flee.

At least, I hoped we could.

We crawled a little farther, until we came to a wide space in the tunnel. Bishop pulled himself up alongside me.

"Kita."

I stopped and glanced over. The harsh shadows in the tunnel obscured most of my vision, but I could see Bishop's face just fine. He had stubble on his chin, and his eyes were clear.

"Don't get quiet on me," he said. "I know you want to— *Ow, fuck.*" Bishop chuckled as he rolled to his side and rubbed at his ribs. "Damn, that one got me good." He tugged on something embedded in his flesh.

After he sucked in some air, Bishop withdrew a sliver of steel. It was at least an inch long, and now coated in his blood.

"Do you see this?" he asked again, holding the sliver into the light of his flashlight. After a single laugh, Bishop tossed it to the side.

I lifted an eyebrow. "You almost sound happy that you got injured."

"I am. A little." Bishop pressed his palm on his injured ribs, stifling the flow of blood. "Pain lets me know I'm still alive. That's always a good thing, right? I'd rather feel something than nothing at all." His smile never wavered, even as he tilted his head back and rested it on a pile of sharp stones.

That was what I appreciated the most about Bishop.

He made being around him easy, even for someone like me.

After a few short moments, Bishop removed his hand from his injury. There was no longer a hole in his body, and the blood had stopped flowing entirely.

Although Bishop and I weren't members of the Iron-Blooded, we both had nanites in our system. They were "gifts" from the brief time we had been held captive by aliens. I shook those memories away.

We didn't have time for reminiscing.

"Try to be careful," I whispered. "Once this is all over, we can have an official date. But you have to promise me that we're both going to make it through this without permanent injury."

Bishop wiped sweat from his face and nodded once. "I promise." Then he pointed at me. "And it's a date. I'm going to hold you to that."

I didn't know what to say. I awkwardly grabbed his pointer finger and shook it. Like a weirdo. I sometimes hated myself for being so . . . embarrassing.

But it didn't bother Bishop. He laughed and then rolled onto his stomach to continue the crawl.

Technically, we had been partners for over a year—living and gathering resources for the Town of Richfield—but I was nervous and slow to advance things and obviously Bishop was growing impatient.

But that would have to wait.

I focused my attention on the task at hand. The tunnel ahead became narrower and more cramped than before. As I squeezed my way through, the rough walls pressed hard against both my shoulders, and it felt like I was being devoured by a stone serpent.

The air grew thicker, and the stink so bad, it made my eyes water.

After I gagged, I managed to squirm my way into a maintenance room. I shone my flashlight around until I spotted a steel ladder that led up toward the arms factory. The rusted hatch into the building appeared untouched, and I hoped it wouldn't be difficult to open.

I stood and rubbed my legs.

The minor scrapes and bruises across my body burned, but not for long. After a few deep breaths, the nanites worked their magic. My skin stitched itself back into place, and the low-key agony faded from my mind.

I turned and watched as Bishop struggled to get himself into the room. His shoulders were so broad, I thought he was going to get stuck, but he somehow managed to wriggle his way into the maintenance room with me.

His white shirt was half-stained with scarlet, and his jeans were smeared in gunk. Despite all that, when he brushed himself off, he was quite handsome.

Or perhaps I was too used to *post-apocalyptic chic*. Anyone who still had all their limbs and teeth was "good-lookin'."

The only thing odd about Bishop was the many tally mark scars he had across his body. His shirt and pants covered most of them, but some were visible on his shoulders and forearms. Each tally mark represented a person Bishop had killed.

I had seen him carve into his body after each battle—it was a ritual he never forgot to conduct.

Bishop carried a handgun that he had tucked into the waistband of his pants. He normally used a rifle, but there was no way his firearm was going to fit through the tunnel.

He glanced up at the rusted hatch. "This is it?" he asked, his voice quiet, but it still echoed around the room.

"Yes," I replied. "If the information I found about the facility is accurate, we're going to emerge into a room filled with sewage tanks. We'll go out the door, travel down a long hallway until we reach the stairs, and then we'll go up one flight, and exit onto a factory floor. That's the most likely location to find stored exoskeleton suits."

"And you memorized the facility enough to know where we need to go if any of that is blocked off? Or we don't find suits?"

I offered a confident grin. "Of course."

He smirked. "Good. Then let's get through this without running into any tally marks, shall we?"

CHAPTER TWO

Bishop ascended the ladder and wrenched the hatch open with a grunt of effort. A thick fog of odor wafted down over us. The smell of rust mingled with the faint scent of oil that had long lost its purpose. I held my breath as I climbed up after Bishop.

My leg didn't hurt as I ascended the rungs. That change filled me with energy and triumph.

Thank goodness for A-tech medicine. I had been crippled for years, but after my . . . visit . . . with the Teth aliens, they had restored my injured body to its original state.

Once in the storage room, Bishop shut the hatch. Our two flashlights were the only illumination available, which got me nervous. If the Iron-Blooded were here, why weren't there any lights on in this room? They had clearly reactivated the factory, and most electronics and computers should've flared to life on their own. Had the Iron-Blooded shut off functionality to certain areas?

No. The factory's electronics were likely malfunctioning.

That was a bad sign.

"Lead the way," Bishop whispered as he readied his handgun.

I crept toward the door and took several breaths to calm my anxiety. Once steeled to our task, I grabbed the door handle and gently pushed it open.

The hallway was deserted.

I stepped out and kept my back against the wall. Not only did the Iron-Blooded have nanites in their systems, giving them enhanced physical abilities and rapid healing, but all of them were trained combatants, armed to the teeth. If one snuck up on me, it would be the end.

Broken piping and twisted bits of metal littered the hallway, remnants of a bygone era when this place had been a hive of industry. The debris made me wonder, though . . . What had happened to scatter so much junk around? And why hadn't the Iron-Blooded cleaned up their base?

Perhaps I would never know. It was likely a fifty-year-old mystery from when the bombs fell.

Bishop turned off his flashlight once he was close to me. He tapped my shoulder and motioned for me to do the same.

Once I switched the light off, I continued forward, creeping through the shadows, my eyes adjusting to the darkness slower than I would've liked. A faint bit of light glowed at the end of the hall, shining down a flight of stairs, and I made my way toward it.

Bishop moved with the agility of predator. Probably because he was one. I was the hacker who had lived in a bunker for years, perfecting my ability to decipher Teth computer codes. Bishop had been busy killing people.

I supposed that made us a good team, because we covered each other's weaknesses.

I softly chuckled at the thought.

Bishop stepped close to me, his warm breath on the back of my neck. "First rule about not getting caught," he whispered, "is to keep quiet."

A scream punctuated his statement, as though the universe had an ironic sense of humor.

Somewhere in the factory, someone had cried out in agony. Their yell sent ice through my veins, and I wondered if we should investigate. The scream lasted a good three seconds, which was two and a half seconds too long for my comfort.

Something terrible was happening, and it drove me insane not knowing what.

Bishop must've understood my feelings, even though I had said nothing. He stared down at me with a hardened expression. "Second rule about not getting caught—don't investigate strange noises."

"What if there are people who need our help?" I asked.

"We have a single handgun between the two of us. How about we find that power armor first, *and then* save some sad sacks."

Heh. That was a good point. We'd be much better help if we actually had the means to fight the Iron-Blooded.

Despite the gnawing dread that ate away at my focus, I pressed forward. We headed to the stairs, just as planned, and then ascended to the next level. The lights destroyed my dark vision and I shielded my gaze as I hesitantly stepped to the top.

Every one of my senses strained to catch any hint of movement.

Besides the screaming—which came frequently, and only got worse with each new cry—I heard nothing else and saw none of the Iron-Blooded lunatics. Instead, we came to a loading garage that was mostly empty. It was an industrial garage, with high ceilings and walls made of stone and steel.

The factory had four garages in total, each placed in one of the four cardinal directions. This was the south garage. As long as I could keep our location straight in my mind, we wouldn't need a map.

Hopefully we wouldn't get turned around.

The lights overhead flickered once. They were powerful A-tech devices that would last for another two hundred years, so long as they were not destroyed, but the wiring in the walls might not be as advanced.

The large doors that led to the heart of the factory were open, though. I quietly hurried over and glanced inside. There was a mechanized assembly line meant to mass create power-armor exoskeletons. Large claws, long motorized belts, and industrial welding tools dominated the interior of the factory. The equipment was all steel gray and bright yellow, with warnings written on the side of everything.

"This place is nice an' spooky," Bishop whispered once he managed to get his own peek.

I pointed to the far line. "There're out of materials," I muttered. "This can't actually create a new suit."

"A shame."

"We should look for a full suit." I turned my attention to the south garage. Then I pointed to some steel crates located in the far corner. "There might be a few here."

Bishop huffed as he turned his attention to the area I had indicated. "And you think the Iron-Blooded haven't pilfered them yet?"

"Only people with interface implants can pilot the power suits."

I grazed my fingers over the back of my neck and then touched the base of my skull. Neuro-implants were fused into my spine that would allow me to control one of the exoskeletons.

I had never done that before, but in theory, I had the capability.

Not many had access to the implants, and they were notoriously difficult to "install" into a human. Before the Forever Winter, it was a simple task done at most hospitals if someone had the need to use an exoskeleton. Since the Forever Winter, though, only a few nations had access to such technology.

Ex Cathedra, the new nation to the east, was one of the few places with a Winter Survivor who could do the operation. That was why Ex Cathedra had their own division of "judges"—soldiers permanently in their power suits who fought raiders, other newly formed nations, or anyone who interfered in Ex Cathedra's business.

Since I had implants, all I needed to do was get into a suit, and then I could pilot it out of this factory. That was Plan A.

If I couldn't get a suit, Plan B was to sneak back out the sewage tunnel.

Another scream brought me back to the present.

My throat grew dry and I swallowed hard. I crept into the large garage and headed for one of the crates. Letters and numbers were painted onto the side of the giant ten-foot-tall boxes. I suspected they were military designations and shipping coordinates.

"You think these boxes have suits?" Bishop asked as he slowly walked around one. He glared at the electronic locks along the edges. "Why would they make so many and put them into these crates? Who does that?"

"Right before the Forever Winter, the United States and their allies had been gearing up for war." I searched the crate until I came to a keypad. The small computer on board was designed with A-tech, and I smiled to myself as I touched the keys. The screen flickered to life.

"War with who?"

"The Vay," I muttered. "The *other* aliens that came to Earth. The Teth and the Vay hated each other, and the United States was caught up in the conflict."

Bishop clicked his tongue in disinterest. He didn't care much for my history lessons.

I didn't blame him. They were depressing. But my need to understand and gather knowledge always kept me digging for explanations and answers.

The crate was likely powered by an atomic battery, a can-sized object filled with radioactive isotopes. The decay of the isotopes generated electricity, and they often lasted sixty years, sometimes longer.

Even if the crate didn't have any power-armor exoskeletons, I could steal the battery and still make out like a bandit.

I tapped at the keypad, putting in commands to bring up the operating system for the crate. The Teth and their A-tech weren't difficult to navigate—so long as the person knew the alien language, Tethlite. It wasn't like English, where you could sound out letters and read it with your eyes. The Teth didn't have eyes, after all.

It was a language of sound and tactile sensations. Using a computer designed by the Teth was an infinitely different experience than something made by humans. I had to feel my way through the menus, basically, but once I had, I knew breaking in wouldn't be difficult.

When the Teth first came to Earth and helped humanity develop A-tech, they had a few simple operating systems that could easily be hacked. The Teth never managed to make improvements because the war wiped most of them out before it could happen. Now the archaic tech was just lying around the wasteland with all its flaws still intact.

Flaws I knew how to exploit.

In a few short minutes, the electronic locks on the crate hissed and released. Bishop flinched and took a step back, his grip on his handgun tighter than before.

One side of the crate went down, and I held my breath as I waited to see the contents.

Empty.

There were hooks for hanging power-armor suits, but they had nothing on them.

Crestfallen, I cursed under my breath and then hurried to the next crate. Bishop stayed close to my side, but when a third round of screams echoed into the garage, he seemed distracted. He stared at the far door while I tapped away at another keypad.

"I don't think we should stay here long," Bishop murmured. "Finish this quickly."

It took me another couple minutes, but I managed to open a second crate. Again, it hissed as one side lowered down to the floor. This one, too, was empty.

I exhaled, confused by our findings. There weren't any more crates capable of holding exoskeletons. Just these two.

"Let me get the batteries." I stepped into one of the crates. "Then we can check one other area."

"Kita." Bishop held his gun close. "I don't think we have time for that." He jogged over, his attention on the far door. "People are on their way."

They were? I glanced around the garage. The crates were still open, indicating our presence. It would take me a few minutes to shut them—did we have time for that? Would it be better if we hid?

I motioned to the interior of the crate. Perhaps we could duck down, out of sight, and hide here.

Bishop grabbed me by the elbow and yanked me out of the box. "Third rule about not getting caught—never pick a hiding spot with no exits." Then he scooped me up into his arms and ran across the empty garage.

He was rather strong, which I appreciated. Although, there was no need to carry me anymore. Bishop had done so when I had a lame leg, but that part of my life was long over now.

Still—I wasn't going to complain. I liked being in his arms.

Bishop ducked into the heart of the factory just as the door to the garage opened. The screaming became louder—and clearer—as someone was dragged inside. Voices carried in the open garage, and the crying echoed around, creating a noise worse than a thousand wailing infants.

Bishop ducked behind one of the conveyor belts. He set me down in a sitting position, and then motioned to the back of the factory line. There was probably an exit in the back, but we would need to make it there without getting caught.

"*Does this room jog your memory?*" a man asked in Tethlite.

I'd recognize the language anywhere . . .

Tethlite sounded garbled and disgusting. Speaking the language required a thick use of the tongue. It wasn't human, even if humans could technically speak it.

Someone moaned in agony. From behind the conveyor belt, I couldn't see what was happening, so I poked my head up enough to peek over the machinery.

Three human men in black armor stood in the middle of the garage. They surrounded a single individual who was huddled on the ground. Blood pooled around the man on the floor, but I couldn't immediately spot any injuries. Where was all the crimson coming from?

The lights flickered overhead.

The Iron-Blooded wore armor that had been dyed black and marked with white symbols. It was equipment made with A-tech from before the Forever Winter. Tough vests, thick pants, and boots that could withstand a bed of nails.

And their clothing also bore a mark . . .

A white painting of a human skull inside of an alien skull's open mouth.

That was their symbol—like how old-school pirates used the skull and crossbones to designate themselves as cutthroats. The Iron-Blooded had a fucked-up sense of humor. They were all humans who served aliens, so clearly, the human skull needed to go into one of the Teth's.

"*Where are the supplies?*" one of the Iron-Blooded asked, his voice icy.

The man on the floor sobbed, clearly unable, or unwilling, to answer.

I scooted up a little higher, just to see more details.

The Iron-Blooded, the one who had spoken, knelt and grabbed the bleeding man. With a pair of pliers—rusty, old *pliers*—the Iron-Blooded proceeded to yank out one of the broken man's teeth. Slowly, painfully, twisting and wrenching until the front tooth popped out of the man's gums and sent blood splattering to the floor.

The scream only grew louder—and then it became gargled.

I regretted my curiosity.

Shivering back empathetic pain, I ducked back down behind the conveyor belt.

"How fucked are we?" Bishop whispered. He held up his handgun, as if to ask the firepower of the enemy group.

"I think they're distracted," I muttered. Then I motioned to the factory floor. "We should go. Quietly."

"*What the?*" one of the Iron-Blooded shouted. "*Look! The crates! Some-one opened them.*"

A loud string of curses filled the south garage, and I knew Bishop and I were quickly running out of time.

"*Alert Commander Dannik! Inform him that we have intruders!*"

CHAPTER THREE

Commander Dannik.

His name was the equivalent of the world spitting in my eye.

He was *here*? Of all places?

While my heart twisted in my chest, my thoughts went into overdrive. If Commander Dannik was here, that meant there probably *was* power armor still stored somewhere in the facility. Dannik led crucial missions for the Iron-Blooded, after all. My gut instinct told me he wouldn't be present if this was just a normal operation for them.

The Iron-Blooded ran around the garage, checking the steel crates and the shadows in every corner.

"*Find them!*" one shouted.

"They're all speaking gibberish," Bishop whispered. He rubbed his ear. "What're they saying?"

Bishop didn't understand Tethlite. That was fine. He didn't need to.

"We need to hurry." I crept toward the back of the room. "They know we're here."

The last time I had seen Commander Dannik was nine months ago, but I knew he would remember my face. We had to avoid him at all costs.

Bishop and I stayed ducked down as we hurried our way to the back of the assembly room. The place had all the welcoming warmth of a graveyard. The dead machines hadn't been activated in over fifty years, and some of the robotic arms—the ones used for moving large pieces of metal—had fallen over, their claws pointed awkwardly in the air like grasping hands reaching for salvation.

I jogged through a thick collection of spiderwebs and then slowed in order to wipe them from my face and hair.

A while ago, my hair had fallen out due to radiation poisoning, but it had slowly grown back in. Now it was pixie short, which was light and effortless to manage—and also easy to clear of bugs and their webs.

Bishop ran into me. After a quick grunt, he said, "What's wrong?" He glanced over his shoulder, his handgun held close. "We shouldn't stay still. We should get back to the sewer tunnel as quickly as possible."

"I know a way," I whispered as I pictured the maps of the facility in my mind's eye.

The sounds of the Iron-Blooded echoed throughout the dead facility. But then the hum of power flared through the factory floor, almost causing me to yell out. Someone had fixed the power problem, that much was certain. Lights flicked to life overhead, and portions of the assembly equipment groaned as they stiffened into working positions.

Bishop glanced around, a slight smirk on his face. "Looks like things are getting more interesting by the second."

"*They couldn't have gone far!*" an Iron-Blooded shouted. "*Post men at all the exits!*"

I tugged on Bishop's elbow and led him behind one of the large assembly machines. The safety lights flashed on the side, indicating it was ready to operate. It didn't move, though. Everything had readied itself into starting positions, but now they were all waiting for commands.

Two Iron-Blooded entered the factory floor the same way Bishop and I had entered. They both carried assault rifles, and they kept their weapons up as though they would need to use them at any second. I had no doubt in my mind they would shoot first and ask questions later.

The moment the two Iron-Blooded dogs were looking in opposite directions, I went to step around the machine. Bishop grabbed my shoulder and kept me back.

"They always travel in threes," he whispered.

Sure enough, a third soldier stepped onto the factory floor a moment later. He would've seen me had Bishop not been on his game.

We needed a distraction.

I turned my attention to the machinery in front of me. There were several computer panels around, each one tied to a major position of the assembly line. I crept close to one and then tapped at the screen. Thankfully, nothing was password locked, and it was made with humans in mind.

There was a visual component, which made navigation easier and faster. I went straight into the menu and activated the robotic arms.

Several of the toppled-over arms stuttered to life, their metal scraping against the concrete floor and creating a cacophony that filled the room. Sparks flew from the aged machinery, and I suspected more of it would crap out in minutes.

But I didn't care. It was noisy—that was all that mattered.

The three Iron-Blooded dashed over to the assembly line, their rifles at the ready.

I was about to turn and run off with Bishop, but I stopped when I realized the machinery menu had several interesting items.

"What're you waiting for?" Bishop hissed. He tilted his head to the side. "Let's go, Kita."

"W-Wait. I found something interesting."

I tapped my way through the menus, searching for all the specifications. The factory was designed to pump out exoskeleton power suits, but it was also configured to create advanced greenhouse supplies.

The type of greenhouses that were built underground using A-tech— the kind that could last centuries without any sort of outside influence. They grew food without any fear of radiation or ambient poison and were sheltered from extreme weather.

I had once fantasized about fleeing to the BC Oasis, the largest underground greenhouse in the world, but there were obviously other greenhouses to find. This factory was creating parts for more to be built.

How many underground greenhouses had been created before the Forever Winter?

Maybe this factory would know.

The factory would keep a shipping list, wouldn't it? A list of places where all the new parts would be shipped off to. Or perhaps a distribution facility that would know the answer.

"*It's just the machines going haywire,*" one of the Iron-Blooded stated. "*Leave it.*"

"Kita," Bishop growled, his body tense. He glanced around the assembly line and groaned in irritation. "I think we lost our distraction. What's taking you so long?"

I poked away at the screen until I arrived at the information I was looking for. There were addresses for the underground greenhouses *and* a shipping facility with parts. However, I didn't have anything to write the information down on. Instead, I stared at the letters and numbers—an old-world address for when the government kept track of everyone's owned property—and tried to memorize everything.

I *could* find these locations. There were ways to use the pre-Forever Winter maps, and I knew them all.

"*Kita*," Bishop whispered, his urgency bordering on panic. "We don't have time."

A second later, one of the Iron-Blooded goons stepped around the machine we were hiding behind. Bishop didn't hesitate. He lunged, grabbed the man's arm, and yanked the villain close. Without missing a beat, Bishop shoved his handgun into the underside of the man's jaw and fired.

Blood and brains exploded across the nearby equipment.

And the floor. And parts of the ceiling.

The Iron-Blooded fell backward, dead nearly instantly from the shot. Unfortunately, now everyone knew where we were.

Bishop grabbed my arm and pulled me along as he ran across the factory floor. The other Iron-Blooded lunatics fired at us, their bullets ricocheting off the machinery all around, the whole room filled with the sounds of a battlefield.

The whistle of a bullet whizzing by my ear caused all the hair on the back of my neck to stand on end.

Bishop charged through a door and dragged me deeper into the factory.

"The other way," I said between huffs. "The exit is the other way!"

I figured Bishop had heard me, but he never slowed his pace. He dashed around a corner, headed through another door, and then pulled me through a large area filled with ancient cubicles, decaying work computers, and a dusty conference table. The overhead lights flickered as they struggled to stay on.

Several doors were positioned around the walls, but I suspected most of them led to personal offices.

Someone entered the room right after us and opened fire.

Unlike the assembly line, there wasn't much to hide behind here.

A bullet sliced through Bishop's bicep, and he staggered forward, groaning in pain. He ducked into a cubicle, yanking me along the way. The gray cubicle walls were only four feet tall—we couldn't stand and run, not unless we wanted to get shot again, and they wouldn't offer much protection.

Bishop grabbed at his injury, chuckling to himself as he applied pressure. He handed me the gun. "They're coming. I need a moment. Cover us."

Normally, I avoided firing handguns, but this was a necessity. I would do what I needed to in order to survive—it was a promise I made to myself, and I made to others.

I held the gun close and waited for the Iron-Blooded to get closer. Bishop reached into his pocket and removed a small amount of gauze. It wasn't much, but enough to soak up some blood until his nanites kicked in and started stitching his body up.

The thug opened fire again, his rifle fire ripping through the flimsy cubicle walls. I ducked down, hoping beyond hope that I wasn't randomly struck. Bishop ducked a bit, but the chaos and danger didn't faze him. He wrapped his arm without hesitating or shaking. We could be sinking into an active volcano and Bishop would be as cool as ice all the way until he fully melted.

The Iron-Blooded soldier momentarily stopped firing. The room smelled of gunpowder and mold, and I knew he was close. My ears still rang from the fury of his weapon.

I glanced at the forgotten workstation and spotted an old ceramic mug. Desperate to do *something*, I reached up, grabbed the mug, and then threw it across the aisle, shattering the cup in the opposite cubicle from us.

The man turned on his heel and opened fire on the empty cubicle.

This time, I wasn't going to waste my distraction.

I stood and shot my handgun twice. The first bullet struck his bullet-proof vest, but the second hit his neck. The bullet shot through his flesh, and he stumbled down onto one knee, clearly caught off guard and now choking on his own blood. While the man was down, I planted my feet, took a second to aim, and shot him through the chin.

Bishop's handgun only had fifteen bullets. We had used it four times. I needed to conserve our ammo.

Once the Iron-Blooded fell to the floor, I stepped forward, intent on stealing his rifle, but I never reached his body. A third Iron-Blooded fiend stepped into the room, no doubt drawn to us by the sound of gunfire.

More would show up.

I opened fire on the man, shooting twice, and he used the door as a shield. While he was hiding, I backed up and motioned to Bishop.

"We need to go," I muttered.

"Heh. *Now* you're in a hurry." Bishop pushed himself to his feet and smirked. "There. Look."

A red "STAIRWELL" sign flickered over one of the back doors. I never turned my back to the soldier across the room. When he poked his head around his cover, I fired two more bullets. Cover fire was important, but our ammo was vanishing fast . . .

Bishop ripped open the door and we fled through it. The Iron-Blooded opened fire, the bullets almost catching me as I escaped into a narrow stairwell.

We could go up two stories, or down one. My thoughts were jumbled, so it took me a moment to recall the layout of the factory. I had to visualize the map . . .

Bishop slammed the door shut behind us and then held it shut. The thick steel of the door was enough to protect us from the bullets, but not forever.

The sounds from the cubicle room shifted from gunfire to shouting.

"*They're trapped,*" someone yelled.

I recognized the voice. Commander Dannik. He had a gruff and icy tone that haunted my nightmares.

"*Use one of the firestorm grenades. It's imperative no one know we're here.*"

Oh, just my luck.

Firestorm weapons were some of the most powerful A-tech used during the wars before the Forever Winter. My blood iced over as I imagined the destructive flames filling this whole stairwell. Bishop and I would be incinerated within seconds, nanites be damned.

"They not chasing us, which is weird," Bishop muttered, obviously oblivious to our impending doom. "Let's pick a floor and go."

Contrary to my earlier thought, I now really wished he would learn Tethlite.

"We need to run," I said, practically tripping over my words in my haste to speak. "The next floor up. *Right now.* Hurry!"

CHAPTER FOUR

I leapt up the stairs three at a time, my legs burning by the time I reached the floor above. Not as much burning as if I were hit with a firestorm grenade, though. Running as fast as my agonized legs could go, I slammed through the second-story door and stumbled inside.

Bishop rushed in after me, his gaze searching our surroundings. Dust motes hung on the air, as though unaffected by gravity.

This was a foreman's office. It once belonged to someone who oversaw the factory. Bishop coughed and grabbed the handle of the nearest door. He threw it open.

A closet.

"That one." I wheezed and pointed to a far door. "I think we can go through there . . ." I hacked back more dust. "And then take the mezzanine floor around to another stairwell."

Bishop nodded. He grabbed my elbow and took me straight across the room, avoiding the large desk and metal cabinets with such speed and accuracy, it was like he had done this before.

He grabbed the door handle, and a loud *boom* rocked the factory. Bishop yanked me through the door, both of us stumbling onto the wire-mesh floor that overlooked the assembly line. White-hot fire exploded from the stairwell and washed into the foreman's office, charring every-thing it touched.

The A-tech bombs were specifically meant to damage carbon-based life. I wasn't entirely sure of the method, but firestorm bombs damaged living matter more than metal, plastics, or ceramics. Bishop shut the door behind us, preventing some of the fire from flowing out onto the mezzanine.

"Damn." He laughed once. "They really want us dead."

"Seems like it," I said, my voice shaky.

"C'mon. We're not gonna be anyone's tally mark today."

We ran along the mezzanine, our footfalls rattling the rusted steel-mesh walkway. Several bolts holding the mezzanine to the wall fell loose as we dashed by, and my throat tightened with ever-growing anxiety. I decided to stop, and I held my arm out to signal Bishop to do the same. He almost slammed into me, but he voiced no complaints.

Shouts from around the factory rang out. The Iron-Blooded were still searching.

"*The ones in the stairwell must be dead,*" someone said. "*Check the rest of the facility. Make certain we have no more pests.*"

Barely anyone outside of the Iron-Blooded spoke Tethlite. They probably assumed their commands and plans remained unknown, even as they yelled them at the top of their lungs. Unfortunately for the Iron-Blooded, *I* knew quite a bit about the Teth, including their language. The Iron-Blooded had no advantage I didn't also possess.

I grabbed Bishop and pressed a finger to my lips. Then I crept along the mezzanine walkway, careful not to rattle it too much. Bishop followed suit, his hot breath on the back of my neck. When we reached some stairs, I glanced out over the assembly floor. Sets of three Iron-Blooded soldiers were diligently searching the corners of the room, careful to sift through every shadow.

I took the stairs as quietly as possible.

Bishop practically slid down the railing. The man was a risk-taker, and I held my breath until his boots softly touched down on the concrete. What if the rusted metal had given out under his weight? What had he been thinking?

He offered me a shrug as he tiptoed by, but then he grimaced and grabbed at his gunshot wound. I gave him a "*that's what you get*" look, and Bishop just gritted his teeth and forced another shrug.

He would drive me insane.

That was fine. At least . . . I wasn't alone anymore. Raiding bizarre facilities for parts was infinitely more exciting, and bearable, with someone to do it with.

The two of us remained hidden behind ruined machines until we could dash to the nearest hall. Then we quietly made our way into the east garage. From what I remembered of the maps, this garage was meant for vehicles. Unfortunately, if we drove out of here, the Iron-Blooded would chase us down in a heartbeat.

We couldn't risk taking a vehicle.

The garage was just like the other. Wide. Open. And there were, in fact, vehicles at the far end.

I turned to run for the door that would lead us back to the *south* garage—and our sewer tunnel exit—but before I could move, I caught sight of an exoskeleton.

My heart practically stopped. It was nearly eight feet tall and made from the most advanced A-tech imaginable before the Forever Winter.

The steel alloy of the power armor was so clean and scratch-free, it practically glittered. I had never seen one of the exoskeletons look so *brand new* before.

It was shaped like a human and meant to fully encase an individual within. There were vents on the neck and lights to indicate the power cell situation, but everything about the suit of armor was cold. Lifeless.

It hadn't yet been activated.

The words JUDGE-X0 and Mark VI were painted onto the front leg.

"Look, Bishop," I whispered, gesturing to the exoskeleton.

It stood next to a transport truck, completely stiff and unmoving. It had likely been placed there by the Iron-Blooded, so it could be loaded and then hauled away. Unfortunately for us, nine of the Iron-Blooded soldiers were milling around the vehicle, each with a rifle. Even if I could somehow sneak over to the suit—which was unlikely, given that the garage was mostly empty, with nothing for me to hide behind—the power armor looked as though it had no power.

If I managed to get inside, I'd just be trapped, with no way to move the suit.

We needed power cells. Or a way to recharge the suit's current power cells. Either way.

Bishop placed a hand on my shoulder. He gently guided me away along the wall, heading for the exit door. "We're not getting that one," he whispered. "If we find another, *maybe*. But not that one."

The Iron-Blooded men hadn't spotted us yet. They talked among themselves, as though they were having an intense conversation. Each stuck close to the truck, some even leaning against the side.

JUDGE-X0 suits were among the best—and I didn't even know they had made Mark VI variants. It must've been one of the most advanced and cutting-edge pieces of military equipment ever produced before the Forever Winter.

I stared at the suit as Bishop pulled me over to the door. Without making a sound, he opened it and dragged me through.

"Focus," he said, keeping his voice low. "We'll get the next one." Bishop shut the door as quietly as possible and then turned to me for directions.

We stood at the end of a hallway, and it took me a second to reorient myself. Once I was certain of our location inside the factory, I pointed to a far door. Together, we headed straight for it, but along the way, we passed a few open rooms, one of which had Iron-Blooded supplies inside. Bishop continued forward, but I stutter-stepped to a halt and then backed up to get a better look at the room.

They had armor, rations, ammunition, and most importantly, a few more firestorm grenades. They had them all stacked on top of black steel crates. No one was around. The Iron-Blooded had several normal grenades as well, but they were much more common—and easy to produce—when compared to the A-tech grenades.

"*Kita*," Bishop hissed from a dozen feet down the hallway. "Why do you keep stopping to window-shop?" He held out his uninjured arm and cocked half a smile. "We probably could've been home by now if you didn't examine every little damn thing."

"This'll only take a moment." I dashed into the supply room and grabbed two firestorm grenades and one normal grenade. I didn't see a bandolier to carry them, however, and all three were far too large for my pocket.

As I searched for a container that wasn't a steel crate, my attention was drawn to the upper corner of the room, right where the wall met the ceiling. A single camera had been placed there. It wasn't something from the old factory—it was A-tech. A spying device. No doubt something the Iron-Blooded had placed here to watch their equipment.

Which meant I had made a terrible mistake.

Bishop—who had obviously hurried back to my position—appeared just beyond the doorframe. He glanced around, nodded in approval, and didn't voice any more complaints. I handed him my gun. Then I reached for another grenade.

The hallway outside the supply room exploded with rifle fire. Bullets whizzed past the door, the light of rifle muzzles coming from the direction of the east garage.

Bishop ducked into the supply room, his teeth gritted, but his lips still curled upward in a feral smile. Although the sudden violence startled me, I wasn't without my wits. I handed him one of the grenades, and the instant there was a break in the rifle fire, Bishop yanked the pin and threw it as hard as he could back toward the enemy.

He slammed the door shut.

We both took cover behind the crates. The resulting explosion of shrapnel shook the unsteady building. Dust and debris rained down from the ceiling, and the dull gray walls grew spiderweb cracks. A loud *clang* of metal echoed throughout the whole factory, and I wondered if the rickety mezzanine had finally fallen from the wall a few rooms over.

Bishop and I leapt to our feet and exited the supply room.

While smoke and dust filled the air, we coughed our way to the maintenance room. Our sewer tunnel was connected to it. Even with my eyes watering, I knew the way. I guided the both of us straight back to the stairway down, and then to the maintenance room we had entered from.

Bishop leapt down the hatch first, barely holding on to the ladder as he went. I slid down after him, but it was difficult while holding the firestorm grenades. Once my feet touched the ground, Bishop took one, climbed the ladder halfway, armed the weapon, and then tossed it into the maintenance room.

As fast as he possibly could, he slammed the hatch shut.

A firestorm grenade exploded in the room above us. The hatch prevented the deadly fire from blasting down the ladder.

With the aid of gravity, Bishop came back down to the ground with a hard grunt. Then he took my arm and ran straight to the hole, where we crawled through. I huffed and wheezed, still carrying a firestorm grenade, a grin on my face.

Maybe Commander Dannik would be incinerated.

I wasn't that lucky, though.

"You're insane," Bishop said as he crawled ahead of me. With a laugh, he added, "I love it."

I choked back my own laugh as I scooted forward. "I think they had cameras in the supply room. I think they know it's us."

"Oops," Bishop playfully said.

Although I was unable to stop myself from chuckling—I was too nervous to emote properly—I replied, "This is serious. Commander Dannik was among them."

"Who is he again?"

"*Bishop.* He nearly killed us at the Hoover Dam."

"Oh, right. That douchebag." Bishop grunted as parts of the jagged wall scraped his injury.

Fortunately, most of the nails and terrible jagged rocks that had been here before had been brushed away by our bodies when we entered. This time around, it was a much smoother experience.

"If they really know we're here, then we shouldn't linger once we get outside," Bishop muttered, his tone icier than before. "We'll get to the buggy and head straight home, all right? Over the rocks, that way they can't follow our tire tracks."

I huffed out an acknowledgment as I dragged my body forward.

We just had to make it through this stinky sewer tunnel.

CHAPTER FIVE

Bishop and I jogged down an abandoned roadway. On either side of us, buildings stood as tombstones, devoid of life, a testament to what once was.

The sky—like all days—was overcast. Thick, black clouds, pregnant with water, hung low, creating a cold and dark atmosphere that many considered *normal*. Books written before the Forever Winter talked about blue skies and warm summers, but I had never seen such things for myself.

Eventually, Bishop slowed. He glanced over his shoulder and offered me a smirk. "Well, that was enough excitement for one day."

I turned around. The Iron-Blooded were nowhere to be seen. They clearly didn't know about our sewer route, but if they found it, I suspected they would scour the whole abandoned city for us.

"C'mon," Bishop said. He motioned to a dilapidated shoe store. It was called *Pumps and Circumstance*, though the colors on the sign had all faded to a dull gray.

The front wall of the store was mostly gone, and it was easy to walk into the building. Most deserted places had a musky stink that lingered, but that wasn't the case with this little gem.

Bishop had driven his buggy straight into the shop and parked in the back. He then moved display cases and racks in front of it, attempting to hide the buggy from any fellow junk hunters. Those scavengers picked through the remains of civilization in the hopes of discovering worthwhile tools, artifacts, or machines they could then lug to a functioning town and sell.

The dim sunlight—what little filtered through the dark clouds—wasn't enough to illuminate the shoe store. Bishop activated the flashlight clipped to the collar of his shirt. The light cast rays upon the piles of debris and shattered display cases.

This place was a graveyard of old shoes and bizarre marketing campaigns that incorporated too many people hiking.

Bishop and I hurried forward. The floor creaked underfoot, as if protesting the intrusion. Remnants of shoe racks lined the walls, their empty hooks like skeletal fingers reaching out for the past.

"So, did you find anything worthwhile in that factory?" Bishop asked as he hopped over a small pile of rotting leather lumps.

"I found information on underground greenhouses and—"

"Oh, *what the hell?*"

Bishop's shout caused me to flinch.

The back of the shoe store had been disturbed. And was now empty.

Bishop ran over to where the buggy should have been and threw his arms up in frustration. He kicked over one of the wooden stands. It slammed to the carpeted floor and dust exploded upward into the air. We both coughed and wheezed as it settled all around us.

"First, I lost my truck. Now, I lost my buggy?" Bishop wiped off his clothing and shook his head. "I'll kill the bastard who did this."

I crossed my arms. "I thought you once told me that all is fair out in the wasteland? And I think you said, specifically—if you're not actively protecting your things, you shouldn't be surprised when they're taken from you?"

Bishop flashed me a perfect smile. "Well, at some point our *thief* will find himself sleeping. And then he won't be *actively protecting his life*, and I'll just up and take that."

I pursed my lips.

His smile slowly faded. "What? You always give me that look when you don't like my plans."

"I just think the buggy isn't worth an entire revenge plot over."

Bishop rubbed his arms, his fingers grazing over some of his tally mark scars. For a long while, he mulled over my comments. Then he turned to face me fully, his flashlight shining in my eyes. "You know all our stuff was in that buggy, right? The rest of our ammo, and our food for the trip back."

Oh, damn.

I hadn't thought about that.

Those motherfuckers.

Bishop snorted back a laugh and sauntered over to me. "Oh, *now* who wants revenge, huh?"

"I-I didn't say that."

He threw an arm over my shoulders. "Well, let's get walking. If we're lucky, we'll find some kind strangers on the road who will be willing to share some of their food. If we're *unlucky*, it's just a two-day walk to the nearest known civilization. Easy-peasy."

After a long sigh, I said, "I wish I had your optimism."

"With God's help, anything is possible."

My mind settled on the fact that the Iron-Blooded would eventually come looking for us. If we were strolling through the wasteland, we'd be much easier to catch than if we had a buggy.

This was unfortunate.

"Don't worry." Bishop turned me around and walked me toward the front of the store. "It'll give us plenty of time to think up the perfect date."

"Date?" I repeated.

"That's right. You made me a promise. We both made it out of the factory alive, so now we get to go on a date."

I held up a finger. "I submit to you that we haven't made it back safely yet."

Bishop clicked his tongue in disapproval.

I knew I wasn't playing this game right. I *should've* said something flirtatious back to him, but I only realized that after I mulled over the conversation after the fact. Clearly, I was terrible at this. Perhaps I could make it up to him. After all, Bishop was the one person who stayed by my side, no matter what. I wanted to be with him, but after a lifetime of loneliness and betrayal, it was difficult to trust.

A whisper of wind rattled through the broken front windows as we exited the store. I shivered back a sense of melancholy and steeled myself to the reality of the situation.

We had a long walk ahead of us.

"So, what about these underground greenhouses?" Bishop stepped onto the cracked roadway and gave me a sidelong glance. "You wanted to get to one before, didn't you? The BC Oasis?"

"Yes." I hopped onto the sidewalk and then strode over to his side. "That's the most famous underground facility in the world. Built before the Forever Winter. But the ones I found addresses for in the factory are much closer than that. And might be untouched."

Bishop shrugged. "I thought we had a good thing going in Richfield."

The Town of Richfield . . .

After everything I'd experienced at the Hoover Dam, I had decided to head back to Richfield. It was a quaint town of a hundred and fifty residents. That was it. They were close-knit, and they had a sturdy wall all the way around town.

They also had a fission battery that kept everything running. And their numbers remained low because they barely let anyone join their little community. There were too many raids, junk hunters, and rail gangs out there who would steal the whole town blind if they were allowed in even for a single night.

Bishop knew people in Richfield and was granted access. Plus, their doctor, Tammy Claire, was a Winter Survivor, so she had mountains of medical knowledge—making it the perfect home for someone looking to survive the wasteland.

But I wanted to do more than survive.

"Remember those alien eggs I stole from the Teth?" I whispered. My boots crunched some old garbage rotting in the gutters.

"I do," Bishop muttered.

"I've been giving our situation a lot of thought since we moved into Richfield. I think we should find a bigger—better—home and hatch the eggs. Then we should start building."

Bishop laced his fingers together and then rested both hands on the top of his head. "And you want to do that in an underground bunker?"

"Well, not quite. If we have access to a massive underground greenhouse, we can build a city around it on the surface." I gestured with my hands, unable to contain all my excitement. I pantomimed tall buildings, and then the flicker of lights. "Imagine it. Our city could be bigger and better than even places like Boulder."

"'Cause we got aliens?"

"Because we won't limit ourselves." I turned my head and met his gaze. "The Teth are stuck on this planet as well. We can't make them our permanent enemies. But if we build a home for them, too, we can make them powerful allies. Like . . . like my grandfather once did."

Bishop laughed. "I thought you hated aliens, Kita?"

"I've reconsidered my position. Ever since I spoke to the architect, I think it's wise for us to live in peace with one another. The only way to do that, I think, is to demonstrate how it can be done. If we raise some Teth aliens ourselves, it should be easy."

"Easy, huh?"

I nodded once.

"Pfft." Bishop shrugged. "All right. So, let me get this straight. Your *new-new* plan, since getting an exoskeleton obviously failed, is to find an underground greenhouse?"

"Yes, exactly."

"And then it's to move the people of Richfield to this new location?"

I smiled as I nodded along with his words. What a relief it was that Bishop understood so well.

"You know those people haven't left their town since the Forever Winter, right?" Bishop chortled to himself. "You'd have better luck asking the sun to pack up and head to a different solar system."

I held up a finger. "This is why we should find the greenhouse first. If we have proof that their new home would be substantially better—and far from the rail gangs—I suspect I can convince them."

Bishop eyed me. Then a grin slowly spread across his face. "Maybe you should let lil ole me handle the talkin'. You're cute when you're flustered, but you definitely get weird when it comes to people sometimes."

I lowered my finger. As we headed up an on-ramp to one of the major highways that used to exist in the old world, I crossed my arms. "Well, if I manage to get my hands on a judge suit, I think more people will listen to what I had to say."

"Because they'd be scared of you."

"Perhaps. But they would listen."

Bishop huffed as he stepped over a shattered piece of asphalt. "Sure, sure, Kit-Kat. We'll add it to our grocery list. *Find another exoskeleton.* Then we'll find the keys to the greenhouse."

"Kit-Kat?" I scoffed as I climbed over the bit of ruined road. I had to step high, and carefully avoid the sharpest parts, lest they slice right through my jeans. "I told you, I'm not fond of nicknames."

"Kit-Kat is cute, though. Suits you."

I didn't know how to respond to that. Was he flirting? Or directly sidestepping my displeasure with nicknames?

Bishop offered his hand. Once we were both on the highway, he stopped and glanced over the ruined city. It was small—the type of old city where every store and business was also a gas station. The factory off in the distance had been the bulk of the jobs for the citizens, no doubt.

The Iron-Blooded still occupied the factory, their vehicles easy to spot among the rubble of the ruined city. Dust kicked up from their tires made it effortless to track their movements along the roads as well. And at least two of their vehicles were speeding around the center of town, zipping across the derelict roads, obviously searching for Bishop and me.

We couldn't stay here long.

"Maybe we should get off the road," Bishop whispered. "I think they might take this route when lookin' for us."

I held my breath for a long moment. "You're probably right."

But if we didn't take the road, our travels would be even harder, and likely take even longer. I wasn't looking forward to that.

"Help!" someone shouted, causing my skin to crawl.

Whoever called, they were close. Perhaps even under the overpass.

"Anyone! I need help!"

The second yell was loud, and echoed across the empty landscape. Would the Iron-Blooded hear it over the sound of vehicles? Would they come looking?

"Just what we needed," Bishop said. "Some idiot screeching." He grabbed my shoulder. "C'mon. Let's find him before he yells again."

CHAPTER SIX

Bishop and I slid down large slabs of concrete until we were under the overpass. It was darker here, and the cracks in the support beams were large enough to make me uneasy.

There were dozens of deserted cars parked along the abandoned roadway. Each had rusted, and the tires were long deflated. The harsh shadows were too thick to see through. It was like staring into a cave.

"Hello?" Bishop called out.

The Iron-Blooded roamed the city with enough ferocity that I heard the roar of their vehicles even when there were several buildings between us. They were getting closer, however.

Before I could voice my concerns to Bishop, someone replied to Bishop's shout.

"I need help," someone said, their tone masculine.

Bishop readied his gun, holding it in both hands, but pointing at the ground. "We're here to help, but we can't stay long. Show yourself or we're leaving."

The slow and steady sound of footfalls echoed under the bridge. A man emerged from the darkest of shadows, his clothing unusual. He wore a long trench coat and a scarf over that, both marked with odd white stitching, as if they were scribbled words. His boots, which were high up on his leg, were caked with grime, and his black hair was disheveled.

Small scraps and splatters of blood speckled his outfit.

He wasn't holding a rifle or a weapon of any kind. As a matter of fact, the man held up both his hands, his fingers flared, his palms calloused, but empty.

His eyes were a little too intense for my liking, though. He had bright green irises, which contrasted heavily with his pale skin, causing them to stand out even more.

It appeared he had dragged himself through a sewer tunnel as well. Or perhaps I was reading too far into things.

"I'm not armed," the man said, smooth and confident.

Which I didn't like.

If he was unarmed, like he claimed, he'd be at our mercy. Logically, he should be more hesitant—more afraid. This man spoke with a tone that told me he had an ace up his sleeve. He wasn't afraid of us.

"What do you need?" Bishop asked, his grip on the handgun tightening. He must've felt the same way I did.

"Do you have any medical supplies? I can pay you in ammo. Twenty-twos."

Bishop clicked his tongue in disapproval. "Tsk. Listen, I don't know if you can hear the ruckus in town, but the Iron-Blooded are in this area and—"

"The Iron-Blooded?" the man interjected; his green eyes widened. Half a second later, he relaxed, his expression back to what it once was. "Damn. Where are we?"

That was a strange question. Perhaps he really *did* come from the underground.

"We're near the weapons facility next to Nellis Air Force Base," I replied.

"Is someone injured?" Bishop asked. "Answer quick. Like I said, we're in a hurry."

The man motioned over his shoulder. "My friend is wounded."

Bishop reached into the pocket of his pants and withdrew the gauze he had used on his shoulder. He held it up for the man to see.

"Do you know where I can find medicine?" the man asked. "My friend . . . needs something for an infection."

The rumble of nearby vehicles caused my skin to crawl.

Bishop reached into his *other* pocket and withdrew a small baggie of antibiotics. Dr. Claire had fermented plenty back in the Town of Richfield, but antibiotics were still a rare and valuable resource.

Trading it to a random man under an overpass seemed like a waste. Our handgun didn't take twenty-twos. We could give him the medicine . . . He was *human*, and he appeared shabby. A little kindness could go a long way out in the wasteland.

"You should give him the baggie," I whispered to Bishop.

He gave me a sidelong glance. "The *whole* baggie?"

I nodded once. "We'll be home soon, and we don't need it right now."

Bishop sighed, but then offered a shrug. "All right."

He threw the gauze, and the antibiotics, a good fifteen feet forward. They landed on the road with a soft *pat*.

The man walked over, knelt, and scooped them up. "Antibiotics?" he whispered. "You just have some on you?" He met Bishop's gaze. "What do you want for it?"

"Nothing."

"Nothing?" the man repeated.

"That's right. Now we'll be leaving." Bishop took a step backward, his gun still held in front of him. "I hope you and your friend make it all right."

The stranger didn't reply. He just held the baggie, his fingers gently caressing the plastic outsides, his intensely green eyes focused so hard, it was like he was drilling a hole through the bag with his gaze.

I touched Bishop's shoulder, and we both jogged away from the overpass, heading south, and away from the weapons facility. The sound of the Iron-Blooded vehicles still rang out between buildings, so Bishop and I left the road and headed for a rocky patch of wasteland to the east.

The Town of Richfield was northeast of here. If we could find some landmarks, we'd be okay.

We just couldn't get caught out in the open. That was a death sentence, especially given our lack of supplies . . .

Night.

Bishop and I sat around a fire he had constructed inside the hollowed remains of a coffee shop, a good day's walk from the weapons factory. One whole wall of the shop was missing. I suspected it had once been a window, but the glass was long gone. Now it was just a tile floor, three walls, and a strong aroma of coffee beans that refused to yield, even to the apocalypse.

The fire was small and made possible thanks to the wooden chairs in the back room of the coffee shop. Bishop had broken them up, piled them together, and used some filters as kindling to get the flames going.

We didn't have any food, though.

Bishop rummaged around the empty drawers of the shop, like he would find a rare and elusive Twinkie. When he pulled out a small bread knife and smiled, I rolled my eyes.

He walked back to the middle of the dining area where our fire was positioned. Then he took a seat next to me on the floor and placed the blade of the knife into the flames.

"I need to add another tally mark to my collection," Bishop said.

"How many?"

"Just one."

I tilted my head. "You threw those grenades. What if you killed someone then? How would you know how many marks to add?"

"I don't count those." Once his knife was hot and glowing red, Bishop pulled the blade out of the heat. He ripped off his shirt and tossed it to the side, exposing his tally-marked torso.

Hundreds of lines.

The groups of five were obvious. He kept them semi-neat, but some were just in random places. His chest. His ribs. His shoulder. Along his collarbones. I rubbed the base of my neck, shuddering in empathetic pain.

"That doesn't hurt?" I whispered.

Bishop chuckled as he brought the knife down to a blemish-free region near his belly button. "Oh, it hurts like a bitch, Kit-Kat. I love it."

He pressed the blade into his flesh, and it sizzled. I cringed as I watched, but I couldn't look away. The scent of cooked meat smelled disturbingly good, and I frowned at the implications. Bishop forced a grin as he allowed the blade to rest in his skin for a moment.

He had to do that. If he didn't keep the hot knife pressed against his flesh, the nanites in his system would repair him before a scar could form. However, if Bishop allowed this wound to sit he would burn the skin enough that the nanites couldn't repair it.

Seemed terrible and foolish, but logic didn't always work with Bishop.

Once he removed the blade, Bishop let out a long sigh of relief. "There."

"Congratulations," I sarcastically said.

Bishop glanced over, his smile coyer than before. Then he rested back on his posted arms, making it easier to get a good view of his stomach. "You wanna kiss it to make it all better?"

"Sure," I replied.

Sure.

Oh, perfect, Kita. Yes, *very* sexy.

Sure. What a response. Way to make him weak in the knees. I should've said something more seductive.

Instead, I had said *sure*.

I turned to face Bishop. If he thought my response was silly, his expression didn't show it. The crackle of the fire was our only music as I scooted closer. Did he really want me to kiss him?

The tally mark was still fresh, but the nanites were already at work, sealing the injury.

It *was* sexy to kiss him on his stomach, wasn't it? I wasn't certain. The look Bishop gave me said he wanted me to, though.

I placed a hand on top of his leg as I positioned myself over his taut abdomen. I brought my lips down close to his flesh. Bishop said nothing. This close to him, my face felt hot, and I wasn't sure if I should break the tension with a joke or just carry on. Did Bishop find this attractive? Or was he making fun of me?

I had never done anything like this before.

After a long minute's hesitation, I gingerly kissed the mark. Bishop was tense. I felt it, even though my lips only briefly touched him. He had let out a soft exhale the instant it happened.

But still—he said nothing. He did nothing.

At that moment, I felt like . . . maybe he wanted me to do more.

My face was close to his belt, and Bishop made no move to remove me from his lap. Why didn't he speak? Would I ruin the mood if I asked what he wanted?

My throat was so tight, and so filled with cotton, I didn't know if I could issue the words, even if I wanted to.

The fire made everything warm. Or maybe that feeling came from the thought of removing Bishop's pants.

With an unsteady hand, I reached for his belt. I unlatched it slowly—painfully slowly—giving Bishop plenty of time to say something, in case he thought this was foolish.

My fingers trembled as I unhooked the button of his jeans.

I couldn't bring myself to look up and meet his gaze. My face burned too much, and my heart pounded too hard. What was he thinking? His silence was uncharacteristic. Should I stop? I had already gone so far.

We hadn't even gone on our first date.

That was such an odd thing to think.

Why was I like this?

The roar of an engine revving was as startling as a corpse at a birthday party.

Lights flared to life in the road beyond the coffee shop as people whooped and shouted, their truck's headlights illuminating the once-dark city.

The gunfire blasted through the streets.

Bishop kicked his boot across the small fire, snuffing it out as quickly as he possibly could. He grabbed me, pulled me toward the wall, and held me close, his breathing husky.

"Is it the Iron-Blooded?" I whispered, my heart going so fast, it was like I had run for three days straight.

"I don't know," Bishop growled. "But I'm going to kill those mother-fuckers for their poor timing."

CHAPTER SEVEN

Trucks tore across the road, their tires squealing.

At first, I thought there were only two trucks, but three pairs of headlights flashed across the outside of the coffee shop. Gunfire came from the last two trucks, and I had lived in this wasteland world long enough to know what that meant.

The first truck was being chased.

I didn't know why—I could make a few guesses, and all of them involved rail gangs mugging random people—but this had nothing to do with me or Bishop. We were just in the wrong place at the wrong time.

A loud *crash* and the twist of metal killed all quiet within the tiny, deserted town. I wanted to know what was happening, because I hated being in the dark, so I crawled over Bishop and glanced out of the coffee shop.

One truck had slammed into a dead streetlight. The front end of the vehicle was dented, one of the tires torn apart, and smoke billowed up from under the hood. The other two trucks screeched to a stop, one on either side.

The driver of the ruined vehicle stumbled out of the cab just as flames erupted from the engine.

Gunshots. So many gunshots.

The driver was dead before I could glean any more details.

"Get out of the truck!" someone shouted to the passengers in the flaming wreckage. "Get!"

"We can wait this out." Bishop pulled me close and slipped deeper into the darkness. "Once they're done robbing those corpses, they'll leave. Probably."

"Is it a rail gang?" I whispered.

It had to be. This whole area had plenty of railroads, and ever since the Forever Winter, punks with some knowledge on how to work a cart or a basic engine could get a locomotive running fast down the tracks. Gangs used the railways to attack any towns that settled along the tracks, and then sped away before the locals could do anything about it.

Some rail gangs, like the one in front of us, hauled trucks from location to location. They would stop their train, unload their vehicles, and then drive around, stealing anything not nailed down.

They were land-based Vikings, basically.

"Who cares who they are?" Bishop huffed a laugh. "They have rifles. We don't. It's a simple equation as far as I'm concerned."

"We have a firestorm grenade."

The rapid fire of more rifles told me whoever the gang was mugging was already dead. Outside the protection of cities, there was no justice unless you made it for yourself.

Killing members of a rail gang wouldn't leave me sleepless at night. They went on murder frenzies regularly.

"You sure you want to use *that* grenade on a group of random thugs?" Bishop huffed. "It would fetch a nice price in any major city. Or kill some real assholes, if we were ever in a pinch."

"Well . . ."

Before I could mull over the benefits of using the grenade, another crash shook the street, this one heavier than the last. Something heavy cracked the asphalt, and I wished we had a light to shine, because the gloom of an overcast night made seeing anything difficult.

The hiss and low hum of A-tech electronics told me that something terrible had entered the city.

When the rail gang had bothered us, I hadn't been frightened. I had seen too many wasteland thugs to be bothered by their interruptions.

But when I heard the stomp of an exoskeleton power suit, I knew we were in grave danger. I couldn't even see it yet, and already my heart was trying to leap up my throat and escape my body. It pounded against my ribcage, my vision tunneling.

"What's that?" one of the rail thugs shouted.

A flash of superheated plasma lit up the road beyond the coffee shop. It was some sort of blade, and it was extending from the arm of a nine-foot-tall suit of power armor. The shine of the metal and the

Mark VI on the leg told me it was the same power suit I had seen in the weapons factory.

I had never seen a JUDGE-X0 suit with a plasma blade before. Normally, they just had metal blades used for cutting a path. This weapon—glowing bright bluish-white with barely controlled heat—was hot enough to illuminate the whole damn road.

It would carve its way through solid steel, there was no doubt in my mind.

And if it touched flesh—that was an immediate *game over*.

"They found us," Bishop whispered, panic in his tone. "The Iron-Blooded never take a goddamn vacation."

I took his arm. "We need to go." The hammering of my heart wouldn't ease.

"There's only one way out."

Through the front, right onto the road with the hulking suit of power armor.

Luckily for us, the rail gang desperately wanted to be our distraction. They all opened fire, the barrels of their rifles lighting up the other side of the road, the fire of the ruined truck an intimidating backdrop.

Bishop stood, grabbed what little supplies we had, and then met me back in the corner of the shop.

The Iron-Blooded soldier stomped forward, the bullets harmlessly bouncing off its advanced armor. Normal guns would have no effect against a JUDGE-X0 exoskeleton. What were those goons even thinking?

With brutal efficiency, the soldier rushed forward, each step of his steel alloy boots shattering the road further. He brandished his plasma sword, and it left a streak of color through the air wherever he moved it, a beautiful tracer for the deadly blade.

Watching the Iron-Blooded slice the first thug was both elegant and horrifying. The plasma was so hot, it effortlessly tore through the gunner. Straight through clothing, flesh, *bone*—the resulting two halves of an adult man hitting the ground in different places bordered on cartoonish.

When the man in the judge armor turned his sights on the five other rail gang members, they did the only intelligent thing they could.

They all ran in different directions.

"Now's our chance." Bishop stood and ran from the shop.

I followed close behind, but in a moment of clarity, I remembered something.

Mark I and II variants of the JUDGE-X0 armor had several weaknesses, including an inability to handle EMPs. The later suits rectified that, but there were some problems the suits could never overcome.

Firestorm bombs—and grenades—had damaged the older models of the armor. Perhaps the Mark VI variant still had that weakness? Could it even be overcome? The suit would have to be airtight, and the filter system, and oxygen system, protected from the deadly flames of the firestorm A-tech.

If the suit wasn't protected, we could kill the pilot inside with our grenade.

That was worth losing it, in my opinion. The man inside would be turned to ash, and most of the suit would likely survive. I could buff out the damage and wear it for myself.

And even if this suit *was* designed to handle those kinds of hazards, there was still a small chance it would be damaged in some way. Perhaps it would cause it to *not* be airtight, or it would mess up the vents and the pilot would need to exit.

It was worth a try.

I pulled Bishop toward another building across the road. We leapt over the sill of a shattered window and then ducked behind it. He turned to me, his eyes narrowed.

"What're we doing?" Bishop motioned wildly to our surroundings. "We can't keep stopping in the middle of perilous situations. The first step to fixing this is to admit you have a problem."

"Let's try to kill him." I pointed to the grenade in his hands.

It took a full two seconds for my words to settle over him. Bishop honestly laughed once. "You're insane," he playfully muttered. "Okay. Let's do it."

"Control yourself, Quern," someone shouted in Tethlite. *"Commander Dannik wants them alive. Look what you've done . . ."*

Bishop and I peeked over the top of the sill. The man in the power armor stood over the corpse of the thug, his plasma blade still powered and humming with energy. I wondered how many energy cells the suit took. Was the blade's power use even the same species as something efficient? I suspected not.

Two Iron-Blooded men dressed in their classic black with white skulls painted across their chest strode down the road. They held rifles, but they kept them down.

"*The architect won't tolerate our failures,*" one of them said, his Tethlite perfect. "*Remember—Dannik wants to question them. Did you hear me, Quern? Keep them alive. Don't make me say it a third time.*"

The man in the suit didn't give an auditory reply. Instead, he answered by shutting his plasma blade off. It died with a soft *sigh* as the power drained from the metal coils. Then it retracted into the arm of the suit.

"I've changed my mind," Bishop whispered as he chanced another glance. "You should've stolen that suit."

I held back a laugh. "Too late for that now. We just have to hope they don't find us."

But then the armor turned on its heel, the helmet visor aglow with power for a short second.

In a distorted and robotic voice, the man inside said, "*There are two individuals in the buildings fifty meters from here.*"

Oh, damn.

The suit had the ability to detect life signs. The Mark V variant wasn't as capable.

One of the Iron-Blooded not in the armor scoffed. "*There are seven of them, then. Hunt them all down.*"

"What's wrong?" Bishop whispered. "You went pale."

Again, he couldn't speak Tethlite. "You need to throw that grenade."

Bishop didn't even question why. He silently observed everything, and as soon as the power armor and people turned to face a direction down the street, away from us, he armed the grenade. Then Bishop threw it as hard as he could. The deadly weapon sailed through the sky in a high arch. Together, we hit the floor and tucked ourselves close to the wall. As long as the firestorm flames didn't get us, we'd be fine.

For the first time in my life, I caught a glimpse of the grenade detonating.

The flames were white and red, brilliant and terrifying. They exploded outward in a flash, swirling around the road, into nearby buildings, and across the Iron-Blooded.

The heat and intensity were so great, the Iron-Blooded caught fire. They screamed, but only for a moment, before their voices were forever stolen. The firestorm grenade made quick work of their flesh. They collapsed to the ground, their clothes also ablaze, but less than their skin, muscles, and insides.

The firestorm A-tech really wanted organic material . . .

When the fire rushed over the JUDGE-X0 Mark VI power armor, the vents closed and sealed, protecting the pilot inside. Then the flames waved over the metal and continued for a short distance before eating all the oxygen it touched and then dispersing.

Quern, the Iron-Blooded in control of the power armor, was untouched. He stepped around the charred corpses of his comrades, scanning the rubble of the city around him. That was typical for the Iron-Blooded—death was commonplace. They were trained from a young age not to care about one another. They only cared about serving their alien masters.

I closed my eyes and rubbed my eyelids. The heat from the grenade had reached me, if only slightly. I shuddered as my imagination painted a picture of my charred corpse found in the wreckage of this town weeks later.

Or worse—if Bishop was somehow killed, and I was left maimed by his scorched body. The terrible thought haunted me and sent a lance of pain through my chest.

I didn't want to lose any more people.

When some of the heat receded, I fluttered my eyes open. Then I peeked over and out into the road, hoping Quern had decided to head after the others.

My heart hammered.

Quern stomped over the corpses and headed straight for Bishop and me.

"We need to go," I said.

But Quern was fast. He crashed into the front wall of our building, his suit so sturdy and powerful, it wasn't even scratched for the effort. The whole damn building shook. Parts of the wall collapsed, and debris went everywhere, filling the air with a thick mist that clogged my lungs.

"Kita!" Bishop shouted.

Quern activated his plasma blade. It was bright enough to shine through the clouds of debris, and it was deadly enough that when Quern swung it, the blade cut straight through a still-standing wall.

Bishop grabbed my arm and hauled me to my feet. I coughed, and my eyes watered.

"Time for an adventure," he wheezed as he pulled me deeper into the building, away from the street, and away from the power armor.

I wished I could speak, because that was certainly the wrong way.

CHAPTER EIGHT

Bishop took off running.

The deserted city was a dangerous obstacle course of collapsing walls, rusty pipes, and fragile floors threatening to shatter at any moment. Bishop—still shirtless—crashed through a window and threw us both into a dirty alleyway.

Quern didn't bother with the window. He bulldozed through the wall, his power armor unaffected by things like bricks and drywall. With one swipe of his plasma blade, he cut his way through the rubble. The hum of his weapon was like a thousand flytraps all working together. Bishop and I were the flies.

It was difficult to see with all the debris in the air. We were caught in a cloud of destruction, but that didn't stop Bishop from charging forward.

Quern stomped along behind us, shaking the whole neighborhood.

As if luck were on our side, one of the rail gang thugs launched himself out onto the street, trying to flee from the rampaging power suit. Quern stopped and glanced over as the thug took off running.

The Iron-Blooded wanted everyone alive . . .

Which meant if it was easier to get the rail gang member, Quern would likely abandon us in favor of a guaranteed target.

I grabbed Bishop's elbow. "Underground," I shouted. "We need to get underground!"

While the power-armor suits were very useful, they were heavy. Going down was easy, but getting back up was trouble. If Quern wanted to round up a few people, the intelligent thing to do would be to grab anyone on the roads. If Bishop and I went underground, it would only slow Quern's pursuit of everyone else.

I just hoped Quern was logical.

And that he didn't know if it was Bishop who had thrown the grenade that killed his allies.

Through the cloud of dust wafting around us, I spotted a manhole not too far off. Bishop must've spotted it as well, because he headed straight for the hole. There was no cover—most had been taken to use for other things—and if we could just get down below . . .

But my insides turned to ice as the road cracked beneath our feet. Quern's stomping was lethal to the neglected roads within this crumbling city.

Right as Bishop and I reached the hole, the road broke. Bits of concrete and asphalt gave way to the sewers beneath us. It was like tumbling into an abyss of darkness. Bishop barely had time to shield me with his body as we fell into the depths of the forgotten city.

When I hit the ground, my head snapped backward onto a piece of unforgiving cement. My head spun. I tumbled into something—a hole. There was so much darkness.

Heavy chunks of road crashed all around us. I closed my eyes, my heart beating so hard, it was taking all the energy my body had left.

The stomping of the power armor continued. I thought Quern would jump down onto us, killing us in an instant, but that never happened. Instead, Bishop's heavy breathing reassured me that we were still alive.

Minutes went by. Dust and rubble settled.

Then the stomping resumed. Closer than before.

Concrete and blocks of cement moved all around us. I kept my eyes closed, my head pounding. The power armor—the hum of the plasma blade was so distinct; I saw it in my mind's eye. Quern cut his way closer and closer.

And then Bishop was yanked from my body.

I wanted to yell out, or grab him, but it was then that I realized my body wasn't replying to my commands. Sluggish and barely breathing, all I could do was rest my head back and exhale.

Everything became black as the stomping faded into the distance.

When I finally opened my eyes, I realized it was day.

It was difficult, because the clouds never really parted to allow for the full shine of the sun, but it was obvious. The air was warmer, and there was more light than before.

My head still hurt, and I was wedged between two pieces of the road. Was that why Quern hadn't taken me? I was too deep in the rubble? It took most of my willpower to yank myself out from the devastation.

It was quiet.

Normally, that would've been a good sign, but dread crept into my thoughts, poisoning me with panic.

"Bishop!" I called out.

My voice echoed in the wrecked sewer tunnels around me. They were the only answer I got.

Although my stomach was twisted with hunger and my head pounded with a deep ache, I climbed out of the pit in the middle of the road and made my way to the sidewalk. My palms bled by the time I managed to stand.

"Bishop," I called out again, my throat raspy. "*Bishop!*"

The wind howled across the tops of the buildings, mocking me. There was no one here. Bishop had been taken. That realization caused my vision to tunnel. What was I going to do? I wrung my hands together, and then fidgeted with the cuticles of my fingernails.

I kept fidgeting as I paced the cracked sidewalk. My fingernails also began to bleed.

"Kita," I whispered to myself. "Pull yourself together. You need a plan."

Plans gave me comfort. I could work with plans, because plans had steps. Smaller goals led to a bigger outcome. What was the first step?

First step . . .

First step . . .

I slapped my own cheek. "Don't get weak. The wasteland kills people who are weak."

The first step was to get back to Richfield. I needed food, supplies, and transportation. I couldn't save Bishop as I was. My stomach was threatening to consume my other organs in order to get sustenance. Once I had supplies—and guns—I would find Bishop.

I glanced around, my sense of direction horribly rearranged.

But once I found my bearings, I headed toward Richfield. One step at a time, and everything would be fine. That was what I kept telling myself.

The trek to Richfield was rough. The roads between cities weren't a place for a lone wanderer. If any of the rail gangs caught me out, by myself, I'd be in trouble. So I walked along the barren wastes, stepping over thorn-covered weeds that grew over the dirt like moss did over rocks.

Gigantic bugs, damn near prehistoric in size, skittered about, darting from one shadow to the next. I needed to avoid them. Some had venom that would dull all sensation in my body and cause me to collapse.

I couldn't have that.

But the worst part about my walk—more awful than the thorns, the insects, and the rough trails—was the loneliness.

I thought I had gotten past that part in my life. Obviously, I had thought wrong.

The sun set, but it was difficult to tell. Only the presence of colder winds really told me what time it was. The overcast skies were a blanket of mystery, shrouding the world in a dimness that seemed to stifle all life.

As I made my way over a patch of brambles, I caught sight of a house in the distance. It had probably been a farmhouse, given the amount of land surrounding it, but since the crops were all long dead, I had no way to know for sure.

The house really embraced the *haunted* vibe. Windows were shattered. The outside paint was cracked and peeling. The front door, swaying back and forth on its hinges, creaked with every movement.

I would've continued walking right past it, except I spotted movement deep within.

Like a deer that heard the crunch of a twig, I froze in place, my eyes wide. More movement. Something went from one room to another.

I ducked down, hiding myself as best I could among the prickly weeds. Something walked out of the farmhouse.

A Teth drone.

Not a drone robot that flew through the air—a drone like ants have drones. A mindless creature that answered the command of other Teth aliens, but otherwise had the intelligence of a dog.

It had all the features of the Teth—four arms, large frame, dull black complexion—but unlike the intelligent Teth, the drone was skeletal, their skin a thin coat over their muscles and bones.

They also primarily walked and ran on all six of their limbs.

They didn't speak or even wear clothing, and this one in the farmhouse sniffed at the ground as though following a trail. It conducted itself no better than an animal.

The Teth were an alien race with castes—a strict social hierarchy that all Teth adhered to.

Drones were the lowest caste in Teth society. They were bred to serve and were controlled through a complex system of pheromones that the other castes released from their pores.

Because they had no higher levels of thought, or even any empathy, drones were the scariest for most people. You could reason with an innovator, or a warrior, or an architect—but you couldn't even communicate with a drone.

The drone dug a small hole in the front yard of the house. The size of the creature bothered me. The drone was as large as three full-grown humans—if the humans were on their hands and knees. It also had claws the size of a spatula, however, and the beast cut through the weeds with little difficulty.

The Teth had no eyes, but their sense of smell and their ability to detect movement and heat were unparalleled. In the past, I would've been quite frightened, but since I now had nanites flowing through my veins, my scent was altered. Most Teth drones would consider me friendly and not attack.

The key word was *most*, because drones that had been given specific commands would still follow them. If this was a feral drone with no commands, I'd be fine, but I didn't want to take that chance.

I slowly scooted backward, hoping to avoid the drone at all costs.

If the beast managed to cut me with his claws, I'd be paralyzed by its neurotoxins.

"What would Bishop say in a moment like this?" I whispered to myself. In a fake masculine tone, I replied to myself with, "Kit-Kat, sometimes it feels like God just wants me to come home early."

My terrible impression actually got me smiling.

I wished Bishop were here.

With a sigh, I made my way around the thorny weeds. I had to stay focused. I couldn't be caught by the drone. Richfield wasn't far. One more night's sleep, and I'd be within spitting distance.

The drone continued to pick away at the ground. Then, it ripped a rabbit from the dirt. The bunny flailed and kicked its legs, but the drone opened its mouth wide and crushed the rabbit with fangs and molars that effortlessly shredded the mammal's body.

Then the drone licked its matte black lips and continued to sift through the dirt.

I held my breath as I crawled *far* around the farmhouse. The prickly bits of the weeds dug into my arms, and I quickly remembered the weapons factory. It felt like the universe was laughing at me.

But then I crept beyond a bramble bush and almost gasped.

A man was crouched there, watching the drone. His eyes immediately fell to me, his body tense, even while kneeling down.

Intense green eyes.

I recognized this man. He was the stranger from the overpass. His long trench coat was on the ground, folded neatly beside him, and his scarf was on top. He wore a black T-shirt, and his jeans were covered in stickers from the weeds.

I let out a sigh of relief. Maybe he could help me? Bishop and I had helped him.

But the man must've thought we were generous idiots, because he reached behind his back and pulled out a silver handgun.

CHAPTER NINE

W-Wait," I whispered. Although it hurt, I forced myself to my knees and held up both hands. "I'm unarmed. Please don't—"

"*Shh*," the man hissed.

I said nothing else.

He motioned me closer with a wave of his gun. Every fiber of my being wanted to leave, but there weren't many options. After I swallowed hard, I scooted closer to him. The man wrapped an arm around my shoulders and pulled me close.

How did I always manage to find myself in such situations? Would a normal person ever get into a situation where they hid in a field of overgrown weeds, trying not to attract the attention of a killer alien, all while a strange vagabond hugged them close?

I suspected not.

"Who are you?" I asked under my breath.

"Brecht," he replied, his voice almost too quiet to hear. "Now stay quiet."

Brecht.

It sounded like someone had thrown letters into a bowl and pulled them out at random. I knew I shouldn't comment, though. Instead, I focused on taking even breaths. If I was prepared, I might be able to escape when Brecht dropped his guard.

He held me tighter, his fingers twisting into the fabric of my jacket. With each passing second, he grew tenser, his attention still on the far-off drone. I turned my head to get a better look. Brecht smelled of whiskey and cigarettes. I didn't like it.

A second drone emerged from the farmhouse.

Then Brecht stood.

He just . . . *fully stood up*. And he took me with him. Thankfully, the drones weren't capable of seeing us. But what was he thinking? I thought he might try to tiptoe away, but that clearly wasn't the plan. Brecht took aim with his handgun and fired.

He fired!

That lunatic filled the area with the *bang* of a heavy firearm. My ears rang afterward, and I pressed my face against his chest.

One drone—the one struck with the bullet—barely registered the attack. They were resilient aliens and designed to persevere, even when damaged. The damn drones had three hearts! And their brains didn't process pain like normal. Although bleeding, the drone ran across the weed-covered field straight for us.

The uninjured drone also joined in, their breathing in sync with one another.

I wanted to shout *run*, but it quickly became a moot point.

A *third* Teth alien sprang from the brambles, but it was no drone. This was a warrior caste—one of the largest in the Teth race. It was hulking and muscular, and when it stood on its two thick legs, the damn beast was ten feet tall.

Its skin was shiny black, glistening in the dying light of sunset. The monster had four arms—two that were thick with muscle and ended in claws, and two that were small, thin, and capable of fine motor skills. The hands on the smaller arms had long fingers for manipulating things.

The warrior kept his *crafting arms* folded and tucked close to his body, but his gigantic, clawed hands were outstretched for the drones. In one fell swoop, the warrior grabbed both smaller aliens and dug his five-inch-long claws straight into their skeletal bodies.

Blood gushed outward, like the drones were secretly watermelons.

None of the Teth had eyes, but they had long heads and mouths filled with sharp teeth. The warrior bent down and crushed the head of the injured drone. The other drone flailed in the warrior's grasp until it finally stopped moving. It had bled to death.

"We need to run," I said, breathless.

The warrior caste was the biggest and the most aggressive. Every warrior Teth was a nightmare to face, and that alien could rip our spines from our bodies as easily as a fisherman rips a hook from a fish.

It turned its head and sniffed the air. Then the beast lumbered over to us, holding both drone corpses like luggage. The warrior wore shorts made of wetsuit-like material. It was nearly as black as the alien's skin and blended well.

The warriors were intelligent and modest when it came to social norms. They didn't like roaming around naked, just like humans.

I couldn't believe it was getting so close. Brecht didn't run. Instead, he lowered his handgun.

"Thank you, Vega," Brecht said. He tucked his firearm back into the waist of his pants. Then he released me, but not until he had given me a rather judgmental once-over.

I rubbed my knuckles, my brain finding this scenario so unlikely, I contemplated the possibility of everything being an elaborate dream.

The harsh winds and stink of blood told me this was real. For a short while, I had no words, just emotions. The warrior—Vega—dropped the drones at Brecht's feet.

"*Why do you have a human female?*" Vega asked in Tethlite.

When the aliens spoke their own tongue, it sounded much different. Humans spoke using their lips, teeth, and tongue. The Teth used only their tongue. They squirmed it around their mouth while they pushed out air, giving their whole language a slurpy and gargled effect.

"*She arrived here on her own,*" Brecht responded, his own Tethlite perfect. That stunned me.

"*She smells familiar,*" Vega said. The alien lowered its fang-filled mouth closer to my pixie-cut hair.

With a shaky hand, I smoothed all the locks disturbed by its blood-soaked breath. The Teth were "touchy-feely," and often remembered every-one they met, either through smell or by tactile sensations.

"*We met her and her mate near the other city,*" Brecht replied. "*They gave us medicine.*"

"He's not my *mate.*" I crossed my arms and practically hugged myself. "And he was taken by the Iron-Blooded."

"You can understand us?" Brecht blurted out. He knitted his eyebrows and glared. "Humans don't normally learn Tethlite. Unless . . . they're one of the Iron-Blooded."

"I'm not with them. And some humans know Tethlite—I do."

Brecht glanced over at Vega, but the Tethlite had no eyes, so the alien didn't glance back. Somehow, though, it seemed they were on the same page. Vega stepped around me, sniffing deep as it did. "*What happened to the male with you?*"

"I already told you. He was . . . taken by the Iron-Blooded." I rubbed my arm. "I'm currently heading to Richfield. Then I'm going to get him back."

"If the Iron-Blooded took him, he's already dead," Brecht stated, his words icy. Even his expression was cold.

"He's not." I shook my head, debating on whether I should tell them everything about Commander Dannik and the orders I overheard. I thought better of it. I didn't know these two, and I didn't have time to sit around and explain things when I had places to be.

Brecht eventually stepped away from me, his steps stiff. "Vega, you should carry the bodies. We shouldn't stay out in the open long. You never know when the CCP will find us."

"*Agreed,*" the Teth alien replied.

The warrior hefted the drones back up with its large hands. Then it sniffed me once more before turning to follow Brecht. The two headed into the field of grass, content to leave me alone, but the mystery of their partnership meant I had to stop them.

"Wait," I called out. Then I switched to Tethlite. "*Why are the two of you together? Where do you come from?*"

My words in the tongue-based language were rusty, but intelligible.

Brecht and Vega stopped. They both turned around to face me.

"We were raised and trained in an underground facility." Brecht placed a hand on his chest, and then placed it on Vega's. "It was sealed . . . until a few months ago. We escaped, but it's been difficult navigating this world. Our families were killed or taken by the Iron-Blooded."

"Really?" I asked with a gasp. "*Perfect.*"

Brecht and Vega became tensely silent. It was only after a moment of reflection that I realized what I had said.

"I-I apologize. I didn't mean *perfect* about the deaths. I'm sorry for your loss."

I had meant *perfect* because if they had lived in one of these underground greenhouse facilities, that meant they might know more about the inner workings and maintenance. This could, potentially, be a huge boon for me. As long as I didn't mess it up. Which I seemed to be headed toward.

Brecht exhaled. "We were told once we reached the surface, we would need to fight for the United States against the CCP, but . . ."

"*But nothing is right about this world?*" I asked.

Brecht nodded once.

"Wait," I muttered. "What is the *CCP?*"

"The Chinese Communist Party," Brecht replied matter-of-factly.

His response almost had me laughing. The United States and China were long gone. He had lived in an underground facility, trained to fight the CCP? This was almost stranger than fiction.

I wanted to ask more about the underground facility—and how many people had lived there—but I knew that wasn't a topic I should bring up after my callous remark. What really fascinated me was the existence of communities still dwelling in the underground greenhouses. If *one* community existed, there was a possibility of others. Where would I go to find information on others? If I had to guess, I would say the computers *inside* Brecht's bunker could tell me.

But I was jumping ahead.

My first priority was retrieving Bishop . . .

That didn't mean I couldn't gather more information and plan for everything once he was safe.

"*We have a common enemy.*" I stepped closer and forced a smile. I wasn't happy, but I wanted to show that I was excited to have met them. "*And I think we have a common goal. My name is Kita Yamasaki, and I'm—*"

"Yamasaki?" Brecht interjected. "Like the famous Dr. *Yamasaki?*"

I nodded. "He's my grandfather."

"O-Oh . . . I had no idea. Forgive me. I didn't realize. If I knew you were related to him, I wouldn't have been so rude."

Few people knew of my grandfather anymore. The fact that Brecht recognized the name, and thought better of me for it, was quite a shock. Despite that, I regathered my thoughts and continued.

"*I'm building a community of humans and aliens,*" I said in Tethlite. "*W-With an underground bunker and greenhouse. If you have nowhere else to go, you should join me.*"

Vega snorted. The alien was so tall, it had to lower its head slightly when it spoke to me. "*Do you have an architect?*"

Vega clearly wanted to cut straight to the chase.

"She doesn't have an architect," Brecht snapped. "That's impossible." But then he glanced at me again. "Although . . . Maybe she does. Since she's Dr. Yamasaki's granddaughter."

"*I don't care who it is. We must seek out an architect. We must.*"

"Architect" was the highest caste of alien, better than the rest in every regard, and their default leader in any situation. They were architects of society, not just buildings, and they were so rare and powerful among their own kind that, of the eight million aliens who originally arrived on Earth, only three of them were of the architect caste.

That was how the Teth got their name. Part of their original architect's name was *Orin'Teth*. That architect had been so thorough that he had invented the Tethlite language and instilled in his kin the need for cooperation and building.

Architects also controlled which of the castes could breed. Back in Teth history, before they were space travelers, before they came to Earth, they lived in tribes, the architect their leader. If the architect wanted more warriors, it stimulated the warriors to procreate by use of pheromones.

If the architect wanted more innovators, it would do the same with them, and so on. It was the only way the alien castes could reproduce. If an architect wasn't involved, or at least the artificial pheromones some Teth had used in a lab setting, all offspring produced by Teth would result in mindless drones.

No one wanted that.

That was why the architects were so important. They controlled everything, and were the only way Teth could thrive as a species.

And I *did* have an architect egg . . .

But I couldn't trust Brecht and Vega with that knowledge. At least, not yet. What if they decided to take the egg for themselves? I wasn't in any shape to fight them—no human could stand up to the might of a Teth warrior with bare fist fighting.

"I'm going to be the architect," I said.

That statement caused Brecht and Vega to pause.

"A human can't be an architect," Brecht eventually stated.

Vega snorted and nodded once. "*You lack the physical capability.*"

"Not for long." Before they could argue, I held up a finger. "I'm friends with Winter Survivors—people who lived before the war. They can help with the reproduction of Teth castes. We can *simulate* the pheromones needed for reproduction. Plus, I have plans. Many, many plans for a civilization unlike any other. If that doesn't make me an architect, I don't know what does."

Those were big words, but I didn't care. If I wanted to make my new city—and civilization—a reality, I needed as many of the Teth as possible. Vega was perfect. Warriors were needed to protect our home while it grew.

And, again, I had an actual architect, so any fears of the Teth being unable to reproduce were unfounded.

But Brecht still regarded me with the same awe as before. Clearly, he thought my wild statements were within the realm of possible.

"Richfield isn't far from here," I said when Vega and Brecht remained quiet. "You should join me. We can travel there, and you'll be safe from the Iron-Blooded and rail gangs."

Bishop was better at things like this than me, but I wasn't useless. I knew how to appeal to someone's best interests—and that was a skill everyone needed, but few ever learned, for some reason.

After another moment of deliberation, Vega said, "*They did give us medicine.*"

"You're right," Brecht whispered. "And she is related to Dr. Yamasaki."

"Was the medicine for one of you?" I motioned between them.

Brecht shook his head. "It was for . . . someone else. Someone not with us anymore." He quickly added, "It wasn't the fault of your medicine. The injuries had been infected too long. Now Vega and I are all that remain of Facility Twenty-Six."

"R-Right."

Vega exhaled. "*If you plan on living side by side with the Teth, then I want to join you.*"

Brecht shot his alien companion a sideways glance. "Very well. We'll go together. Show us to your town."

CHAPTER TEN

It was . . . *awkward* . . . traveling with two individuals I knew little about.

As a small person—and a woman—and someone who had been crippled for many years, I had a deep-seated mistrust of random people. Teth aliens were also low on my trust list, but Brecht and Vega seemed different than most wanderers out on the road.

Brecht didn't leer or make many comments other than to point out our environment. Vega was the same, though like all in the warrior caste, it stayed close, and loomed over us, its muscles tense, ready for combat at a moment's notice.

My fear for Bishop's safety multiplied in my thoughts, growing like a fungus that just found a corpse. I didn't want to imagine what the Iron-Blooded were going to do to him . . .

They would begin with an interrogation, and knowing Bishop, he would throw insults into their faces until *they* broke and finally killed him.

I shook my head and shivered.

"Are you okay?" Brecht asked. He touched his knitted scarf as he spoke, his eyes narrowed in concern. I hadn't realized he had been staring at me.

"Yes. I . . . I'm sorry. I'm worried about my friend."

"He is your mate, isn't he?"

"I . . . Well. Sure. Let's just say that." I had been the one to first deny it, but that had been a knee-jerk reaction. I had been alone for so long.

"Sorry for your loss." He spoke in the exact same way I had spoken about his dead family.

I didn't reply.

Bishop would come home to me, no matter what. Brecht wouldn't believe me if I said it, though, so I kept my fierce determination to myself. The Iron-Blooded would regret what they had done—I just needed to come up with a plan.

Thankfully, the roads close to the Town of Richfield were littered with abandoned buildings, vehicles, and cellars. When the sun faded, and the overcast sky grew darker, I pointed to a collection of rusted trucks. Four of them created a basic shelter, with three of them acting as the walls of a triangle, and one, half on top of the others, functioning as the roof.

I recognized the vehicle fort, and knew we were close to home.

It was actually the *second* vehicle fort that had been constructed in this area. The first one had been made out of cars that still had atomic batteries inside. According to the stories they told in Richfield, a group of travelers had decided to have a bonfire party near the old vehicle fort, and one thing led to another, which then led to an explosion.

So now there was a crater next to the current truck fort. People used it as an improvised toilet.

Nothing crosses all ages, races, and genders like stupidity, or so Bishop would often say.

Brecht glanced up at the sky. "When will the weather get better?"

"Better?" I asked.

"When we were younger, we watched educational vids. They said *weather* changed on the surface. It could be dangerous, or peaceful. But since we've left, the weather . . . is always the same."

He stared at the sky with an expression that bordered on childlike wonder.

"Earth's atmosphere has been clouded ever since the firestorm bombs," I whispered. "The nuclear fallout messed things up, and then the weather satellites around Earth were permanently altered. Whatever educational vids you watched are . . . out of date, to say the least." I forced a chuckle.

Brecht frowned, not amused by my statements.

When we reached the rusted trucks, Vega stepped forward. With the nose of a hunting hound and the ears of the most alert rabbit, the Teth alien searched the area. Once Vega was finished, it dropped the two dead drones on the ground and then motioned for us to get close.

"How did you know we were stopping here?" I asked. Vega couldn't see me point, and I hadn't said anything.

"These vehicles have a distinct scent. Several people have stopped here to rest, and your fatigue—and sweat—tell me you're both ready to retire."

Perhaps his nose was *better* than a hunting hound's.

I ducked under the truck roof and took a seat on a tarp that was nailed down to the dirt. Brecht took a seat near the entrance to our improvised hut. He withdrew an electric lighter from his coat.

"If we had something to burn, we could cook these," Brecht said, staring at the drone corpses.

"I will find something." Vega stood tall and then lumbered away from our position. Its steps were heavy, and its silhouette impressive as he headed toward the sunset. "We shouldn't eat the drones," I said.

Brecht shook his head. "We have nothing else. They have a foul taste, but once they're cooked, we'll have plenty of meat."

"We'll be in Richfield soon."

"We were instructed to eat three balanced meals a day."

I almost choked on my stifled laughter. With a raised eyebrow, I quirked a grin. "Lots of people here in the wasteland go a couple days without eating. As long as you have water, you'll be fine. Plus, we don't know what these drones have eaten. Contamination can spread in the food we eat. If the drones had radionuclides, you're putting yourself at risk by consuming them."

Brecht turned to face me. We huddled close, in our truck fort, and he stared with an intensity I wasn't used to.

"How do you know that?" he asked. "I mean, how do you know so much about radiation and the weather?"

Again, I wanted to laugh. The type of information I had spouted was elementary. I was like a twenty-four-year-old answering second-grader questions—the answers came easy, but they were nothing to be proud of.

"Everyone knows not to eat the Teth drones," I said, keeping my sarcastic commentary to myself. "Everyone. You must know information like that if you're going to survive out here in the wasteland."

Brecht nodded once. When he turned away, he touched his scarf. "We were taught that once we made it to the surface, a whole new world would be awaiting us. The United States would have regained power, and we'd need to sniff out all the remaining CCP soldiers. We were also told all the hazards would be cleared away."

"Your greenhouse facility just opened after a certain amount of time?" I asked. "Once food ran out, I assume?"

"We had a large greenhouse." Brecht sighed. "We grew our own supplies with a carefully controlled system. Plants, animals—we even had a water filtration system that took moisture from the surrounding area outside of our facility. We could've lived there forever."

Now that we were talking about the facility, I could potentially bring up their roles and functions. Did they help maintain the facility? Was Brecht an engineer? Or perhaps someone who knew the inner workings of their computer systems?

This was shaping up to be a major boon.

If only Bishop were here to share in my delight . . .

"Do you mind if I asked what happened?" I asked. "Exactly."

"We were supposed to wait for a signal from the outside, but the signal never came. The doors—and the seals, and locks—all failed one day."

"I see."

"Contaminates from the outside crept in. We had to venture out before it was time. That was when the Iron-Blooded attacked. They took people. Killed most of us. Vega, Lessa, and I ran, but Lessa didn't make it. Now we're here. No home. No family. No understanding of the world."

Brecht probably wasn't an engineer, then. And he probably wasn't a handyman. He was less useful for my burgeoning plan to build a perfect civilization of aliens and humans, but I wasn't going to give up hope.

However, our conversation died. Brecht didn't seem the talkative type, and by the time I was done imagining an underground city where I lived side by side with aliens, I realized we had been silent for several minutes.

What would Bishop say here?

He was charismatic, and I gritted my teeth, fighting back the urge to charge out into the wasteland and go get him with my bare hands. No—I had to get supplies in Richfield. Then I would get him. Instead of dwelling in fear and anxiety, I needed to channel his positivity.

Thankfully, Vega returned, the alien's heavy footsteps heralding its return long before I saw it. The Teth stopped at the entrance of our truck fort and then sat down. Once comfortable, the massive alien folded its muscled arms, and then its thinner, smaller arms unfolded from around his chest.

The "crafter arms" were the second set of arms all the Teth had. The alien's spindly hands held out shrub branches and dry grass, which I assumed were for us to start a fire.

"*I found no trees,*" Vega said, its garbled language quiet, as though trying to whisper. "*This kindling should help you start a small flame. Perhaps we can smoke small pieces.*"

"We're not going to eat anything," Brecht said. "Kita says it's unsafe, and we'll be at her community soon."

The Teth snorted and dropped the kindling. Then it moved the dead bodies of the drones, pushing them into the crater next to the trucks. Once the bodies slid down the incline and splashed into the waste, Vega returned to the entrance of our truck fort and resumed sitting.

The warrior's body was so large, it blocked anyone from seeing into the fortification.

"*You don't have to worry,*" the alien said to me. "*Brecht is kin of different blood. I will keep you both safe from the CCP and the Iron-Blooded.*"

"*Thank you,*" I replied. "*But you should both know that the CCP doesn't exist anymore. You don't have to worry about them. Just the monsters that roam the wastelands.*"

Brecht stared for a long time, his expression slowly shifting from shock to resignation. Clearly, his perception of the world was changing too fast to truly grapple. He went silent afterward, his eyes unseeing.

Vega scooted closer to me, and even moved an arm around behind me.

In reality, it was awkward having one of the Teth protect me. The last time I had interacted with them, they were all out to kill me.

Brecht rested on the dirt. I curled up into the other corner, my stomach grumbling. It wouldn't be long now . . . I tried not to think of Bishop as I closed my eyes.

The Town of Richfield was surrounded by heavily fortified walls. They were made of steel, bricks, and debris, creating an ugly amalgamation that I considered an eyesore, while at the same time appreciating its utility. The wall prevented slapdash attacks by the rail gangs.

I approached the wall with Brecht in tow, but we had left Vega a few roads down.

The gates into the city were operated by A-tech and powered with atomic batteries. Normally, they would open as soon as Bishop and I drew near, but this time, the guard on duty—*Old Man Tim*—poked his head up over top the wall.

He wasn't old, just in his early thirties, but Tim had earned the name *Old Man* when he refused to do or try anything new. His motto was often *it's good enough*, whenever someone tried to offer him improvements for his life. Everyone joked Tim acted like an old man.

"Kita," Old Man Tim called from the wall. "Who's your friend?"

"His name is Brecht, and I need to bring him to see DC. It's urgent."

"Oh, all right. DC is in her clinic. One moment."

DC.

That was how most people referred to *Dr. Claire*, the town's sole Winter Survivor. She was the one everyone in the town looked to for guidance, since she was so knowledgeable about everything, from medicine to history.

If DC said that Vega and Brecht were safe, they would be allowed to stay in Richfield. If she didn't want them here, I wouldn't be entirely sure what I would do other than leave immediately.

"Stand back," Old Man Tim called out.

The fifteen-foot-high door opened outward to allow Brecht and me inside. The screech of metal on metal was harsh, but short. Once opened, Brecht and I walked forward.

"This is a standard town?" he whispered as Old Man Tim watched our every step inside.

"No, not normal. It's safer than other places in the wasteland." I motioned him to stay close. "The other cities and towns are a lot more . . . hostile."

"Wait, Kita," Old Man Tim shouted.

I turned on my heel. "Yes?"

"Where's Bishop?"

"He's busy," I replied.

"Ah. Gotcha."

Bishop often gallivanted off and did whatever he pleased. He was known as a *junk hunter* by most everyone in town—someone who gathered up old-world tech and brought it to places to sell or refurbish. It wasn't uncommon for him to disappear for weeks on end.

I hurried into town, my heart heavy.

Richfield had been built before the bombs, but all the buildings had been repaired using the debris from other cities. The citizens of Richfield attempted to hide their patchwork via thick coats of paint, which made everything look . . . extremely similar.

The town looked as though it had once been a quaint oil painting.

"I like this place," Brecht whispered.

"Good, because I want my final city to have this same feeling of safety." I motioned him to pick up his pace. "Quickly. We need to speak to DC, get our supplies, and then head out."

The citizens of Richfield went about their daily lives as Brecht and I hustled by. They hung laundry on lines, went about farming, and cleaned the streets to keep them safe. The old concrete and asphalt before the For-ever Winter had been shattered, but patched, keeping it smooth, even though you could see repair lines spiderwebbing throughout it.

I pointed to the town's clinic. "Brecht, there's our destination."

It was nothing more than a single-story community center painted white. It defied expectations as well as a bowl of cottage cheese.

"It's amazing," Brecht breathed, his eyes wide. "It looks *just like* build-ings from our educational vids."

"O-Oh, well, if this impresses you, I can't wait to see your reaction to places like Boulder City." But in reality, I never wanted to return there ever again. I had made a lot of enemies. "Wait," I said. "How long have you been outside your facility?"

"Only a few months." Brecht swished back his dark hair. "We kept mostly to the underground tunnels for weeks after escaping, and only managed the courage to get to the surface a couple days ago."

That knowledge shocked me. They stayed underground? Didn't they know that was dangerous? Radiation settled in low areas and bugs the size of dogs roamed some of the old tunnels.

"Why?" I asked.

Brecht rubbed his neck. He didn't look at me when he said, "I was afraid of the sky."

"The *sky*?" I repeated.

"I . . . hadn't ever seen it before. And I had lived my whole life with . . . a ceiling, let's say. It's disconcerting to have . . ." He nervously glanced upward, and then half a moment later, returned his gaze to the clinic. "So much *openness* above me. Even now, after a few days of dealing with it. The sky feels unsafe."

Brecht did seem jittery. I had thought it was because he wanted to get used to the wasteland, but apparently it was because he was just a weird human who had lived a completely different life than the rest of us. I needed to keep that in mind. Brecht wouldn't think the same way as others.

Sort of like me.

The door to the clinic opened, and out ran a little girl. She stopped dead in her tracks the moment she saw me.

I couldn't stop myself from smiling.

"Chelsy!" I held out my arms as she ran straight for me.

CHAPTER ELEVEN

Chelsy, the eight-year-old girl, ran straight into my arms. I smiled as I hugged her tight, her little fingers twisting into the fabric of my dirty shirt. She held our embrace for a long minute before breaking away.

She wore a pair of old jeans with large pockets. Chelsy reached deep into one and withdrew a small notepad. Then she quickly wrote down a few sentences and handed it to me, her blue eyes practically alight with joy.

The note read: *I missed you! Where is Bishop?*

I handed the paper back to her and shook my head. "Um. I'm sorry. He's busy. I'm going to go get him, though."

Chelsy's dark hair had grown to her shoulders. She was young, and growing, so despite the fact she had cut it short a while back, it was already flowing with the wind.

With a squinted gaze, she turned her attention to Brecht. Chelsy tilted her head, obviously questioning his presence. I stood straight, patted my clothing off, and then motioned to my traveling companion.

"This is Brecht. He's a new friend of mine."

Chelsy wrote something and then handed it to the man. Brecht stared at the paper as though it would set his hand on fire if he touched it. With an awkward step backward, he shook the paper away. "No, thank you," he said, his voice gruff. "I don't want to play any games."

Chelsy held her arm out, completely straight, stretching as far as she could in an attempt to hand the man her note. She even waggled to the paper for a moment, her expression stern.

Brecht glanced at me. "Is she deaf? Tell her to stop."

"She's *mute*, not *deaf*," I stated. "And she speaks using her notes."

"I thought we didn't have time for this." Brecht stepped around behind me, distancing himself from Chelsy even farther than before.

His avoidance bordered on fright. He gave Chelsy odd glances and then urged me toward the clinic.

Chelsy slowly lowered her arm and took back her note. She squished her lips together in an exaggerated show of disapproval before giving me one more quick hug.

She then pointed to the far schoolhouse.

There were only a few children in Richfield, but everyone here took care of them. The schoolhouse was the nicest building in the whole city, even better than the walls set up around the hot springs.

"I'll be back in a few days," I said.

Chelsy nodded and then took off.

Although I didn't say this to Brecht, Chelsy was my adopted daughter. She reminded me of my late sister, and I had basically assumed responsibility of Chelsy the moment her father died in front of me.

Brecht and I resumed our trek. We entered the clinic, and the smell of soap invaded my nostrils. The front room was empty, so I headed to the back. DC had an honest-to-goodness medical office, complete with an IV, multiple needles, and several pairs of disposable gloves, though it was just one large room. Her operating table and tools were standard—nothing A-tech—but everything was lovingly cared for.

DC, who sat behind a small desk, glanced up from her computer.

She was beautiful. All Winter Survivors were, in my experience. They had lived before the fall of mankind, and most had been given medical upgrades that made them youthful, and healthy, for much longer than normal.

DC was seventy-four years old, but she appeared to be in her twenties, with a cute heart-shaped face, and long golden hair.

"Kita?" DC asked. "Is everything okay?"

I hurried to her desk and placed my hands on the edge. "I don't have much time," I said. "Bishop is in danger, and I have to go help him."

DC's eyebrows lifted to her hairline. "Why are you here, then?"

I gestured to Brecht. "I found a couple survivors out in the wasteland, and I want them to stay with us in Richfield. At least . . . until I find a place for us to all move. This is Brecht. He has a friend named *Vega*, but it might be a hard sell to get Vega welcomed by, uh, our community."

I was spouting everything as fast as possible, but it couldn't be helped.

"Is he ill?" DC stood from her chair. She was taller and statuesque. Everything about her seemed constructed to be as appealing as possible. "I could help almost any disease. We have the antibiotics."

"It's not that." I stood straighter, wondering how I would word this.

No one said anything. Not even Brecht.

"Vega is one of the Teth," I whispered.

In reality, this situation was doubly perfect. I wanted to test out how DC would react to the idea of aliens joining us. She had never spoken terribly of the Teth, but she obviously avoided the subject. So did most people living in Richfield, as a matter of fact.

It was easier to pretend the past never happened than to actually deal with it. If they kept within their walls, and never interacted with anyone else, they could pretend forever, I supposed.

However, my goal wasn't to solve the wars of the past—it was to build a bigger and better future. Humanity and the Teth struggled to get along, and even now, there were groups like the Iron-Blooded who had a twisted relationship with the aliens beyond the stars.

If I could fix that, we could have a grand city that would eventually blossom into an unstoppable nation. Probably long after I died, but that wasn't going to stop me.

"I can convince the others to allow a Teth to stay with us," DC eventually stated. She fluffed her blond hair, her eyes falling to the table as she obviously mulled over the situation.

"You're not afraid of it, are you?" I asked.

DC shook her head. "Most Teth—besides their drones—were friendly enough when I met them. That was back in my youth, mind you." She waved her delicate hand. "I thought all the surviving Teth were anti-human now. Or they had become tyrants who ruled over humans, like with the Iron-Blooded."

"I've met a couple that weren't like that. Vega is one of them."

"But why?" DC held a hand to her chin. "There's little benefit to taking a Teth into our city. The Teth are very communal in their thinking. There's a good chance the architect of the Iron-Blooded will demand Vega join his ranks, and if Vega has no architect its bonded with, it could turn on us."

"Vega is my kin of different blood," Brecht finally interjected. "That means it considers me family."

DC nodded once. "Oh, I know what it means. And from my personal experience, it's more likely Vega will just take you to go serve the architect. You see, the Teth love their hierarchy, and a random human—even if family—isn't on the same level of authority as an architect."

Brecht motioned to me. "I thought we were going to get a *human* architect."

That caused DC to pause. She glanced over at me, her face youthful, but her eyes hard from a long life of suffering. I didn't like making eye contact with people, and I glanced away a moment after she challenged me to explain with her single stare.

"I'll handle that aspect after I save Bishop," I said. "And I doubt the Iron-Blooded will take Vega before I get back, so I don't think we have anything we need to worry about."

"We're running low on ammunition," DC said.

She was warning me.

If it came to a fight with those lunatics, we would lose.

"I'll get us more supplies." After a deep breath, I added, "And I *will* get us a suit of judge armor."

"You *didn't* get a JUDGE-X0 exoskeleton?" someone billowed, the anger in their voice akin to a gathering storm.

I hadn't realized someone else was in the clinic. I whirled around on my heel, my heart racing, but calmed once I noticed who had joined us.

Judge Gascoigne.

Well, just *Gascoigne* now. A name like that suited her. It was tough and rugged as she was, and as she strode into the main medical office, everyone straightened.

Gascoigne wore a tight pair of black shorts and a matching sports bra. Scars crisscrossed her muscular frame like hieroglyphs etched by the hands of the apocalypse itself. Her eyes surveyed the room with an intensity that cut through the shadows, and she stopped to glare at Brecht as though he were some sort of blemish on the wall.

"Oh, Gascoigne, how are you feeling?" DC asked. "I didn't see you this morning."

"I was getting prepared," Gascoigne muttered. She shot me a glower. "*Someone* said they would be bringing back an exoskeleton power suit. I wanted to make sure we had everything set up to house it."

Gascoigne had the neural connectors on the back of her neck that allowed her to wear judge armor as well. Everyone could see them—Gascoigne kept her brown hair cut shorter than most men kept theirs. She had once *lived* in a suit, since it could be used to filter blood, but after she received medical attention, and her old suit was destroyed, she had gone without.

That obviously bothered her. Gascoigne wanted a suit more than anything. That was one of the reasons I had gone out with Bishop in the first place—she had pressured us to get this done sooner, rather than later.

Gascoigne folded her arms across her chest, and her defiant stance accentuated the corded strength in her sinewy form. Her lips curled with a caustic edge as she said, "When were you planning to tell me you had failed?"

"I just got back." I shook my head. "And I need to leave again, anyway. The Iron-Blooded took—"

"Feh." Gascoigne sneered. "Those Iron-*Chumps* are still giving us troubles? After you blew up one of their headquarters? You'd think they had learned their lesson."

"*You blew up one of their headquarters?*" Brecht asked in Tethlite.

I nodded once, but the alien language offended Gascoigne. She immediately tensed.

"Oh, you're one of the Iron-Blooded, aren't you? Listen, I'm not gonna let some sad sack like you do—"

I held up my hand. "No. Bishop was taken by the Iron-Blooded. Brecht is just a friend."

This information ended our conversation. Gascoigne wasn't someone to quibble over details. She took a deep breath, but retained all her anger.

I turned back to DC. "Okay, here's my plan. I'm going to gather supplies, and one of the buggies, and then head out to get Bishop. After that, we'll stop by Richfield to discuss future plans. I want us to find an underground greenhouse."

"Oh?" DC sat at her desk. "You haven't given up on that dream?"

"I think, with the right facility, we can make a grand city. Especially if we incorporate willing members of the Teth. *If* you can start convincing everyone around here that's a good idea, I would appreciate it."

DC blinked.

I understood—I was asking a lot of her. And I wouldn't want to be in her shoes.

"How will I do that?" she asked, sweetness in her voice.

"With Vega. The alien is agreeable, and Brecht is correct. Vega thinks some humans are kin of different blood. Just take the Teth alien around town to everyone, and please emphasize how the last batch of crops have been weaker. If everyone in Richfield is on the same page by the time I get back, that would make this whole process faster."

Gascoigne ran a hand over her face. Her expression, so hard-set and angular, pierced straight to my core. "You're not leaving me behind this time," she said, no question in her voice.

"You *want* to go?" I asked.

Gascoigne had been weak and sickly when we first brought her to Richfield, but since then, she had done nothing but train her body. She ate properly, stretched, exercised, and went on long runs. Her muscles were a product of hard work and self-hatred, and I sometimes wished I could convince her to rest.

"You left me behind when you went to the air force base, and now you lost Bishop." Gascoigne huffed. "Clearly, you needed me there. So now, we'll go together, get your boy toy back, and also get me a judge suit. Got it?"

I was going to answer, but Gascoigne didn't wait for that.

She turned on her heel and headed for the door. "Good. Now gather your supplies. I'll be waiting by the gate."

CHAPTER TWELVE

When Bishop and I had set out to get the judge armor, we had packed light. My original plan had been to slip into the weapons factory, get the goods, and leave as quickly as possible without getting caught.

But not having enough supplies had obviously been one of my mistakes.

This time would be different. I couldn't overstock, but I also couldn't leave myself defenseless. And if Gascoigne was coming with me, I needed to make sure she had enough supplies as well.

There was a supply shed in the middle of Richfield. It housed all the important items, including the town's sole fission battery. I didn't care about that, though. I went straight for the supplies I would need for my journey.

Well, after I ate a sandwich. It was tastiest stale bread I had ever had in my life. Every flaky crunch was a godsend.

Then I headed to the supply shed and picked out the things I would need for the trek.

I arranged everything neatly before I packed it away in my satchel.

Two heavy handguns with some .45 ammo.

My hand flashlight. Who would travel the wasteland without one?

A single EMP grenade. It was the only one we had. It had a short omni-directional range, but the burst of electromagnetic energy would disable all electronics that didn't have specific protection. It would even disable some older models of the judge armor. Lastly, it would also harm nanites—a hit with this kind of weapon would kill anyone with the nanites in their bloodstream. The tiny robots would die, and clog their hosts' blood vessels. That included me.

Food. Dried bars of granola, and other preserved offerings. Enough to get me by.

A water boiling system. A tiny thing I could light when needed.

Bandages and gauze. More antibiotics. I even took an extra baggie, just in case I needed to barter again.

I grabbed the sturdiest pair of boots I could wear. Normally it was difficult for me—my feet were tiny—but they were required for any long trek. Just in case. The wasteland had a lot of bizarre perils that involved broken glass.

Then I grabbed a lightweight blanket.

I could already hear Bishop. *Kit-Kat, you don't need that—I'll keep you warm.*

It made me smile. Somehow, he was still entertaining me, even while being held captive by the Iron-Blooded.

Obviously, I packed a multi-tool—a small device that functioned as several smaller tools, including a screwdriver and a tester for atomic batteries.

As I rummaged through everything in my satchel, counting it all again, I realized I didn't have anything of Bishop's. For some irrational reason, that worried me. It was as if . . . he could easily be forgotten. I didn't like that. It caused me more anxiety than I cared to admit.

So I thought about the real problem at hand: the Mark VI JUDGE-X0 exoskeleton.

"Think, Kita," I muttered to myself. "Think."

Without knowing its specs, I couldn't defeat it. Well, I could try things randomly until something worked, but that wasn't a real strategy. I would need something else—something more actionable.

The real answer was to return to the Nellis Air Force Base and dig through the computers. There was a good chance the Iron-Blooded had taken Bishop there anyway. But what if they hadn't? Did I have enough time to go to the air force base and gather information before tracking down Bishop? Did *Bishop* have enough time for that? But if I couldn't defeat the Iron-Blooded, what chance did I have? It was a weapons factory, after all. Even if the Iron-Blooded weren't there, perhaps I could find something worth using against them.

The only trade-off was time.

Which I basically had none of.

The door to the supply shed slammed open. I tensed as I whirled around into a standing position. Gascoigne stood in the doorway, her eyes icy.

She was the exact opposite of subtlety and delicate femininity. Gascoigne had swapped out her normal ensemble for a pair of tattered jeans, a stained white shirt, and a leather jacket that had seen more action than a rail gang shootout.

Her boots were larger than mine, and they looked like they barely fit her.

She also carried a semiautomatic rifle, which really upped her threat levels.

"What's taking you so long?" Gascoigne asked, her voice measured.

"Nothing." I picked up my satchel and pulled it over my shoulder. "I'm ready."

"Then get your ass in gear."

She threw the door open wide and allowed me out into the center of town. We both turned to head for the vehicle hangar—the only one Richfield had—but I stopped the moment I noticed the crowd of people by the well. They were gathered around Vega, the hulking warrior-caste alien. At least twenty people had formed a circle around the Teth, pointing and whispering. Vega hardly moved. Its shiny black skin glistened a bit, even with the overcast weather, and since it had no eyes, its head was positioned squarely forward, which was odd.

Someone stepped close to Vega—a sixteen-year-old boy by the name of *Justin Riddle*. I had never interacted with the kid much, but Bishop had described him in such a colorful way I would never forget him. He was the "cocky kid who thinks he has the entire female population riding his nuts."

I supposed that description was accurate because as Justin approached Vega, he turned to a small group of teenage girls and gave them a wink. Some of the girls giggled, but a few brightened with anticipation. Then Justin swished back his perfectly tousled brown hair and flashed them a confident smile.

His demeanor told me he was a man who had a vocabulary consisting of fifteen words and ten of them were some variation of, *"How you doin'?"*

Not my type.

Never my type, actually.

Only once Justin was finished with his showboating did he touch Vega's massive bicep on one of the work arms. When the alien tensed, Justin leapt away, as though he had been electrocuted, even though I knew he hadn't been.

"Whoa, do you see how dangerous this thing is?" Justin loudly said. "I can't believe we're letting him stay with us."

Vega snorted. Then it reached out with one of its little crafter arms and touched Justin's hair. Justin let out a shrill scream and threw himself on the ground. If he could urinate, I assumed he would've.

Part of me understood—the Teth drones were frightening monsters that would tear you apart with their claws. But Vega wasn't a drone.

The crowd of Richfield denizens gasped and backed away. One man rushed forward and helped Justin to his feet.

"I am Vega," Vega said in English, its words wet and practically a sequence of slaps with its tongue. "I am one of the warrior caste, here to protect my kin of different blood."

The entire crowd held their breath. A few took several steps backward, their twitchy movements akin to frightened animals.

"Mary, get our guns," I heard someone whisper.

I hurried over. "Hey! Listen, everyone." Once near Vega, I reached a hand upward to touch its shoulder, but I was too short for that, so I awkwardly patted one of its massive elbows. "This Teth warrior was raised by humans, and is far different than the rumors about aliens you might've heard. There are informational vids on the Teth, and their lifestyle, in the schoolhouse. I recommend you all watch those this evening. Maybe twice."

"Why?" someone in the crowd asked, though I couldn't identify who.

I wanted to tell them it was because we would need to find a way to coexist, but I figured that would be met with negativity.

"So we don't run into any problems," I eventually stated. "Vega will be a guest. It needs your utmost respect."

"Did you just call him *it*?" Justin said as he got to his feet. "*That's* disrespectful."

"The Teth are hermaphrodites, you fuckin' boob," Gascoigne chimed in. She strode over to the group, and everyone backed away. She always wore an expression that indicated her displeasure with everyone and every-thing. "*It* is a fine way to refer to them."

No one shot back with any sort of comment. Most people in Richfield didn't much care for Gascoigne.

"We'll watch the vids," an older man in the crowd said.

Vega exhaled. After a moment, the alien turned to me. "*I see the humans will follow your guidance,*" Vega said in Tethlite. "*And it seems you have a female of the warrior caste with you.*"

I almost snorted out a laugh at that comment.

"What did it say?" Gascoigne snapped.

"It thinks you look tough," I replied.

She rotated her shoulder, held her rifle closer, and shrugged. "I'd look a lot *tougher* in judge armor."

Chelsy emerged from the crowd and approached Vega. In the past, Chelsy had taken an odd liking to Teth drones. Since the drones were mute, she half identified with them. I had even fashioned her toys based on their likeness—which I thought was bizarre but who was I to tell her no?

Chelsy stepped close to Vega. The alien was ten feet tall, and she wasn't even half that. The differences in them were numerous, I could list them all day, but the most striking was how frail Chelsy seemed next to the muscled body of one from the warrior caste.

She said nothing. She couldn't.

Vega touched her hair with its small crafter hand, tangling its fingers through her dark locks.

"Don't touch the kid," Justin shouted. "Stop him!"

I held out an arm. "It's okay. All the Teth are blind. This is how they interact, even with one another."

"B-But their claws! They paralyze people."

I shook my head. "Just the drones. Not any other caste. You're perfectly safe." Although not from Vega's massive muscles. But I wasn't about to admit that.

"O-Oh."

The whole crowd of people watched as Vega carefully caressed Chelsy's head, then her cheek, and finally her neck. Once finished, Vega lowered its massive head, and mouth of finger-sized fangs, until it was close to Chelsy. At first, people in the crowd grew visibly nervous. They fidgeted and pointed, but no one acted on their concerns.

Instead, Chelsy took her turn.

She touched Vega's head and ran her palms across the alien's shiny skin. Normally, the Teth didn't like to be outside, since it dried out their epidermis, but the warriors were built a little sturdier than most.

Chelsy touched Vega's mouth, poked some of its sharp teeth, and scratched its head as though it were a dog.

Then she placed her forehead against Vega's. Since she couldn't speak, it would be extremely difficult for her to communicate with the Teth, but that didn't seem to stop her from liking it.

"This is weird," Justin muttered from the crowd.

"This is entirely normal." I stepped between him and Vega. "Again, I urge you all to watch the informational vids on the matter. The Teth aren't our enemies."

"Yes, they are," an older man in the crowd said.

He was *Scrapyard Pete*, our resident handyman. I just called him Pete, since it was shorter, though it bothered him for some reason.

Pete was in his late forties, and had retained some of his youthful vigor, even though he had been born during the Forever Winter. His tall stature and confident gaze set him apart from the others, and he was always as quick as a whip.

"They're our enemies," he said. Pete pointed at Vega. "If these fuckin' aliens hadn't landed on our goddamn planet, we wouldn't be in this mess."

"Which is true," I said, "but so what? Nothing will change what happened, all we can do is focus on moving forward. Having Vega—and other Teth—around, will make life easier."

"Or they'll try to run everything, like they did when they got here." Pete thumbed the tip of his nose. "You see this *beast*? It could kill anyone here without a second thought. It doesn't even need no gun nor grenade. What kind of monster is it? Why are we just welcoming it with open arms? We fuckin' send away *humans* all the time because they might be no good."

His points resonated with the crowd.

It was true. Richfield had maintained its "normalcy" because of its long-standing refusal to admit anyone in without a solid recommendation.

"L-Listen," I said, some of my confidence waning. I gulped down air and thought about Bishop. I didn't have time to argue. "Richfield hasn't changed its way in thirty years, and in that time, it has almost been ransacked and destroyed by outside forces. We're getting weaker, not stronger—so we need to make changes. And we can start by making one that'll be helpful. Vega is strong. Give it some work. Give it a chance. You'll see."

I wasn't good at speeches—but I was good at faking it. Lying had been the name of my game for many years. It had been one of my only tools to use against the darkness of the wasteland.

"We do have lots of scrap metal to haul," Pete said as he rubbed his scruffy chin.

"Good," Gascoigne said with a grunt. She grabbed my shoulder and pointed my whole body toward the vehicle hangar. "Pete, handle it while we're gone. We'll be back in a few days."

"Can I go, too?" Justin asked with a dopy smile.

Gascoigne gave him the once-over and sneered. "Never."

"B-But I never get to leave!"

The crowd of people sided with Gascoigne, many of them shaking their heads. "It's dangerous," one man said. "Worse than before. Ever since Boulder City ran into all those problems. People have been raidin' and lootin' more than ever."

Justin scoffed and stomped his foot. He wanted to argue, but there was no point. Not in Richfield. Everyone was tight-knit and knew everything about everyone else. They wanted to protect their young people—there weren't many here, after all. Even if they were annoying.

"Sit down and relax," a woman said to Justin.

He collapsed faster than a deflating balloon.

"Wait!" someone else shouted.

I glanced over my shoulder.

Brecht pushed himself through the crowd and walked over to me. With his expression hard-set, he asked, "May *I* go with you?"

"Why?" I asked.

He opened his coat and flashed his handgun. "I was trained in sharp-shooting to fight the CCP. And since they're no longer a threat . . . I want to use my skills against the Iron-Blooded now. They took everything from me. And if you're really opposed to them, we *are* allies."

"Who are you?" Gascoigne interjected before I could answer.

"I'm Brecht Cortez. From Facility Twenty-Six."

"What the fuck is *Facility Twenty-Six*?" Gascoigne whipped her attention to me. "Do you trust this knob?"

I nodded once. "I think it would be a good idea to take him."

Gascoigne sneered. She stared at Brecht. "He's so pale, he looks like he's been dead for weeks."

"He lived underground his whole life," I muttered.

Brecht took the insults well. He hardened his expression and waited.

The citizens of Richfield guided Vega away from us, showing it toward the main scrap pile near the walls. Chelsy remained by Vega's side, which I appreciated.

"Fine," Gascoigne finally stated. "You can come with us. But *I'm* driving."

CHAPTER THIRTEEN

The Town of Richfield had exactly five electric vehicles capable of running. Three of them were buggies. Well, two now, since Bishop and I had lost one. The other two vehicles were hauling trucks. Since these were too large to effectively stealth around with, we took another buggy.

It was a lightweight automobile with off-road tires, suspension, and very little bodywork. We didn't have doors, just a cage of bars around four seats and a steering wheel. The very back had a cooler the size of a coffin strapped to the bars that acted as a trunk. It was the largest part on the whole vehicle, and it rattled every time we went over rough terrain.

At least the engine hummed along, nearly silent, as we crossed the desolation. A few days ago, on foot, this had been a nightmare, but with a vehicle, it was nothing.

"We need to head back to Nellis Air Force Base," I said. "Do you know the way?"

Gascoigne, in the driver's seat, nodded once.

That was good. I hoped beyond hope that Bishop would be there. It would make this whole ordeal easier. Especially now that we had weapons.

Brecht, in the back, gripped the sides of his seat as though he were going to be thrown from the vehicle at any moment. He didn't seem . . . comfortable.

"The Iron-Blooded might still be there," I said. The wind from our travels washed over us. We had no windshield, and I was thankful my hair was short. A few ambitious strands of hair poked me in the eyes occasionally, though.

"We'll handle it when we get there," Gascoigne stated. Then she poked at the radio until she found the only station that worked in the area.

Typically, music played at this hour, but once the crackling static of the radio faded, we were treated to some man's joyful statements.

"Hey there, listeners! You're tuned in to the wasteland's one and only source of entertainment. I'm your host, DJ Slam-A-Damma-Ding-Dong. Well, my friends just call me *DJ Slam*, while the ladies just call me *Damma-Ding-Dong*, if you catch my drift."

I thought that would've offended Gascoigne. Instead, she stifled a laugh and smiled.

"Is *this* what passes for entertainment up here?" Brecht asked.

Gascoigne shot him a glare. "Shut up. I'm listening."

"Another wave of raiders swept through Dodge City last night, leaving destruction in their wake," DJ Slam said, his tone entirely too upbeat for that kind of news. "Local residents say they've been after atomic batteries as of late, though no one can explain why. At least ninety are confirmed dead as a doornail, most of which slowly bled out over several hours."

"That's horrific," Brecht muttered.

"Welcome to this unrelenting holocaust of dreams we call *the waste-land*," Gascoigne sarcastically replied.

Brecht leaned his head back, and the wind whipped through his dark hair. With his eyebrows knitted, he asked, "You don't have a . . . a . . . leader? A nation? A people?"

"Not here," I said, my words gobbled up by the wind a few seconds after I uttered them. I had to speak louder, just to maintain the conversation. With water being ripped from the corners of my eyes, I continued. "To the east is Ex Cathedra. It's a gigantic nation that covers most of the flatlands between the two largest mountain ranges."

"They're at war on bother borders," Gascoigne said with a snort. "Which is good for us, because Ex Cathedra is the last place to use JUDGE-X0 suits in their military. Since they're wearing themselves thin, they won't be bothering us. But if we come across any judges, we need to leave. Immediately."

I ignored her ominous statement. "To the west of here is United Cali-fornia. People call it *U-Cali* for short. They've made their territory on the coast, on the *other* side of the smaller mountain range. For the most part, they're also militaristic, but people say they feel safe there."

Brecht scoffed. "Why?"

"Because U-Cali kills all raiders and aliens." From the rumors I had heard, they also destroyed all A-tech that was written in Tethlite, even if it could otherwise be useful. They wanted to remove the alien footprint from Earth.

Not wanting to be depressing, I motioned to our surroundings. "This barren territory in between the large mountains and the little mountains is referred to as *the wasteland*. It's ruled by no one."

"Is there a reason for that?" Brecht asked.

"It's a desert," I said.

Gascoigne huffed. "It's also desolate. Rocky. Practically unusable. Only idiots stay in a place this unforgiving."

Brecht leaned onto the back of Gascoigne's seat, his grip on the vehicle still tight. "Don't *you* live here?"

"Heh." She glared at the oncoming wind, unbothered by the way it whipped across her. "I stand by my statement. If I had been smart, I would've offed myself a long time ago." Gascoigne sighed. "But here I am . . . saving some junk hunter."

"Ex Cathedra . . ." Brecht closed his eyes. "We didn't learn about that in our educational vids. All we learned about was the United States and China. How they both grew to power."

"Neither exist anymore," I muttered.

Brecht sighed. "What about the Vay? I was taught to fight them, too."

The Vay were *other* aliens, similar to the Teth, but war hungry. Although I knew of their existence from my grandfather, and historical documents, they had landed on another continent. I had never seen one personally.

I shook my head. "You don't have to worry about the Vay."

"So . . . these other nations . . . they sprang up from the United States?"

"Ex Cathedra and U-Cali didn't come into existence until after the Forever Winter," I muttered. The tales of the formation were filled with strife. I had hated it whenever my father and grandfather had told me about it.

"Buckle up, folks," the radio host said, the man's chipper voice a harsh juxtaposition to the world around us. "The rest of today's news will make you appreciate that extra can of irradiated beans in your stash!"

Brecht frowned.

"First up, it seems those Iron-Blooded loons decided to stage an impromptu *shopping spree* at the rowdy town of Boulder. Eyewitnesses report that they made off with enough canned goods and ammo to last for a *second*

Forever Winter. So, heads up! If you see a band of Iron-Blooded headed into your local town, just remember that sharing is caring, but not with them."

"I've run across so many of them," Brecht said. "I—" He was slammed on the seat back as the buggy went over a hill and then slammed back down. The man rubbed at his chest and gripped the vehicle even tighter than before. "I . . . I can't believe how many Iron-Blooded there are."

"Speaking of those alien-worshipping freaks," DJ Slam said, his tone turning quizzical. "Get ready to have your Geiger counters go haywire! Remember that quaint little town just a few clicks from here? *Pesto*? Or something like that. Well, apparently, our extraterrestrial friends decided to pop in for a visit, and let's just say their version of '*Greetings, Earthlings*' involved a few too many gunshots and piss-poor diplomacy."

I held my breath.

The sounds of the radio drifted away as I dwelled on Brecht's statement. The Iron-Blooded *were* everywhere lately. They had even stationed themselves in that weapons factory—seemingly out of nowhere. Now they were raiding cities and the Teth themselves were killing people?

No.

They likely didn't kill people. They captured them. To grow their ranks.

But why?

"Kita?"

I didn't know why, and I had a terrible feeling that I needed to find out.

"Kita."

"Hm?" I asked.

Gascoigne glowered at me. "We're almost there. You ready?"

I glanced up at the sky. It was still afternoon, but the clouds were denser than usual. "I studied the guard routines of the Iron-Blooded on that factory for days. If we approach now, they'll be doing a wide sweep of the surrounding city and base. We can either go in on foot, or drive closer in an hour or two."

"And you trust this guy?" Gascoigne tossed her shoulder in Brecht's direction. "Because he seems like a quivering lump of jelly that's just stinkin' up the place."

"*Hey*," Brecht barked. He didn't release his death grip from the buggy, though. "I've never ridden in such a wild vehicle before. I'm perfectly capable of holding my own. I've had to fight the Iron-Blooded since I arrived in this wasteland."

The conviction in his words told me he had been genuinely offended by Gascoigne's comment.

"I believe you," I said.

Brecht glanced over to me, his scarf flowing behind him as we drove.

"Just because he *can* shoot a gun doesn't mean he'll shoot it for *us*," Gascoigne commented. "When things get rough, is this boob going to stick it out or flee?"

"I have a grudge against those monsters." Brecht's fingernails dug into the leather of the seat. "They're obviously doing something. They raided our facility, killed or captured everyone I know—took the eggs in our crèche. They're evil. I might not know the both of you, but I *hate* the Iron-Blooded."

Gascoigne wobbled her hand back and forth and then shrugged. "I suppose that's a good enough answer. Fine. Stick close to us and follow our instructions. If you don't, you're on your own, but if we stay together, we have a wildly better chance of making it home alive."

"I understand."

My heart sank as soon as we drove to the edge of the city.

The Iron-Blooded had left the weapons factory. Their armored vehicles were nowhere to be seen. The streets in the surrounding city were quiet. The factory itself was as dead and cold as the day after the bombs dropped.

I wanted to scream in frustration, but I kept that to myself. Instead, I dug my fingernails across my scalp, feeling the pain and remembering what Bishop said about living. Sometimes life was a lot of pain—but at least we were alive.

Was he still with me, though?

Gascoigne parked the buggy just outside the south garage, her expression set in sardonic irritation. "I take it they're not here," she said.

"That's fine, it's fine, everything's fine," I said, practically vomiting the words—more for myself than anyone else. I grabbed the cage of the buggy and hopped out. "I need to go inside and access the computers. You two wait here."

Gascoigne switched the vehicle off. She slid out of the driver's seat and hefted her rifle. "Watch the vehicle," she barked at Brecht. "I'm going inside no matter what."

Brecht, eyeing Gascoigne, hesitated for a long moment before shooting me a nod. He pulled himself into the driver's seat to guard our vehicle, and I appreciated that he was willing to listen to my command.

With the swagger of someone who had seen one too many battles, Gascoigne sauntered over to me. She offered a cold glare, and then motioned to the factory with a swing of her weapon.

"I'm not leaving you alone," Gascoigne drawled. "I've seen what happens when you make impromptu plans."

"Well, thank you. I suppose."

I didn't trust Gascoigne like I trusted Bishop, but she had never betrayed us since allying with Richfield, so I decided to contemplate the possibility that she would gun me down now that we were alone.

The trunk of our buggy rattled. Gascoigne whipped around, her rifle at the ready. To my surprise, Brecht did almost the same thing. He turned around in his seat and grabbed his handgun in one swift motion, like he had done that action a hundred times before.

Both of them kept their weapons pointed at the coffin-sized trunk.

It stopped moving, shaking back and forth.

"Who's in there?" Gascoigne shouted. "Come out now, because I'm not afraid of wasting bullets."

The trunk lid popped open, and out rolled the teenager, Justin. He tumbled onto the dirt and then stood, his hair screwy and his hands shaky. With a bright smile of perfect teeth, he forced a laugh. "Hey."

That was all he said.

Hey.

What an intellectual.

My first rule to lying—tell them what they already believe first, then everything that came after seemed more plausible. If Justin had given us a lie about how stupid he was, and how he got lost in our trunk, I might've believed him, but instead, our stowaway just stood there, waiting for someone else to speak.

What were we going to do with him?

He didn't even have a weapon.

And I wasn't about to turn around to drop him back off. There was no more time to waste. We had to get to Bishop and rescue him, and this teenage stowaway wasn't going to stop me.

"Why am *I* dealing with this?" Gascoigne lowered her weapon. "That's the one question I ask myself every goddamn day."

"Why did you follow us?" I asked.

Justin shrugged. I waited, silent and persistent. Why would some random teen do this? Justin shrugged a second time, his gaze falling to the dirt. "I just . . . wanted to get out of the town. They never let me leave Richfield. You and Bishop go all the time. And if Bishop is in trouble, I want to help."

His reasoning irritated me. Didn't he know it was dangerous out in the wasteland? He must have, but still he insisted on following us.

"You wanted to impress some girl, didn't you?" Gascoigne asked.

Justin didn't reply. He sheepishly rubbed the back of his neck and shrugged a third time.

Now it all made sense. He probably told some young girl in Richfield he would head out and get her something. Bishop told me that was all the rage a few years back—for young men to prove themselves by becoming junk hunters to find some rare jewelry or something to give their girlfriends.

But junk hunting was dangerous.

Well, to be fair, *everything* was dangerous these days.

"Just let me stay with you," Justin said, cutting into my thoughts. "I can be useful. I can carry things."

Gascoigne turned on her heel. "Wait in the buggy, boy. We'll be back in a moment."

"You're going to make the men wait in the car?" Justin motioned to himself and Brecht.

"I'm *ordering* one trained soldier, whom I trust, to guard our vehicle and one *idiot* to stay in our only zone of safety." She shot him an icy glare. "But if you'd rather walk your fancy testicles out in front of us to act as a meat shield, by all means. Be my guest." She dramatically motioned to the weapons factory.

Justin gave her offer serious thought—for some reason.

After a gulp of air, he shook his head and leapt into the buggy behind Brecht. The two stared at each other for a long moment, neither speaking.

I sighed and then joined Gascoigne.

Together, we headed into the factory with me in the lead and Gascoigne trailing behind. I hated having people behind me when I walked. Some sort of rabbit instinct told me to keep glancing over my shoulder to make sure everything was okay.

This bothered Gascoigne. She glared every time my eyes caught hers.

"Do I have something on my face?" Gascoigne asked, curt.

"N-No." I hurried forward through the southern garage, my attention on how empty it was. The steel crates were nowhere to be seen. Had the Iron-Blooded taken them all? They'd had trucks when last I was here.

The good news—trucks left marks across the mud and dirt of the wasteland and were easy to track.

The bad news—they had been moved to a more secure facility. An Iron-Blooded base.

Once we entered the factory floor, I took note of our surroundings. It was easy thanks to the overhead lights. Not only that, but the machinery was still operational. The claw hands and conveyor belts were lit up, but unmoving. It told me our enemies had left the power on, which was disconcerting.

They had been intent on hiding their presence here. I had heard them say so. Why leave blatant evidence of their work?

My heart hammered.

I had lived too long not to know a trap when I saw it. They probably left the power on to attract individuals. Something in this factory was a trap. I knew it deep in my core.

The computer panel I had accessed before wasn't far from us—about fifty feet—but the floor was covered by debris that hadn't been there before. Fragments of the walls, broken up cubicles, and multiple barrels' worth of nuts and bolts.

I took a cautious step forward, pushing the debris to the side before placing weight on my step.

"Hold up," Gascoigne commanded.

I stopped cold. "Yes?"

"Did you hear that?" She pointed her rifle at the far wall. "There was some sort of scratching."

"I doubt it's a person."

"Heh." Gascoigne shook her head. "You know how many critters live in shitholes like this? That's the number one secret killer of soldiers in Ex Cathedra. It's not the enemy. It's the damn diseases everyone keeps catching from God only knows what."

"Maybe rats?" I whispered.

"Maybe." Gascoigne sneered. "Could be drones?"

"No. I think the Iron-Blooded left us a trap. Something is wrong with this place." I cleared more of the debris, slowly and painfully, and found a small fist-sized orb of machinery. With my breath held, I backed away. "There are A-tech grenades in here," I whispered.

Gascoigne spotted the spherical orb and groaned. "Those things will go off if they're moved even slightly. And if you've spotted one, there are definitely dozens of others."

Good thing they were Teth-designed weaponry. Since the race was blind, they rarely ever designed weapons with sight-based detectors. This was a motion-based weapon. It would detonate the moment it was jostled.

I glanced into my satchel. The EMP grenade would likely deactivate the A-tech, but it would also harm the factory's computers, and then I would get nothing for my efforts. I couldn't use the EMP here.

So I turned my attention to the conveyor belts. If I walked across them, I could reach the computer panel without touching the floor.

"I'll be right back," I muttered as I hauled my small body up onto the belt.

Gascoigne eyed me while I crawled along the line, slowly heading to my destination. "You look like a fucking child."

"It gets the job done," I muttered.

She rolled her eyes, but kept her weapon up regardless. From what I knew of her, she wasn't the type of person to let her guard down. When more scratching came from the walls, she gave it her full attention.

While Gascoigne fretted over the rats in the wall, I managed to make my way to the computer panel. I stayed on the conveyor belt as I reached over and tapped away at the screen.

What I needed was a way to defeat the Mark VI exoskeleton. And I wanted a solution that didn't involve destroying the suit in the process. It was a tall order, but if I managed to find it, I'd feel a lot better about storming into an Iron-Blooded facility to retrieve Bishop.

As soon as I had that, we could leave.

Something on the wall *popped*, and the clink of metal on metal filled the factory. I glanced over. A swarm of rats, at least a dozen, spilled out of a floor vent that had been busted open. The little brown and gray rodents hurried into the factory, some of them leaping over the debris—and the motion-detecting grenades.

If one of the rats landed on one, this whole place would become a storm of shrapnel, or worse. The A-tech weaponry often had nasty surprises.

"Gascoigne!" I shouted.

"Why am *I* dealing with this?" Gascoigne growled as she took aim.

CHAPTER FOURTEEN

Gascoigne opened fire. Not in a spray-n-pray manner, but in a methodical one-shot-per-rat way that left the rodents splattered across the far wall. The squeaking and squealing were only drowned out by the raucous rifle fire. I flinched when she turned her weapon in my vague direction, but Gascoigne never missed—or even got close to shooting me.

The rats darted off in different directions. I pointed to the ones scurrying toward the grenades. Gascoigne focused her efforts, but the echo of her rifle fire was quickly stealing my ability to hear. With my hands over my ears, I grimaced with each shot.

All the intelligent rats darted back into the vent. The simpleminded rats leapt into the factory's machinery, ultimately getting themselves crushed between moving cogs and gears. The one rat with enough testosterone for three grown men ran at Gascoigne herself, only to face down a bullet and lose.

By the time this war was over, I would never look at the rodents the same ever again.

Thankfully, the rats were either dead or gone, and while the blood was still setting into position, Gascoigne reloaded her rifle.

I took in a deep breath, the smell of gunfire just as present as the copper tang of blood on the air.

"That was . . . impressive," I said.

Gascoigne narrowed her eyes. "Are you done yet?"

That was all she said. She didn't thank me for the compliment or even ask if I was okay. She just wanted to know when we could leave.

"I'll hurry." And then I returned my attention to the computer.

But just as I said that, I heard the creak of the factory door. I figured it was the Iron-Blooded. Fortunately, I wasn't *that* unlucky. No—it was Brecht. He stood in the doorway, his handgun at the ready. Justin stood by him, his eyes wide. The two entered the weapons factory, both glancing around.

"I heard gunfire," Brecht said.

"Tsk," Gascoigne replied with a click of her tongue. "I told you to watch the vehicle. You disobeyed orders *and* you didn't help me gun down the pests? What a terrible combination."

Brecht lowered his weapon. "I apologize, but I wasn't sure what you were shooting at."

"Did you see that lady?" Justin gestured with excited energy. First to Gascoigne, and then to the blood-splattered walls. "What a warrior woman! She came in here, swinging her fallopian tubes like nunchucks, showing all those rats who's boss!"

"*Shut up*," Gascoigne snapped.

He did.

And then I stopped paying attention to them, even after they started up a conversation about what they all should be doing. I needed to focus on the task at hand. What did I need from this factory? Information. Desperately.

I hurried through the menus, searching for everything I felt was relevant. First, I went straight for the Mark VI schematics. What sorts of weaknesses could I find? Fortunately, the old-world governments loved to take notes. Unfortunately, they weren't always thorough.

The notes for the JUDGE-X0 Mark VI weren't difficult to find, but they were scattered and complicated. Reading just happened to be one of my strongest skills, though, so even though there were pages of information, it didn't take long to consume them.

The Mark VI was meant to use the most advanced A-tech the Teth had to offer, which was interesting, to say the least. Plasma blades and super heat-resistant plating made the whole suit far more dangerous than the previous ones. Normally, the judge exoskeletons had normal steel alloy blades, which were useful as utility tools and not typically weapons. That wasn't the case with the Mark VI. It had a blade that could cut through almost anything.

But apparently, it was extremely taxing on the battery cells. Normal suits of power armor were already costly in terms of power, but the Mark VI spiked when the blade was in use.

"Fascinating," I whispered as I continued to read.

Apparently, if the blade was on *too* long, the battery cells could drain at a rapid rate, and then the whole suit would cease to function.

Was that a weakness? Yes. Was it useful? Not so much. That meant I would need the enemy to use their most powerful weapon for a prolonged period of time without dying. I couldn't think of a single strategy in history where something like that had been effective.

But perhaps if I trapped the pilot and suit behind a thick wall . . .

Or drew more power from the blade, in some way, to force the battery cells to drain even faster. I would need to think of something.

I bit my pointer finger on my left hand as I used my right to sift through the remainder of the computer's information. First, the inventory list for the factory.

There were a lot of raw materials listed, including grade-316 stainless steel, various prefabricated exoskeleton parts, and spare atomic batteries, all of which were promising, but they could've been pilfered already. There were even more greenhouse fixtures and repair kits, and I knew I had to have it all, if they remained.

I clicked through the security cameras, and while half of them were too damaged to function properly, it appeared the north and west garages still had some supplies. More than enough for my future plans.

Perhaps I could send word to Richfield . . . The buggy had a radio. If they would come here, gather the materials, and hide them in town, I'd be prepared for the next phase.

The most important piece of information I found came at a shock, however.

No exoskeleton battery cells were created at this factory. Instead, they were made in a separate location—a special lab that focused on energy containment. I thought back to when Bishop and I had infiltrated this weapons factory. The Mark VI suit had been inoperable because it had no batteries. Less than a day later, the Iron-Blooded tracked us down, the suit fully powered.

Perhaps . . .

They had moved locations to get battery cells. Could they be waiting there with Bishop?

"We need to go," I said.

Gascoigne shrugged her shoulder at Justin. "What're we doing with Fuck Nugget over here?"

"*Hey*," Justin balked. But he didn't follow that up with anything.

"He wanted an adventure, didn't he?" I left the computer and crawled onto the conveyor belt, my eyes drawn to the crimson rat blood. The squeaks of the remaining rodents echoed out of the vents, and I knew that if we wanted the factory to remain semi-intact, the vent would need to be closed.

"Where are we heading?" Brecht asked.

"Back to the buggy," Gascoigne snapped. "Assuming it's still there, since everyone guarding it just up and left."

There was no follow-up to that. The levels of tension were high, and I hated the fighting, but I wasn't about to contradict Gascoigne. She was right. We needed to protect our things. Our last buggy had been stolen, after all.

"Gascoigne, can you seal the vents before we go? To keep the rats out of this room?"

She glowered at me, but didn't question my request. Instead, she went straight about doing it, which I appreciated. Perhaps she knew my reasoning.

The drive to the labs would only take us a few hours.

The wrecked streets, littered with deserted cars, sheds, and barrels, was like navigating a maze, but Gascoigne took it all in stride. She never tapped the brakes as she swerved between the stationary obstacles, her icy attention on the road like it was her nemesis and she intended to drive across in perfection as a sign of dominance.

Justin and Brecht sat in the back. Brecht's white-knuckled grip on his seat was visible from the rearview mirror, and Justin's excited grin could be seen from the moon.

Music played on the radio, and I wondered how long it would take the residents of Richfield to move all those supplies. They hadn't been keen on my request when we radioed over to them, but they eventually agreed.

It was only a matter of time until I had everything I needed.

Then the music came to an end, and the low hum of the engine dominated. That was, until the DJ came back on the airwaves.

"Hey there, my favorite listeners! It's me, DJ Slam, bringing you all the greatest hits from before the Forever Winter. Did you like that last tune? It was by someone named Kill-a-Watt, or some shit, and he's probably spinnin' in his grave."

"This is such a bizarre source of entertainment," Brecht whispered.

"I love DJ Slam," Justin said.

Gascoigne sighed before nodding as well, as though agreeing with Justin about anything caused her physical pain.

"In Ex Cathedra, the broadcasting is controlled," Gascoigne said, her tone somber. "They only play propaganda, or approved music. Someone like this DJ Slam is refreshing."

She was right. Ex Cathedra would never allow someone as . . . eccentric . . . as DJ Slam on the radio.

"More news comin' at you quick," DJ Slam said. "A few callers have told me about underground facilities where, and get this, apparently people have been living for *decades*. Can you believe it? Underground mole people, who have never seen God's glorious earth for themselves. I thought I had heard everything, folks, but this is a strange new tale that I'm not even sure is true."

Justin leaned onto the back of my seat. "I really like when he reads stories late at night."

"Because of all the erotica?" Gascoigne quipped.

"W-What? I didn't say that!" Justin punched her seat, though it was with a weak wrist. His face was red when I glanced over my shoulder, and I chuckled, if only because it wasn't *me* who was the most awkward here.

"That's my favorite part of the show, too," Gascoigne eventually admitted as she narrowly dodged a rusted vehicle. "I think DJ Slam writes them himself."

Brecht muttered prayers under his breath, shaking his head as we sped along. He clearly wanted no part of this conversation.

With a sigh, I settled back into my seat. Bishop would've had a grand time discussing the bizarre nature of the wasteland's radio theater. If only he were here . . .

We drove by an old medical center on our way to the labs.

It was a sprawling complex that had once been a bustling hub of healthcare. The old signs, faded, broken, or rusted, stood near most doors. There was a dentist's office, a general practitioner's office, and a place for surgeries.

Gascoigne altered our course to go wide and around, and that turned out to be for the best. The moment we drove through the large parking lot, where a few battered vehicles huddled together like survivors in a storm, we spotted members of a rail gang skulking through the shadows.

They were here waiting for someone to come looking for medicine. That was when they would strike. They'd leap from the darkness, kill or maim the individual, and then rob them of all their worldly goods.

"Should we stop to get medicine?" Brecht asked.

I shook my head, my pixie-short hair tickling my ears as the wind whipped by. "We'd get into a fight, and we don't have time for that."

"I doubt there's any medicine there, anyway," Gascoigne growled.

And she was right. A place like this had probably been picked clean during the Forever Winter.

I glanced out beyond the medical center and spotted the railway where the gang had probably come in. There was no train there now, but it would come back to pick them up, no doubt in my mind.

I kept this place in mind, just in case we would need to avoid it. My imagination told me we'd have to run from this lab with Bishop in tow, but I wasn't entirely certain, and I definitely didn't want to run into rail gangs like last time.

CHAPTER FIFTEEN

The lab was far larger than I thought it would be. It was a gigantic building—three buildings, really—all attached with corridors and surrounded on all sides by an empty parking lot. The exterior of the building was a patchwork of reinforced steel and makeshift barriers—evidence that people had gotten here before us.

A large sign sat just beyond the parking lot. It read: POWER-WAY LABS, THE LEADING PRODUCERS OF ADVANCED BATTERY TECHNOLOGY.

That was how it went before the Forever Winter. Once the Teth arrived and shared their advanced knowledge with humanity, several companies sprang up to invent bigger and better things. The Teth had strange limitations, due to their physiology, and since humans enjoyed using their eyeballs for simple tasks, most A-tech was just a product of human ingenuity mixed with this hyper-advanced alien tech to make new human-friendly devices.

An entire lab dedicated to making improved batteries probably wasn't uncommon before the firestorm bombs dropped.

Gascoigne pulled the buggy up into the shadow of the sign before killing the engine. The parking lot, barren and cold, appeared lifeless. But something wasn't right. There were no animals here, and when I glanced to the fields beyond the parking lot, I noticed dozens of rusted vehicles.

Someone had cleared the parking lot.

So there would be nowhere to hide when approaching or leaving the building. And the complex had several lights on inside, though they were tiny and difficult to see.

The Iron-Blooded were here. My gut wasn't wrong. They were just hiding.

"What're we doing?" Gascoigne asked. "We going in through the front door?"

Justin leaned his head out the window of the vehicle. "What is this place?"

"It's a lab to create batteries." I tugged his shirt until he leaned back into the buggy. "We really shouldn't get caught by anyone. I think we should turn around, find a place to park our vehicle, and then search the perimeter."

Gascoigne nodded once. Then she started the vehicle, turned it around, and drove out into the graveyard of deserted cars. She pulled the buggy into a patch of trucks, and once again switched off the engine.

"They might already know we're here," she said.

"If they know we're here, they'll send someone out to come get us." I poked my head up over the cage of our buggy and glanced over the wreckage of old vehicles. The parking lot remained quiet and empty. "I think they're inside, and have warning systems in place to indicate if someone is approaching. Having active guards to watch this whole complex would be too much wasted manpower."

"What's the plan?" Justin whispered.

I pointed to him. "You'll guard the vehicle."

"With what?" He shrugged and patted his pockets. "Do I get a gun?"

"No."

Justin squished his face up in comical disgust. "I can't protect our vehicle without a firearm. I need something. You saw those rail gangers! I have to be able to fight back."

Gangers was a new word I hadn't heard before.

I sighed as I headed for the trunk. Technically, I had brought the two extra handguns. If I gave one to Justin, he would protect our belongings . . .

I picked up the .45 and examined the outside. It was a heavy handgun. The kind with a lot of kick. Would he be able to handle it?

With a frown, I handed him the gun, butt end first. "Here." Once he took it, I added, "It'll be loud if you fire it. Everyone will know where you are. Only shoot if you have to, understand?"

Justin offered me a sarcastic salute. I hated it.

Was he taking this seriously?

"You should reconsider his role," Gascoigne said. She turned to the boy. "The kid has a reaction time of two to three business days. You can't give him a deadly weapon."

"What?" Justin cradled the firearm close to his chest. "I'm a man. I can handle this." After a second of mulling everything over, he finally barked, "*Hey!* I'm plenty fast."

Gascoigne motioned to him with a shrug of her shoulder, as though he'd proved her point beyond a shadow of a doubt.

"What's a *business day?*" Brecht asked. "I don't think I've heard of that before."

"It's a phrase my commander would say," Gascoigne muttered, her gaze dark.

I ignored their banter and pointed to Brecht. "If you're really a sharpshooter, I'll need you. My plan is this—we're going to cause a distraction, get into the lab, find Bishop, and leave. No detours. No stopping for revenge. No gathering extra information. Just in and out."

"That's what she said," Justin quipped.

No one laughed.

Brecht coughed.

Justin slid back into his seat with a dramatic roll of his eyes. He might've been a hit with girls his own age, but to me, he looked like a pouting infant. Strange what certain people thought was attractive. I never understood.

"You'll stay with the buggy?" I asked.

Justin huffed. "I'll *try.*"

Gascoigne grabbed him by the collar of his shirt. Justin gasped as the ex-judge yanked him from his seat and pulled him close. "Listen here, you piece of shit. If this vehicle goes missing, I'm going to shoot you myself and blame it on raiders, do you under—"

"*Whoa, whoa!*" I leapt between them and pulled Gascoigne's hands from Justin. I wasn't strong enough to literally pull them apart, but the moment I got involved, she released the teenager. "It's okay. Calm down. We're fine. Justin will watch the vehicle. Won't you?"

Shaken, and obviously disturbed, Justin slowly nodded his head once. "Y-Yeah." He leaned back in his seat and rubbed his chest. "I will. I promise."

Gascoigne met his gaze with something far more serious than she had ever given me.

Scaring him into a pile of jelly wasn't going to help us. We needed him confident and filled with courage, not blubbering before our enemies arrived.

"Nothing will happen while we're gone," I told him. "You'll do fine."

Justin nodded again, but offered no other words.

"Normally, I have Vega with me," Brecht whispered, ignoring the conflict with the boy. "Vega causes distractions, and I do the shooting. That's our tactic."

I reached into the trunk and withdrew my satchel full of supplies, along with the EMP grenade. It was fist-sized and had the letters E-M-P painted on the side in bright orange. There were hundreds of tiny words as a warning underneath them, but they were so scrunched together, they almost looked like lines.

"*This* is our distraction," I said.

"*What the hell is that?*" Gascoigne hissed. She flinched away from it, sneering. "Are you fucking insane?"

"Why are you panicking?" Brecht grabbed his gun, but he didn't draw it. He stayed tense and ready for a fight, obviously confused. "What's going on?"

Gascoigne pointed at me. "That'll kill us, you know. *Anyone with nanites in their bloodstream.*"

"Yes, I know." I pointed to the tiny lettering. "There's a small range on this. The trick is to hit the Iron-Blooded with it. And the building. It'll kill some of them, take out the electronics in the area, and allow us to run inside."

Brecht relaxed a bit. Justin, who had just been curious, leaned back into his seat. Neither of them had nanites. They didn't have to worry about this. Which was perfect. Brecht could be the one to throw the grenade while Gascoigne and I hid.

"Does your mate have nanites in his blood?" Brecht asked.

Which was a great question. I knew where he was going with this.

"He does." I held the grenade with a tight grip. "But again, it doesn't have a wide range. This is a localized device meant for shutting down enemy tanks and small outposts like towers. If we hit a portion of the lab where I suspect the generator is, we should be able to hinder the Iron-Blooded and give us the advantage. I'm . . . I'm going to take a risk and assume they're not holding Bishop in the same room as they're storing all their valuable electronics."

"Wait, did you just say *your mate*?" Justin asked.

Brecht nodded. "Fairly common terminology used between Teth and humans to indicate our proclivity for lifelong partners."

With a snicker, Justin nodded once. "Nice. It's really animalistic. I like it."

"This EMP grenade is our best bet," I said, ignoring all of Justin's commentary.

"It'll also knock out our car if you set it off too close." Gascoigne continued to sneer at the object, obviously discontent.

"We'll go to the other side of the complex." I jumped out of the buggy and landed in the dead grass. The stink of rotted tires and old gas lingered in the air. I waved it away as I snuck around the ruined truck.

Brecht and Gascoigne followed, each of them with their own weapons. Before I left the buggy, I grabbed my own .45 handgun, along with the last of my ammo. I had thirty bullets, and I knew if I ran out, I was definitely going to die.

"Let's go," I said.

We hurried through the field, and then around the outside of the parking lot. While we hurried along the perimeter, not a single thing around us moved. There were no people, no birds, no rats or other rodents—it was just us and the shadows of a waning day creeping across the landscape.

"We watched a lot of educational vids on battery manufacturing." Brecht glanced over his shoulder and then returned his attention to me. "The power required for A-tech is far higher than anything humans had created on Earth prior to the Teth arriving."

As we made our way around the back side of the complex, the sun set. The clouds became pitch black, and almost all light was stolen from us. Fortunately, there were a few lights on around the fortifications that surrounded the labs. Another sign the Iron-Blooded were here. They really didn't want anyone sneaking up on them.

"Do you know anything about draining batteries?" I whispered as we finally made it to the back portion of the lab, far from our buggy.

Brecht nodded once. Then he shook his head. "I mean, yes. They told us how to maintain battery cells so they remained fully operational for long periods of time. I suppose, if we did the opposite of their recommendations, we would ruin them, but why would you do that?"

"N-No, that's not what I meant. Never mind."

I had wanted something to disable or break them in some way, but perhaps that was just wishful thinking. Although I knew the solution to defeating the Mark VI exoskeleton, I didn't really have an actionable plan, which worried me. But I also couldn't wait forever. Bishop needed me *right now*.

We had to go in and find him. We had to.

At the edge of the empty parking lot, staring out across the darkness to the lights flashing on the side of the lab, I held my breath and waited. Once we threw the EMP, the lights would go out, and all the electronics in the nearby area would be useless. Not my flashlight, thankfully, since it lacked any high-tech programmable parts. It didn't have any tiny circuit boards to fry, meaning we could get some light, if needed.

At times like this, I wished I had some sort of night vision, but that wasn't an option.

"It's going to get really dark," I whispered.

Brecht exhaled. "I'm used to that."

"Really?"

"I lived in an underground facility my whole life. Whenever we had sleep cycles, it was always pitch black. No one could see. It doesn't worry me."

Gascoigne shook her head. "Forget that. What's the next step? After you throw your EMP, I mean."

"Run inside." I pointed to some windows on the side of the building. "I assume this place has electronic locks. That'll make getting inside through the doors difficult." I rummaged through my satchel. "I have some atomic batteries. They should survive this EMP grenade . . . I believe. Then we can use them to power battery-operated objects, like my multi-tool. I mean, atomic batteries are basically just tiny Faraday cages, right?"

I glanced to the others, hoping they would confirm my suspicions.

Both Gascoigne and Brecht stared at me as though I had spoken a foreign language.

"So we can use the batteries to power computers?" Brecht slowly asked.

I shook my head. "All the computers will be fried."

"Why do we need batteries then?"

"Certain objects can be powered with just batteries. Like . . . a vacuum. Or certain kinds of lights."

Again, the other two stared, their eyes searching mine. They had no idea what I was talking about.

"You want us to use a vacuum?" Gascoigne asked.

I ran a hand down my face, my frustration mounting. "Never mind. Forget I said anything. Let's just focus on getting into the building."

"Will our guns be okay?" Brecht asked.

"Yes," I said, trying to hold back a sarcastic remark. "EMP just stands for *electromagnetic pulse*. It'll harm all machines and electronics with small parts capable of overheating or frying. Your gun doesn't have that. Neither does Gascoigne's rifle. They're . . . old-school. But computers, door locks, lights, and other complex machinery will be disabled. Do you two understand?"

Gascoigne gritted her teeth. "I don't care about any of that. We'll be killed if we're caught in the blast. I can't state that enough."

The parking lot was at least two hundred feet from the building to the grass. The localized grenade didn't reach that far, but just to make sure, we could hide in the field.

I handed the EMP grenade to Brecht. "I told you, we'll be fine. Brecht, you're going to take this and run across the parking lot to *that corner* of the lab. See there? See where the pipes are on the side of the building?"

The pipes were built into the far corner, and blended well with the patchwork defenses. They were the cable boxes meant for the electronics of the building. The EMP would send a pulse that would disrupt everything if we could hit it just right. The pulse of power would travel through most electrical pathways and fry whatever it surged through.

"Are you ready?" I asked Brecht.

He nodded.

"Good. Then run. Gascoigne and I are going to go in the opposite direction. We'll meet again once all the lights are out."

CHAPTER SIXTEEN

Gascoigne and I ran as fast as we could out into the grass.

Once upon a time, with a bum leg, I never would've been able to run this fast. Now, thanks to the alien tech in my system, I ran like the wind. I even kept up with Gascoigne, who was more muscle than empathy these days. Although, cardio was applicable here. She'd had a lot of that, too.

A few rusted cars stood in our way, but we tumbled around them just as the grenade went off. I heard the *boom*, and I tensed just in case, but I never felt the shockwave. We had done it—we were far enough away to avoid the pulse. My heart beat fast, but at least it was still beating.

The lights across the lab flickered and then died. Darkness swept over us in one frightening swoop. I held my breath as the hum of electronics died down. In the distance I heard a sharp alarm shriek and then end a second later.

Old-world warning systems. They didn't do much for us now.

"We need to move," I said.

Gascoigne grunted, but I couldn't see her. Through memory of our surroundings, I made my way around the cars and across the grassy field. When I reached the parking lot and my boots hit the cracked asphalt, my vision had somewhat acclimated to the darkness.

A tiny sliver of moonlight crept through the overcast skies, providing a merciful amount of light. I saw everything as silhouettes. Dark shapes that danced through a black void.

Gascoigne hurried beside me. Our huffed breaths and footfalls wafted across the empty parking lot. We almost rushed straight into the patchwork barrier around the lab, but managed to slow before hitting the metal posts. Brecht was already there, and reached out to touch my shoulder.

"There's a window over here," he whispered.

I appreciated his quiet voice. The sounds of panicked yelling echoed within the giant lab. The Iron-Blooded who *weren't* caught in the EMP were still alive, and now they were struggling to figure out what was going on. This confusion was our golden opportunity.

We needed to get inside as quickly as possible.

"Hurry," I whispered back.

Brecht guided us to the window. Before I could say anything, he aimed his handgun at the center of the glass—shielded me with his arm—and then fired. The resulting *bang* rattled me to my bones. I hadn't been prepared, and it brought back memories of my late sister.

That left me cold for a moment.

Gascoigne smashed the remaining glass with the butt of her rifle. Then she removed her leather jacket and threw it over the sill. With rough hands, she grabbed me and practically tossed me inside. I stumbled into a standing position, my breathing shallow. When she went to help Brecht, he stopped her.

"I can handle it," he snapped.

"Stop bitchin'," Gascoigne growled back.

Brecht leapt into the lab without help. Although I couldn't see him fully, it was obvious that he was rather athletic. And he landed next to me, in the dark, without much trouble. His boot crunched across the glass as he slipped into the room and made his way along the wall.

After Gascoigne joined us inside, I felt my way to the door. Thankfully, it popped open when I turned the handle.

The hallway beyond our room was black and silent. Shouting deeper in the labs rang out from the vents, but I couldn't make out the words. Someone was shouting orders, confusion evident in their tone.

I stepped forward and my boot hit something. With a shaky hand, I switched on my tiny flashlight and almost leapt backward into Gascoigne. A body was on the floor. Several, actually. Each individual was dressed in the black armor of the Iron-Blooded, their shirts and pants marked with their symbol: a human skull inside of a Teth skull.

A few of the bodies twitched, but there was no blood.

That was because their nanites had stopped functioning, causing strokes or heart attacks for everyone here. It must've been a scary forty-five seconds, but I pushed that from my mind.

These bastards didn't deserve my pity. They had taken Bishop from me—and they had tried to take my life more than once.

But seeing their equipment gave me an idea. I held out my arm and then knelt next to one of the dead men. "Let's . . . take their clothing."

"What?" Brecht immediately asked. "Is this a common thing you do here on the surface?"

"N-No. I just think it would be beneficial."

Gascoigne snorted. "That wasn't a part of the plan."

"This is an evolving plan," I muttered.

She shook her head. "Why take their clothes, though? I'm with the underground shut-in. I don't see the point."

"If we're dressed like them, we can probably move through this lab without conflict, even if they have their own flashlights and shine them on us." I grabbed the man on the floor and yanked him onto his side. "It'll be easier to save Bishop. Come on. Help me."

The other two exchanged skeptical glances. The shouting in the vents was angry and loud, and I understood their hesitation. If someone found us while we were changing, that would be the worst of all worlds.

I ripped off the Iron-Blooded soldier's body armor, shirt, belt, and pants.

They were way too big for me.

When I flashed the light on the man's paling body, I noticed a bizarre number of scars. Not like Bishop's scars, which were short tally marks made with a knife, but long and gnarled scars, from jagged blades or claws. The man must've had over a dozen.

"Here." I handed the clothing to Gascoigne. "These will probably fit you."

"Are there any female Iron-Blooded in their ranks?" She cocked an eyebrow. "I've never seen one before."

We all exchanged glances this time. Now that Gascoigne had mentioned it, I couldn't recall seeing a single woman, either. Then again, I had a seen a few near the architect, so perhaps they weren't usually in vanguard positions.

"It won't matter," I said. "Hurry and change. It's dark, and you, uh, well . . ." I regretted my words, but finished with, "You look like a man already."

Gascoigne slowly exhaled, but she didn't rebut my statement. Instead, she ripped off her shirt, unhooked her belt, and then kicked off her jeans. She had just as many scars as the Iron-Blooded soldier, perhaps more.

Although, without most of her clothes, she appeared more *womanly*.

To my surprise, Brecht watched Gascoigne the entire time while she changed, his attention fully on her movements. He wasn't leering, per se, he was more fascinated, like he had never seen anyone like her. I had to agree. Gascoigne had taken her physical health to a whole new level—and she had done it quickly thanks to the regenerative abilities of the nanites in her blood.

Gascoigne pulled the Iron-Blooded uniform on and then shot Brecht a glare. "Well? Get to it."

The man loosened his scarf, and then removed his jacket, shirt, and belt. Unlike the other soldiers, Brecht had no scars whatsoever. His smooth skin, defined muscles, and noticeable abs made him the perfect candidate for some sort of old-world men's clothing magazine.

Gascoigne watched, but she didn't have the same interest in her eyes that Brecht had with her. No—this was revenge watching. She stared, and analyzed, and never looked away, as though to be as intimidating as possible.

I grabbed the smallest Iron-Blooded soldier and changed while they were busy.

When Brecht reached for his pants, he met Gascoigne's gaze. "Would you like to help?" he asked. I suspected Brecht was being sarcastic, but that didn't stop Gascoigne from walking over, grabbing his waistband, and unzipping his pants. All while staring him dead in the eye.

Was this flirting?

Or a sexy game of chicken?

I felt awkward for even observing.

So instead, I tightened the chest armor of my stolen uniform to hide the bagginess. Every corpse on the floor was much larger than I was, and if it weren't so dark, I suspected my disguise wouldn't count for much. Thankfully, we had the shadows on our side, and they were a powerful ally.

As Brecht finished dressing, Gascoigne stepped back and smirked. "Anyone ever tell your pants it's rude to point?"

He half smiled as he tightened the armor around his chest, but offered no comeback for her quip.

Once Brecht was finished with his armor, he tucked his scarf into his shirt. Then we pushed the undressed bodies into a dark room, took their rifles and ammo, and then headed down the hallway, my flashlight our only guide. We traveled deeper into the building complex.

This place was massive. Although I could hear Iron-Blooded here, I had yet to see any who were alive.

A loud *burr* and *hum* coursed through the walls of the labs, causing a slight vibration. We all came to a stop and glanced around. My attention snapped to the ceiling when a few emergency lights flashed to life.

This had been a high-tech lab before the Forever Winter. They had a built-in backup system for electricity, and lights that wouldn't be affected by an EMP.

Not many, though. We were surrounded by harsh shadows, the atmosphere more gloom than light. I switched off my flashlight and turned to face Gascoigne. With her body armor and short haircut, she easily passed as a male Iron-Blooded thug. Only upon closer inspection could someone notice her smaller chin and lack of Adam's apple.

"You follow behind us," I whispered to her. "I'll stand in the middle. Brecht, you take the lead."

Hopefully, nobody would look too hard at my physique. I was mostly flat-chested, and I suspected I could pass for a boy but hardly a battle-hardened soldier.

Together, we ran down the long corridor, the white walls virtually unscathed, even after decades. Framed posters on the wall, some depicting batteries being used in household appliances, retained an aura of humanity's forgotten era.

The emergency lights overhead bathed everything in an eerie, clinical glow, however. The once happy families looked a little *too* happy with the harsh shadows playing across their faces.

This place felt like a time capsule.

We turned a corner, and Brecht froze. I slammed into his shoulder, but Gascoigne stopped in time and grabbed me.

Only a few feet away, three Iron-Blooded soldiers stood poised in this new hallway. All three of them tensed; one even steadied his rifle at us. They all hesitated, however, staring at us for a short, and anxiety-filled, moment. It was dark, and it was obvious we didn't look quite right.

"*Have you spotted anything?*" the first Iron-Blooded asked in Tethlite, his words slow.

"*Dead bodies,*" Brecht replied, his Tethlite equally as fluent. "*We haven't seen any intruders, but there was a broken window on the east side of this building.*"

I thanked whatever gods were watching that Brecht knew the alien language. The moment he had started speaking, the Iron-Blooded soldiers relaxed. Tethlite was "their" secret handshake, after all.

"*Where are you headed?*" the soldier asked. "*All the building's comms are out. We don't have instructions.*"

"*We're searching for survivors.*"

"*You should check by the barriers. Outside.*"

That was the exact opposite of where we needed to head. We couldn't go back. Not now. Not when we were so close to finding Bishop. I gripped Brecht's shoulder from behind, hoping to convey my urgency.

"*We boarded up the window,*" Brecht replied. "*What if they have more EMPs? We need to tell the commander what's happened.*"

The Iron-Blooded all straightened their posture and stared with hardened expressions. "*EMPs?*" one whispered, his voice tight with worry. "*That's what did all this? EMPs?*"

Brecht motioned them down the hall. "*We should all go together. Come on.*"

Perfect. An excellent lie.

Brecht was going to have them lead us deeper into the lab. They would take us straight to the heart of their operations, I was certain of it.

The three soldiers nodded before turning on their heels. They took off down the hall, and we followed, the dim lighting flickering once.

CHAPTER SEVENTEEN

The three soldiers led us to one of the industrial labs. Gigantic A-tech machines were frozen mid-job. They were behind safety glass, and in the process of constructing the exterior of battery cells. The cells themselves were the size of soup cans, and often used for power armor or armored vehicles.

The room smelled of burned chemicals, and I suspected the machines had been actively constructing batteries up until we blew the power. The lab's backup energy couldn't make the machines work again—their circuit boards had been fried.

Three women stood around the machines, behind the glass, each with their hair cut short, and their shirts marked with the Iron-Blooded logo.

Here were their women.

They appeared to be tinkering with the machines, trying to salvage parts. They were scientists or engineers.

That made sense they were separated from the men. Teth society worked around a caste system. As aliens, they lived more like bees or ants—everyone had a role at birth. It was difficult for them to realize humans could be anything, with a bit of training. The Teth probably forced the women to stay behind and work on intellectual pursuits while forcing the men to be combatants for them.

"*It was an EMP,*" one of the Iron-Blooded soldiers said to a woman engineer.

She frowned and then backed away from the machines. "*There's no saving this, then,*" she said in Tethlite. "*We only finished half a dozen. They're barely charged.*" She pointed to the other side of the room.

A few tables were pushed up against the wall, and various parts were scattered across them. Six completed battery cells were piled together near the edge, each with a small light on the side that indicated they were at less than 10 percent capacity.

"*Architect Riven won't be pleased,*" one solider muttered.

I knew that name. That was the Teth architect I had met at the Hoover Dam. I had been hoping he died in the explosion, but obviously that had been wishful thinking. I had also hoped he would take his aliens and leave the wasteland, but that was another mistake I had made.

"*Are there more EMPs?*" the woman asked.

The soldier shook his head. "*We have no word yet.*"

I tapped Brecht on the shoulder and whispered, "Ask about human captives. See where they're being held."

There wasn't a natural segue for that conversation, but I needed to know. Where was Bishop?

"*What about the prisoners?*" Brecht asked one of the other men. "*Do you think someone is here to free them?*"

That was the worst comment he could've made. Now they would be *prepared* for us, if they took his suggestion as a legitimate one.

"*It's a possibility,*" the soldier replied, his voice gruff. "*We need to inform Commander Dannik.*"

Brecht motioned to the door. "*We'll head to the prisoners now. See what the situation is.*"

"*Take the innovators,*" the soldier said.

Who were the innovators? I didn't see any aliens here.

Brecht was dead silent after the command. I could practically hear his thoughts through his blatant confusion. If I spoke, to answer, they would all know I was a woman, and our cover would be blown.

And Gascoigne couldn't reply—she was both a woman *and* completely checked out of the conversation. She didn't speak Tethlite, so she was actively staring at the wall with a vapid expression, her eyes unseeing. She only snapped back to reality when she realized I had glanced her way.

Which meant Brecht needed to answer. I prayed he would find an acceptable response.

"You *should take the innovators,*" Brecht said, a hint of indignation to his voice. "*We might stumble upon the intruder. They may have more EMPs.*"

The other Iron-Blooded exchanged quick glances. Then the man nodded once, agreeing with Brecht. "*Let's go,*" he said to the women. "*All *innovators, stay between my squad. We'll escort you to the architect's wing and speak with the commander."*

The women—the engineers who had been working on the battery cells—crowded close to the Iron-Blooded.

And this all made sense to me now. That was how Teth designated women. *Innovators.* And the men here were probably designated as *warriors.* The same titles given to castes of the Teth.

The three Iron-Blooded rounded up the innovators and headed for the door. Once they left, it was just me, Brecht, and Gascoigne.

Iron-Blooded always traveled in threes, after all.

"What's going on?" Gascoigne growled.

I headed over to the tables with the batteries and scooped up the completed cells. They didn't have much power, but perhaps I could use them in some way. I didn't want to leave without them. Of course, I didn't have my satchel on me, so I resorted to shoving them into the pockets of my new cargo pants.

"We need to head to the prisoners," I said.

Brecht motioned to the door. "I have no idea where they are. No one said. And I can't ask them—that would've revealed I wasn't one of them."

"It's fine, it's fine. We'll find them. We just have to search."

With our batteries, we hurried into the hallway. Small, automated robots slid out from charging ports built into the wall and began vacuuming up dust in the corners of the corridor. We stepped over them as best we could—each was about the size of a dinner plate—but they buzzed and beeped as we got in the way of their pathing.

This lab had enough power to maintain cleaning robots throughout the Forever Winter? Was that why everything looked so neat and pristine?

What was powering this place? My hopes grew as I imagined a fission battery tucked away at the bottom of the building complex. However, even if it was there, I knew I couldn't go for it. The Iron-Blooded had thoroughly claimed this place, and all I wanted was Bishop. My highest priority was escaping with him in my arms.

When we heard sounds from another hallway, I pointed toward them. We turned down a hall with multiple windows on one side and doors on the other. Iron-Blooded soldiers and innovators were rushing out of the rooms and heading deeper into the building complex. We shuffled into their ranks, and no one questioned our presence.

At least thirty humans were here, which surprised me. How many people were with the Iron-Blooded? This wasn't their only outpost . . . I wished

I had counted the number of people at the dam, but it hadn't been on my mind at the time.

The soldiers led us to a storage room in the middle of the building. It had been locked, but when got near, I noticed it had been blasted open. Clearly, after the EMP went off, the Iron-Blooded made their own solutions to their problems.

The storage room was massive, with high vaulted ceilings and access to the emergency generator. It also had a garage door that led to a loading and unloading zone. The door was open, allowing me to see the three trucks all lined up and ready to take off. The headlights were on, which meant these trucks hadn't been hit by our EMP and would function just fine.

The smell of burned hair irritated my nose, and I wondered if someone had been zapped during the pulse.

"*Get onto the trucks,*" one of the soldiers said to the innovators in Tethlite.

The Iron-Blooded searched around the garage, obviously looking for intruders, and I decided now was a good time to investigate. I broke away from Brecht and Gascoigne, and made sure to stay out of the headlights.

Instead, I headed to the back of the trucks to see if I could spot anything useful—or people who were being held captive.

The first truck carried the Mark VI suit of power armor.

My eyes widened as I climbed into the back. It was dark, more so than the garage, but the power armor was still obvious to me. It was distinct, and sleek, in a way more of the JUDGE-X0 exoskeletons weren't.

And it was so big, the suit had to be crumpled into the back of the truck, like a full-grown adult trying to fit into a children's-sized plastic car. The legs were tucked up close to the chest of the power armor, and the arms were wrapped around.

A single Iron-Blooded soldier stood in the truck alongside the armor. He turned to me, his expression hard.

With a voice as deep as I could muster—even going so far as to cough and rasp up my words—I said in Tethlite, "*I have new batteries.*" I reached into my cargo pants and held one in my hand.

It was the first lie I had thought of.

The man must've found this was acceptable, because he motioned with his rifle at the armor.

I walked around to the back side, my hands shaking. This wasn't part of my plans, but I wasn't going to waste this opportunity. Most JUDGE-X0 exoskeletons had their power cells either fitted into the spine or the chest plate, because both were extra reinforced to protect the pilot. The Mark VI had its on the spine, thankfully.

And everything was open. That was the default setting for whenever the suit wasn't being operated, to make sure no one got stuck within.

I poked at the first battery, and it popped out with a *chiss*. When I glanced at the power indicators along the side of the battery, I realized it had more than 80 percent juice left. I slid my almost empty battery into the suit of armor to replace the first, and then I repeated that process with the last two cells in the suit. Now the Mark VI was almost drained, and I had three perfectly viable batteries all my own.

With a quick nod, I left the truck. The Iron-Blooded man said nothing to me.

I had briefly given thought to just sneaking into the power armor, but I never would've gotten into the pilot's seat without the enemy soldier shooting me through the skull. And one shot would summon the others. At least now, perhaps the enemy would run out of power at an inopportune time.

The second truck already had several women piled inside. They eyed me as I passed by.

Then I reached the third truck, and saw their supplies. Rifles. Ammo. Grenades. Batteries. And that was when I realized they didn't have Bishop here. My heart sank into my stomach and my vision tunneled. I had been trying to stay optimistic, but now it seemed like perhaps I would never see him again.

I was too late.

"*What're you doing?*" someone barked at me in Tethlite.

I straightened my posture and glanced to a man standing on the back of the third truck. He had his rifle in both hands, but the barrel was pointed at the ground.

"*Where are the prisoners?*" I asked, my voice painfully raspy.

The man shrugged with one shoulder. "*Those pieces of shit we found wandering the wastes? Dead. Their bodies are out in the ditch.*"

CHAPTER EIGHTEEN

His statement hit me like a punch to the gut. While my mind had already gone over the possibility, my heart didn't want to admit it.

"*Ditch?*" I asked.

The man motioned to the garage door that led outside. I walked a few paces, until I was at the edge of the building, and stared out into the back parking lot. A barricade had been positioned around all the garage doors, and a ditch had been dug near the base of one. Through the darkness of night, with only a small amount of light from the trucks garage, I noticed the unmistakable outlines of arms, heads, and legs.

Naked and discarded, the bodies of people the Iron-Blooded had killed were outside in the darkness, waiting for the early morning grackles to come feast on their flesh.

Why did the Iron-Blooded do this?

They took people and "recruited" them to their cause. Architect Riven had been trying to take humans off Earth, but after I had destroyed their ship, perhaps Riven was now attempting to gather a small army. The Iron-Blooded had been stealing supplies, after all. How many people did they need? For what?

I suspected everyone in the ditch had declined their offer to join.

Bishop would've declined.

Well, he was also one of their major enemies since he helped me fight back against Architect Riven.

I should've known he wouldn't have lived. This whole mission was a farce to begin with. I was just deluding myself into thinking I could save him.

Exhaustion and dread clouded my thoughts. Anger crept in, like cracks across a smooth surface, forming from overwhelming outside pressure.

I tamped down the feeling. I couldn't grieve here. I couldn't. There would be time later. If I lost focus, and cried or collapsed, I was as good as dead myself.

With sluggish movements, I walked back into the garage, past the three trucks, and straight to Brecht and Gascoigne. They waited as though they were guarding the door, and only left their post when I drew near.

"Did you get any information?" Gascoigne whispered.

"He's dead," I intoned. "This was . . . all for nothing."

The other two said nothing at first. They exchanged a quick glance before Brecht nodded.

"I'm sorry," he said. "I had been hoping some people from Facility Twenty-Six were here, but . . . if they're dead . . . perhaps we should sneak out while they're busy loading their vehicles."

His words circled my thoughts, but the situation wouldn't leave me. The Iron-Blooded, and their Teth allies, were the scourge of the wasteland. They'd proved it at the Hoover Dam, and now they had taken Bishop from me as well?

If someone opened the door to violence, they couldn't complain about what walked through.

I'd make them regret hurting me. *For hurting so many people.*

That resolution caused my blood to go cold, and my thoughts to sharpen. I glanced back at the third truck.

"We need to get on that one," I whispered. "As guards. We're leaving with this convoy."

"What about Justin?" Brecht asked.

Gascoigne shot him a glance. "Who's *Justin*?"

"The boy we left in the buggy."

She snorted and smirked, though it was all callous. "Oh, right. I forgot about that boob."

"I've noticed your train of thought is better described as a dilapidated bus," Brecht quipped.

At first, I thought Gascoigne was going to snap at him, but it actually took her a moment to process the insult. Afterward, she playfully glared at him.

But I didn't have time for this.

"We're leaving him." I motioned to the truck. "C'mon. We'll come back for him afterward. But first, we head out with the enemy."

With our plan set, we walked as a group of three over to the truck. The Iron-Blooded soldiers were too engrossed in their activities to notice us, their commands and chatter drowning out our movements.

As we reached the vehicle, a bead of sweat ran down my temple. My heart raced as I grabbed a crate of ammunition and hoisted myself up into the truck, doing my best to mimic the actions of the Iron-Blooded soldiers. Gascoigne and Brecht followed suit, blending in seamlessly. They looked like thugs in the dim lighting.

"*The architect wants us to leave,*" someone yelled. "*This lab has been compromised. We're returning to the nest.*"

The lone guard in our truck eyed us at first, but after a while, someone called him, and he shimmied between the gun racks and leapt out the back. We were the three guarding this truck now. Just us.

It wasn't long before the truck's engine roared to life. It pulled out of the lab's garage, along with the other two trucks, and someone slammed the back down and locked it. Once in the dark, I switched on my tiny flashlight.

Being locked in the truck was fine. We had rifles. We could exit this vehicle whenever we wanted.

A twinge of guilt gnawed at me. Justin would be fine, wouldn't he? No turning back now, though.

"This wasn't in the plan, either," Gascoigne quipped. She kept her voice low, and the rumble of our truck almost masked her words entirely.

"Like I said, this is an evolving plan." I pointed to the front of the truck, where the cab was. "Once we're away from the lab, we're going to take out the driver, and then take out the other two trucks."

"We're taking all this," Brecht said, motioning to the supplies.

"That's right."

Gascoigne chuckled. "Good."

"The third truck has some judge armor," I said.

Gascoigne nearly stopped breathing, excitement twinkling in her eyes. "No joke?"

"I'm certain the pilot will be in the truck as well." I shook my head. "But if we keep control of this truck, we might be able to outrun him."

That wasn't what Gascoigne wanted to hear. She cursed under her breath and threw up a single hand. "Why do *I* have to deal with this shit? Always me. *Always.*"

As our truck rumbled across the wasteland, the tension inside the vehicle grew palpable. I counted the seconds, trying to figure out how far we had traveled from the lab. I tried to remain vigilant, every bump and jostle of the road amplifying my unease.

Brecht rubbed his arm. "I would've rather fought the Chinese," he whispered.

"Heh," Gascoigne said with a huff. "I was just starting to like you. Don't get weak on me now."

The comment caused Brecht to redden in the face, and the two of them eyed each other for entirely too long.

"Everyone take a grenade," I said as I shoved the lid off one of the crates. "We'll need them."

Both did as I instructed.

The convoy of trucks raced its way forward, picking up speed, with only the sound of the gravelly crunch of tires on the rocky terrain as entertainment. It was almost time. I signaled the other two with a motion of my fingers. We exchanged nervous glances, Gascoigne's fingers itching to reach the trigger of her rifle.

Once I was certain we were far enough away, and the trucks had taken a turn, I signaled Brecht. He shot the back of the truck, destroying the lock, and then lifted the shutter door open. We were the lead vehicle. The driver of the second truck in the convoy stared at us with eyes so wide, his whites almost engulfed his irises.

The second and third trucks slowed, clearly wanting to distance themselves from us. Our truck continued to speed forward.

Where were we?

We had driven off the main roads and were now heading across scrubland. Rocks and dead plants dappled the landscape.

Gascoigne turned her rifle and fired at the driver's side of the cab, her bullets slamming through the metal of the truck, piercing the driver, and then shattering the windshield.

At first, our truck swerved erratically. The squeal of the tires, and the momentum, caught me off guard. I was slammed into a crate, and a rack of rifles collided with my hip. I cried out, but I wasn't too badly injured.

But then our truck came screeching to a halt. I assumed the corpse of the driver had a heavy foot and loved the brake, because everything lurched forward. Gascoigne and Brecht grabbed hold of whatever they could, but I was left to the whims of physics.

Not only did my hip hurt, but my arm was slammed up against the side of the vehicle.

"We need to get out of here," I shouted, my voice tense. "Hurry! Before the other trucks catch up."

Gascoigne and Brecht leapt out of the truck. They hit the rocky ground and then ran around the sides of the vehicle.

I glanced around, still confused by our location.

We were near a bridge. It had probably once been built to bypass a river, but now it was just a sad canyon of red rocks. The fall was at least twenty feet, and I was thankful our dead driver hadn't careened us all off the edge.

The second truck came barreling at us, though.

Clearly, it wanted to fix the driver's mistake and push us off the edge itself.

But Brecht didn't miss a beat. He pulled the pin on his grenade and threw it straight at the windshield. The resulting explosion of shrapnel was entirely too close; I heard the slam of metal in the dirt around us. I shielded my eyes, but peeped a moment later.

The second truck lost control completely, its tires screaming in protest as someone slammed on the brakes. The vehicle hit the side of the bridge, crashed through the metal railing, and then toppled over the edge, tumbling down into the rocky canyon. Sparks and dust filled the air. The third truck swerved to avoid us, but Gascoigne threw her grenade as well, causing them to spin out.

Instead of crashing into the canyon, the third truck maintained its course and parked in the middle of the bridge.

Three soldiers poured out of the vehicle. One ran to the back.

Two opened fire.

Gascoigne and Brecht returned it.

I ducked behind our vehicle, my shoulders bunched at the base of my neck. I had a rifle, but my body throbbed in agony. I needed a moment to recover. Unfortunately, a moment in combat felt like years.

Amid the mayhem, I peeked around the side of the truck. That was when I caught sight of the judge armor stepping out of the third truck. Perfect. I had been counting on that lunatic to fight us.

Brecht and Gascoigne covered me as I scrambled into the cab. Brecht managed to snipe one of the Iron-Blooded firing at us, and I counted all my blessings I had competent allies. Then I pushed the corpse of the driver aside and shouted, "Get in!"

With frantic movements, Brecht and Gascoigne hauled the corpse out of the cab as the Mark VI armor stood and then turned to face us. Bullets *plinked* across the outside of our stolen vehicle, and I flinched as I grabbed the steering wheel.

The judge armor was an intimidating beast, all gleaming metal and advanced weaponry.

"We're going to die," Brecht whispered as he snapped his seat belt tightly across his lap.

"Hang on." I reversed the truck.

The power armor marched toward us, each step of its heavy frame cracking portions of the road. Could our damaged truck outrun the machine?

"You have to keep firing at it," I said as the suit of armor picked up speed. "Use everything you have. Don't let up."

"*We can't fight it,*" Gascoigne shouted.

"I know. Just keep its attention. Aim for the helmet! *Anything.*" I floored the gas pedal and whipped the truck around.

CHAPTER NINETEEN

I sped away from the power armor. Gascoigne leaned out the passenger side window, and then hauled herself onto the top of the cab. What was wrong with her? I almost shouted at her to get back inside, but I had to focus on driving.

Brecht leaned out the window and fired his rifle, his bullets ricocheting off the Mark VI armor. It was like trying to take down a mountain with a handful of playing darts.

The enemy truck with only the one Iron-Blooded soldier flared to life and drove off after us, leaving the bridge and then hitting the dirt as fast as the electric engine could accelerate.

Our truck shook as I hit several shrubs, the thorns and branches smashing across the hood of my vehicle. Leaves and twigs flew into the cab, and I silently cursed the broken windshield.

The Mark VI pursued us—which was my intention—but with each *slam* of its run, my blood pressure went ever higher, to the point I thought I might pop.

We just had to keep it busy long enough for the batteries to drain. If the pilot used its plasma blade, all the better. But if the armor caught us—we were done for.

I weaved around a rock, and Gascoigne slid across the roof of the cab.

"Sorry," I whispered, though I knew she couldn't hear me.

Then Gascoigne started firing. I watched everything through the side mirrors, including the power armor and truck gaining on us. Her shots peppered the armor's helmet. Sparks flew from its metal exterior.

Brecht aimed at the enemy truck, and the Iron-Blooded driver returned fire.

More bullets *plinked* against the back of our vehicle. Some of our valuable cargo flew out and crashed across the wasteland. The Mark VI suit and the truck had to swerve to avoid a crate.

Then Brecht stopped firing. He just leaned out the window, took aim for a solid five seconds, and fired a controlled burst. The driver of the enemy truck lost most of his face, and the interior of his cab was painted a new shade of scarlet. The vehicle flew left and then crashed into a group of small boulders, its engine smashed.

Then the power armor caught us.

The suit reached for the back of the truck and grabbed part of the trailer. The strength of the suit caused the steering wheel in my hand to jerk, and I struggled to keep the vehicle going straight. Gascoigne fired at the helmet, relentless in her efforts. Even when she needed to reload, she did so with the practiced speed of a veteran.

My truck groaned under the strain, sparks bursting from the hood as it fought to maintain its speed.

The Mark VI suit held out an arm, and the plasma blade flared to life from the wrist. The bluish blast of superheated plasma was enough to illuminate the night. Its ominous hum of power drowned out the sounds of our truck struggling to accelerate.

The armor pilot slammed the blade into the side of the trailer and then dragged the blade down to the back tire. It exploded and my back axle basically melted. It was almost impossible to maintain the truck on a smooth course. We skidded to the side, but I refused to give up the vehicle.

I slammed on the gas and kept going, despite the truck's groaning and shaking.

"*What're you doing?*" Brecht shouted.

"Keep firing!" I motioned to the mirrors. "Keep it attacking us!"

Brecht, shaken, took a moment to reload his own rifle before leaning out the window. He fired in a wild manner, raining bullets across the side of the Mark VI. The pilot drew back his plasma blade, and then slammed it closer to the cab, as though trying to end Brecht. The heat was strong enough that *I* felt it from the driver's seat.

Brecht threw himself away from the window, his back hitting my side.

Gascoigne maintained her suppression fire from the top of the cab, and when the power armor drew back its arm a third time, I knew she was the target. Instead of continuing my forward path, I pulled the steering wheel as hard as I could in the direction of our ruined tire. The truck jerked all the way to the side, and Gascoigne slid off the top of the cab and hit the rocky terrain with a shout.

The power armor stumbled, and the truck almost toppled over. The sizzle of the plasma blade flying through the air was enough to cause the hair on the back of my neck to stand on end.

But then the blade sputtered and the plasma went out, leaving the suit with just a steel alloy blade.

The truck skidded to a stop and then every symbol known to man flashed across the dashboard. Something about maintenance, the engine, the temperature, and needing an oil change were all blinking furiously at me.

Brecht threw himself out of the cab, and I clumsily rolled out of the driver's side and onto the dirt. When I sprang to my feet, my heart pounding, I realized my plan had worked.

The Mark VI fell to one knee, and the suit *hissed* as it peeled open, revealing the pilot inside. This was standard procedure for whenever the batteries were drained—again, to prevent the pilot from getting locked inside.

"Brecht, get him," I shouted.

The man nodded to me and then ran over. The Iron-Blooded soldier inside was wearing the same black cargo pants and shirt as the rest of them, but he had no chest armor, likely because it wouldn't fit with him into the power armor. He slid out of the suit as Brecht drew near, and then he reached for something at his waist.

Brecht fired once.

The bullet grazed the man's hand. Blood splattered onto the Mark VI's leg, and the man shouted as he cradled his injured limb.

"*On the ground,*" Brecht said in Tethlite.

The command seemed to shock the pilot. He glanced at Brecht, and then the truck, before he decided to comply. With shaky movements, he got onto both knees and waited.

I ran across the desolate terrain, pushing aside shrubs, until I found Gascoigne. Wasn't too far from us, but I was worried about her.

"Gascoigne?" I asked as I ran to her side.

She was on the ground, resting on her side, one hand on her rifle and one hand on her hip. She glanced up at me with a sardonically disinterested expression. "Am I dead yet?" she quipped.

"Oh, thank goodness you're all right." I knelt next to her and patted her legs, fearing her bones were broken. "I'm sorry I threw you off like that. I was afraid you were going to get cut by the plasma blade. I, uh, panicked."

"Feh." She rolled her eyes. "Don't worry about me. I had most of my major organs quit on me at one point, and I'm still here. God has a cruel sense of humor."

"I'm *not* going to lose anyone else," I said, my tone betraying my desperation.

That must have resonated with her, because her face shifted into something neutral and a lot less uncaring. Gascoigne rubbed her hip, forced herself into a standing position, and then groaned when she took her first step.

"Fuck me," she muttered. After a long sigh, she added, "Why do I have to get old?"

I stood and patted the dirt away from my pants. "We should . . . we should get back. The power armor is ours, and if we have any supplies left in the truck, that's ours as well."

Gascoigne snorted, a genuine smile creeping onto her face. "Good. I need a new suit. Walking around in this disgusting body made of flesh only reminds me of my limitations. I crave the certainty of steel."

"This suit is mine," I said.

Although I knew Gascoigne wanted to regain her title of *judge* by donning a new suit of power armor, I refused to let her take this one. I needed it. Bishop had died for this armor, and there was still something I needed to do.

Gascoigne shot me a sidelong glance. Then she shrugged. "You promised I'd get one. I'll hold you to that. Eventually—I get one."

"You'll have one. But this one is mine."

"Fine."

She made no other arguments. Which was perfect.

Together, we walked around the shrubs and made our way back to our ruined truck. The blade holes and sparking engine were almost comical. The truck looked like it had been chewed on by a kaiju bear and then spit out onto the wasteland.

The Mark VI armor was still there, kneeling and open.

Brecht and the pilot stood a few feet from it. Brecht had the barrel of his rifle against the man's temple. The Iron-Blooded soldier kept his injured hand close to his chest. His handgun—which had probably been tucked into his waistband—was now in the dirt, a few feet from him.

"Thank you, Brecht," I said as I walked over. "Did this man say anything?"

"His name is Quern." Brecht pushed the tip of his rifle a little harder into the man's temple. "But he hasn't told me anything else."

Quern . . .

That was the same pilot who took Bishop in the first place.

I marched over to him, my anger returning like a slow simmer. I wanted to maintain my calm, but a flood of emotions was threatening to break through my willpower dam.

"*Quern,*" I said in Tethlite. I stood in front of him, and stared down to meet his gaze. "*Where did you take him?*"

"*Him?*" Quern repeated, his voice quieter than I had been expecting.

He was muscled, and his black hair was cut short on the sides of his head, but left longer on top. His darker skin matched his clothing well, but his eyes were lighter, which was intriguing, just because it was rare for someone of his complexion.

"*You took . . . someone . . . from the city outside of the air force base.*" I ran a shaky hand through my short hair. "*Where did you take him? Did you take him to the battery lab?*"

I needed this to be confirmed. I needed to know.

Quern slowly took in a breath and then exhaled. "*No, that's not where I take rail gang scum.*"

Rail gang?

There had been a rail gang there when Quern attacked. Had Bishop claimed to be with them?

My heart stopped beating for half a moment. Maybe Bishop was alive. Maybe. *Maybe.*

I knelt to get eye level with Quern. "*Where did you take him?*" I whispered, my hope blossoming into something that would fuel me all throughout the night.

I wasn't going to let Bishop down.

"*That isn't for you to know,*" Quern replied, icy and confident.

Brecht shoved his rifle harder into the side of his head. Quern didn't change his expression, though.

I stood, my hands shaky.

"What's going on?" Gascoigne asked in English. "All I hear when you speak that bizarre language is *slrp-slr-slrrp-slrrip-slrp.*" She sounded like someone sucking down spaghetti.

But before I could answer, I spotted three other vehicles heading in our direction. They weren't trucks—they were jeeps. It was difficult to see, but their headlights shone bright in the night, illuminating each other, and showing silhouettes of Iron-Blooded soldiers in all the vehicles.

"*Did you call for backup?*" I asked.

Quern smirked. "*You're fucked now, scum.*"

I turned my attention to the Mark VI. "We'll see about that . . ."

CHAPTER TWENTY

I hurried around the back side of the power armor. The spine casing was open, revealing red blinking lights around all the empty battery cells. I poked one, and with a harsh *chiss* noise, it popped out and hit the ground sizzling.

All the batteries were hot and spent. I poked the other two, and watched as they fell to the ground with the other.

Then I reached into my pants and withdrew the good batteries. Each of them had more than 80 percent of their energy left, and I slid them into the spine of the suit before hustling around the front.

Quern watched with a hard, and almost disbelieving, gaze. He clearly didn't think we were going to have access to his power armor.

After a long breath, I stepped up into the suit. When the suit was kneeling, the cockpit was like a throne. I sat in the chair, and leaned my head back. The connectors on my neck slid into position, and the suit did the rest. A harsh *click* rang in my ears as the suit fastened itself to my body.

I gritted my teeth as a harsh pulse shot through my system, like a shock of static electricity that went from my nose to the tips of my toes.

Then the suit jostled as power followed through all the limbs. I tucked my arms into the "sleeves" and then pushed my feet down into the legs of the suit. Soft padding tightened around me, holding me in place as the power armor hissed and closed, encasing me in pure technical power.

The helmet fitted itself over me, and the padding around my head tightened until there was no space left between me and the suit.

For a second, everything was black. Then the helmet flared to life, and I saw the world through a computer screen. I saw . . . everything.

The JUDGE-X0 exoskeleton highlighted the terrain, warning me of rocks, drop-offs, and uneven surfaces. A thermal scan told me the ambient temperature, and even highlighted Quern, Gascoigne, and Brecht. Another scan told me our truck's engine battery was rapidly draining of power.

The three jeeps were closing in, and the readout of my surroundings highlighted their approach.

The user interface for these power suits was so sleek and easy to see through, when I focused on the vehicles, I *just* saw the vehicles, but if I needed the numbers—like the approximate distance from me—I could focus on those instead.

"Welcome, Kita Yamasaki," a soft feminine voice spoke into my ear.

That startled me more than the shock of power from the connection.

"H-Hello?" When I spoke, my voice was projected to outside the power armor.

Gascoigne knocked on the leg of my suit. She was so short . . . I had never been up this high.

"What the fuck are you doing?" she shouted. "We have company. *Handle them.* Or else get out of the damn judge armor and let *me* deal with this mess."

The JUDGE-X0 suits didn't have firearms built into them. Instead, they were meant to hold oversized mortars, short-range missile launchers, and high-powered Gatling railguns. But those were all accessories I didn't have access to.

After I gulped down a breath, I took a step forward. The mere *thought* of walking caused the power armor to act. I stepped forward, and the readout on my helmet told me everything was functioning at near 100 percent.

"Oh, god," I whispered.

That wasn't blasted out to the world—it stayed within the suit.

"Your heart rate is elevating beyond normal levels," the same feminine voice said, her tone somewhat robotic. "This JUDGE-X0 unit history indicates this is your first time piloting this suit. Would you like to run through the tutorial?"

"No," I said.

The jeeps sped toward me and they opened fire on my truck. Gascoigne, Brecht, and Quern took cover behind the trailer. Well, Quern didn't go willingly—he was dragged into position by both Gascoigne and Brecht, both of whom seemed like they were trying to rip his arms out by the shoulder socket.

I took another step forward, and I realized the neural connectors in the back of my neck were sending my thoughts into the suit's computer. It was reading my movements before I even made them. And the computer—which had known my name—was somehow also gathering other information about me.

But at the same time, my head felt fuzzier and fuzzier.

All the JUDGE-X0 exoskeletons had a neural feedback loop that prevented the pilots from experiencing fear and extreme anxiety. It was to prevent the soldiers from cowering in the midst of high-powered combat, and with each passing second, my heart beat slower and I felt . . . excited.

Two of the three jeeps drifted by my feet. Again, it was odd being so high up. Looking *down* to view vehicles wasn't my natural state.

The third jeep came to a stop under me, and the three soldiers leapt out and used the jeep as cover. They thought I was on their side.

"*What're you waiting for?*" one of the Iron-Blooded shouted in Tethlite. "*Get them! We'll back you up.*"

I hated hearing their voices, and the suit's power over my thoughts seemed to amplify my rage. Bishop was in trouble. Why was I dealing with this?

"Would you like relaxing music?" the female voice asked.

"Yes," I said through gritted teeth.

"Accessing the local radio."

An upbeat melody started up, the tune straight to my ears. It was a lively song, something from before the Forever Winter, and after a deep breath, I lifted the leg of the power armor and slammed it down on the first Iron-Blooded soldier near me.

The suit was large, but not colossal. It did, however, weigh a few tons. The man was crushed under the sheer amount of weight focused on a single point—the heel of my stomp—and his insides squirted out of the seams of his clothes.

The other two Iron-Blooded whipped around, their faces contorted in sheer horror.

I punched down onto the second, and my steel alloy knuckles effortlessly broke the man's skull. If I hadn't been plugged into the suit—and my emotions manipulated by the programming—I probably would've been disturbed by how easily his skull shattered under the force of my blow.

But right now, I felt nothing.

The music picked up in joyful tune. Words entered the song.

> *Well, I met you in a soda shop, hair all neat,*
> *Your poodle skirt swaying to that jukebox beat!*

The third Iron-Blooded tried to run, but I stepped forward and used my right hand to punch him straight into the rocky terrain. He exploded like a ripe tick.

That was when I thought about the blade. The readout on my helmet blinked, and it seemed my mere thought was all it took to activate the weapon. The bluish-white plasma flared to life, creating a weapon unlike anything I had ever wielded before.

"Warning," the woman said in my ear. "Use caution."

"I will," I whispered in delight.

The music continued with its jolly tune.

> *You ordered a root beer float with extra sass,*
> *That's when I fell head over heels, oh what a gas!*

The two remaining enemy jeeps peeled out in their attempt to accelerate. Once their tires found traction, one sped toward the bridge, and the other back where it had come from. I chased the second—all it took was a thought. My suit started *running*, and I took in the information as quickly as I could, the environment becoming a blur in my peripherals.

It didn't take long for me to reach the vehicle. They fired their rifles at me the entire time, but the bullets did nothing.

I slammed my plasma blade down into the center of their jeep, cutting and melting my way through the frame. Then I sliced outward, completely cleaving through one of the Iron-Blooded, his dying scream cut off halfway through, like a TV suddenly switched to mute.

Without much care, I grabbed the driver and squeezed. The power armor tightened and squished the man's body between the cold metal fingers.

> *You're my sugar dumplin', my honey pie,*
> *My wonderful songbird, the twinkle in my eye!*

The final Iron-Blooded tried to run. He tried.

I jumped off the jeep and landed near him, the ground quaking from the weight of my armor, and the sheer force needed to move at such speed. The man fell over. He garbled out some sort of plea for mercy, his Tethlite barely coherent. With little concern, I lifted my blade arm up, and then crashed it down onto the man, burning through his armor, his flesh, his bones, and even the dirt and rock beyond him.

Within seconds, he was long past dead.

I stood and ended the plasma blade. For some reason, the helmet's display didn't have the suit's battery cell levels. I had to think about the batteries in order for the information to present itself. All three batteries currently had 73 percent left, and that fell in line with what I had learned about the Mark VI.

Too much plasma blade really would drain the suit.

The music ended as I turned around. The third jeep had driven away and never looked back. Probably a wise choice.

"Hello, late-night listeners," DJ Slam said over the radio, his voice distinctly different now that I was listening to him directly in my ear. "I hope you enjoyed that little number. It should set the mood for reading hour, if you know what I mean. I have spicy tales for all you night owls. One of the stories even features owls, because why not? Don't kink shame me."

I lifted my hand, the suit's arm touching the helmet from the outside. There was no amount of money or resources in this world that could convince me to listen to DJ Slam read erotica.

"*Turn it off*," I hissed.

The radio cut out. I took another deep, and calming, breath.

Then I walked over to the truck, my vision of our surroundings heightened thanks to the Mark VI. We had strayed away from the main highway, and this was some sort of backwater road, but the asphalt had mostly worn away, leaving a seemingly barren landscape behind.

Gascoigne stepped out from behind the truck. She snorted as she surveyed my devastation.

"Nice," she said.

That was it.

When I replied in a normal speaking voice, the suit broadcast my words to the outside world. "Thank you."

"Now what?" Gascoigne asked. "I'm sure these Iron-Blooded lunatics are gonna send more people. Eventually you're going to run out of juice. We need to find a charging station—or head back to Richfield."

It was odd "listening" to the sounds around me through the power armor. It was all filtered through an advanced sound system that eliminated any white noise or ambient sounds. Speech came through to my ear crystal clear—better than when I wasn't wearing the suit.

"First, we're going to get information out of Quern," I said.

I stomped my way over to the truck. Brecht waited there with our captive, and both men glanced up at me with slight fear in their eyes.

With slow movements, I strode over to Quern and then stopped next to him. "You're going to tell me where Bishop is being held. If not, I'm going to run a few experiments that all involve how much stress a human body can handle when being pulled apart by a suit of power armor."

CHAPTER TWENTY-ONE

We should just take Quern with us, Kita," Gascoigne said. "We're out in the open, and you're our crew's only overworked brain cell. We can't afford to have you busy."

I hated the idea of wasting even *more* time, especially since I had almost given up on rescuing Bishop. Why had I believed that random Iron-Blooded guard? I should've investigated more thoroughly.

I lifted the arm of the power suit with a mere thought, and then pointed. The second truck, the one that had slammed into a boulder, could potentially still run. If we transferred our goods to the back, including the Mark VI, we could drive back to Richfield.

Gascoigne followed my gesture and hustled over to the truck. While she yanked out the body of the dead driver, Brecht glanced over to me, his expression bordering on indignant.

"I'd like to think I'm also a functioning brain cell," he muttered.

Gascoigne managed to start the banged-up vehicle. The electric engine sparked as she reversed it away from the boulder and then drove toward us. Once she backed up the trailer to our ruined truck, she hopped out of the cab and began hauling crates from one vehicle to the other.

She stopped and then motioned me inside.

When I stepped into the truck, the whole vehicle groaned in protest, the metal screeching. The crash had banged it up bad, but the truck managed to hold together as I ducked down and slid into the trailer. I fitted the power armor inside, and then thought about leaving. The helmet flashed a red warning, and then everything unfastened.

The padding around my body loosened, the front opened up with a harsh *hiss*, and the spine casing around the batteries popped open with a *plink*.

It took me a moment to realize my body was now so much smaller. I hauled myself from the seat of the power armor, and the connecters on the back of my neck sprang free. Another static shock shot through my body. I shuddered and then rubbed my arms.

"That was amazing," I whispered.

Gascoigne, standing just outside the trailer, snorted back a laugh. "You'll get addicted. Trust me."

I rode in the trailer with Brecht and Quern. The truck shook with violent energy whenever we passed over so much as a pebble, but I preferred to stay close to the exoskeleton—and my enemy. I kept Quern's gaze for what felt like an hour of driving, our cramped trailer barely illuminated by my tiny flashlight.

It grew hot and almost humid, probably due to our breathing, but I pushed that from my mind. I didn't care.

Brecht had done a good job of restraining Quern. The Iron-Blooded soldier had his arms secured behind his back by metal wiring stolen from another truck. He sat with his back against the wall of the trailer, and Brecht inches from him, rifle at the ready. I sat against the opposite wall, one knee up, my fingers laced together in front of me, my body tense.

"*If you tell me what happened to my friend, we'll stop the vehicle and let you out,*" I said in Tethlite, keeping my eyes on Quern's. "*You can return to your architect in one piece.*"

Quern smirked. "*You can fuck off.*"

"*What's your cause?*"

"*To rebuild the world. Better than ever before. No wars. No fighting. Everyone has a place, and everyone in their place.*"

I tightened my grip on my hands, my fingernails digging into my knuckles. "That's my goal," I said in English. Then I shook my head and switched back to Tethlite. "*Architect Riven tried to abandon Earth. He's only staying because he has no other choice.*" I glared at Quern. "*So, forgive me—I don't trust that alien has his heart in this Plan B.*"

Quern must've known about the plan to leave because his expression shifted into something curious. He tilted his head to the side, and then the truck shook, and he almost fell over. Brecht slammed the barrel of his rifle into the man's side.

"Better than living a life of filth," Quern said as he straightened his posture. Then he spit in Brecht's direction, though the saliva never touched the other man. *"The Teth still have a wealth of information. Once their A-tech is assembled, we'll rebuild better than ever—while you all fight over the trash that rots in the sands of the Mojave."*

"We'll see who does it first, then," I said, my mind on the underground greenhouses. With a defiant glare, I stared at the trailer floor. "Because Architect Riven doesn't know Earth like us humans, and I intend to beat him to the punch."

Quern didn't reply.

Which was fine. He was an idiot—nothing more than a brainwashed puppet.

"I'm going to assemble my own Teth," I said. *"And we'll grow larger than Riven ever will."*

My last statements seemed to confuse Quern again. He hadn't been expecting my proclamations. To be honest, I wouldn't have believed me a few years ago, either.

The truck rumbled and shook, but this time everyone was tossed around. My shoulder was slammed into the Mark VI, and Brecht had to brace himself in the corner of the trailer. Then the truck just . . . stopped. We lurched forward, and Quern hit the floor face-first. I almost laughed. Almost.

A few moments later, and the back trailer door was flung up and open. Gascoigne stood there, her lips curled in a silent snarl. She glanced between us and then snapped her fingers.

"The damn engine is having issues. We'll be lucky if this jalopy makes it a few more miles."

I scooted across the floor of the truck and slipped out the back. After brushing myself off, I thought back to our travels here. There had been a medical complex infested by members of a rail gang. I had thought we would need to avoid the place, but perhaps we could use it to our advantage.

"Do you remember when we drove by the rail gang?" I asked Gascoigne. "Do you think you could get us back there?"

"Why?" she snapped.

"Because I think we should . . . take the train."

Gascoigne chuckled after that comment. When she smacked my shoulder, I almost toppled over. "Fine. We'll hijack ourselves a train. But first, you should blow the brains out of our captive. We can't keep dragging around a vulnerability. And *fuck* those Iron-Blooded lunatics."

I agreed with her sentiments, but I needed Quern's information. Then I glanced down at my clothing. We still wore Iron-Blooded armor, and now we even had one of their vehicles. That got me thinking about how I could use this to advantage. Could we use their radio? Could we call someone within the Iron-Blooded using their tech?

What had Quern said to me?

He hadn't taken Bishop to the battery lab—because that wasn't where he took *rail gang scum*. Which implied the Iron-Blooded took the gang members somewhere else. Perhaps somewhere specific.

"I have an idea," I whispered, my tone hopeful.

"You're going to blow his brains out with a nail gun?" Gascoigne quipped.

"W-What? No. Just . . . watch them. I'm going to investigate the truck."

She nodded and took a position near the truck. I hurried to the front of our dilapidated vehicle and hauled myself up into the cab. The radio had seen better days. It was a steel box with bronze accents, fitted perfectly into the vehicle's dashboard. Classic knob dials had been added to the radio to give an older aesthetic, but everything was scuffed and faded.

But this antique-looking radio wasn't the prize. Underneath it was some sort of A-tech communicator, complete with a tiny touch screen. It blended with the steel of the radio, and was easily overlooked, especially since it was a small, hand-sized piece of tech.

These communicators were meant to stay connected to similar devices, typically on a protected network. It likely used Tethlite to operate, making them useless to normal humans who didn't know the alien language.

Thankfully, I wasn't normal.

When I poked at the communicator, the screen blinked red. A sign for a fingerprint lit up, and I held my breath.

This device would only turn on for a registered member of the Iron-Blooded.

Good thing we had one in the back.

I leaned out the window. "Gascoigne," I called out.

She walked over, her rifle held at the ready. "We shouldn't stay here long." Then she eyed me. "What do you need?"

"I need one of our captive's thumbs." I met her gaze, and with our silent look, I told her I was dead serious. "Bring it to me real quick, won't you?"

CHAPTER TWENTY-TWO

The screams of fully grown men bothered me more than others. Anything that could elicit such a pained wail from a hardened combatant was obviously something I should fear, and the deep, primal, animalistic part of my brain told me I should avoid it at all costs.

So I sat patiently in the truck's cab, staring out the broken windshield, my heart beating harder with each strangled sob. I actively thought about turning on the radio and listening to DJ Slam's rendition of the *devil's tango* rather than the horrors of torture, but thankfully, it ended quickly.

Gascoigne came sauntering up to the driver's side door. Her Iron-Blooded uniform was wet with blood, but the black material made it difficult to tell. When she reached my window, she handed over a severed thumb. She had sawed into the palm, creating a bloody stump of a finger that resembled a raw chicken wing.

With a shaky hand, I took Quern's thumb. The hot, sticky vital fluids upset my stomach. I held back a gag as I pressed the severed finger against the communicator screen. Once the A-tech had scanned Quern's fingerprint, the device flickered to life.

People were already speaking on the other end.

"And then we lost contact with the transport," someone said in Tethlite. *"Reinforcements are on their way to investigate. The innovator wants as many details as possible."*

"Send warriors. We'll cover more ground."

"We'll relay your suggestion."

Then the communicator went silent. The screen still shone with information, so I knew there were still Iron-Blooded listening on the other end, but they had nothing more to discuss.

I decided to test my new plan—tricking them into giving me Bishop's location.

My second rule of lying? Make a simple statement without too many details. People will always fill in the holes with their imaginations.

"*A rail gang attacked while we were en route,*" I said in Tethlite, using my most masculine soprano. "*We took captives. Please advise.*"

I tried to mimic the matter-of-fact tone the other Iron-Blooded had used in their brief conversation. If this didn't work, I'd just shut off the communicator and try something else, but I kept my fingers crossed and my breath held, hoping they would give me what I wanted.

"*Take all rail gang captives to the work camp,*" someone answered back, almost irritated. "*The quarry near the Valley of Fire.*"

The Valley of Fire sounded like a mythical location straight out of a fantasy novel, but I knew the truth. It was once a park—some sort of national park for the old-world government. From my recollection, several sand mines and rock quarries had been created around it, since the minerals in the area were so prevalent.

Were the Iron-Blooded using the old rock quarries? Had they taken rail gang captives there to work?

If they had, that was where Bishop was right now.

I practically laughed as I said, "*Roger.*"

Then I switched off the communicator and turned to Gascoigne. She was busy wiping the blood from her outfit. She turned to me with a lifted eyebrow. "Well?"

"Did Quern say anything?" I asked. "When you were, uh, chopping off his thumb? About the captives, I mean."

"He said *slrrp-slrr-AAAA-slrrr-AAHHH.*" Gascoigne comically flailed one hand around. Then she snorted back a chuckle and narrowed her eyes into a sadistic glare. "I just assumed he was begging me to stop, but if you want, I can ask the other alien-speaking chump if those slurps and gargles meant anything important."

"N-No. That's fine. We don't have to discuss it. I think I have all the information I need."

"Where to?"

I motioned to the south. "We're still going to take the train. Just south.

To the Valley of Fire. Then we're going to raid a rock quarry and get Bishop back."

Gascoigne laughed once. Then she rubbed her eyes and shook her head. "Damn. You and your *ever-evolving plans*. Do you hear yourself sometimes? This was a smash-and-grab rescue mission up until it turned into a whole desert raid."

"I won't be stopped," I whispered. Then I met her gaze. "Are you with me?"

Gascoigne, like Bishop, seemed to like it more when I was serious. She didn't flinch or back down. "I'm with you. But I'm driving. Scoot over."

"Tell Brecht to load Quern back up in the trailer first."

"You don't want to do it?"

I rubbed my neck and half shrugged. "I don't want to see the damage. I'd rather that stay in my imagination."

"Tsk." Gascoigne turned away and headed for the trailer. "Weak."

Gascoigne managed to drive our broken truck for another couple miles. It sputtered and complained the entire way, worse than an old man trying to run up a steep hill. It rocked back and forth no matter how smooth the terrain, and after a few minutes, my head ached.

When Gascoigne parked, we hopped out of the back and were greeted by the dim light of morning. Only the strongest and most determined of sunbeams broke through the overcast skies, and I found myself smiling when I spotted the distant dentist's office tucked away in the medical complex.

Beyond that, parked at a commercial railway, was a small train. It was the type made from A-tech—machinery that would live through any apocalypse. It was an electric engine with one passenger car, and one boxcar attached to the back. The passenger car had most of the windows boarded up, and obviously belonged to a more commercial train before being scavenged.

The engine and boxcar were black and industrial gray, whereas the passenger car was sleek and faded white. They only matched due to the numerous bullet holes along the side of each one.

Gascoigne adjusted the side mirror until the reflection showed the shadow of someone hidden behind a rusted car in the far parking lot. "Our rail gang buddies are still here," she drawled. "Lucky us."

"I'm going to get into the exoskeleton." I gave her a long look, wondering if she would protest. When Gascoigne said nothing, I added, "I think you should wait here, with Brecht, and watch our stuff."

"Whatever you say, boss."

I didn't like the way she said the last word, but now wasn't the time for arguments. Everyone was tired. We had already fought our way through a group of Iron-Blooded lunatics. Now we had to fight our way to a train through a group of gangers. Life wasn't fair, but I wasn't about to give up now.

I stepped out of the cab and walked around to the back of the truck. With a heft and a grunt, I threw open the trailer door.

Brecht and Quern were still in the back. Quern had seen better days. He was dappled in a cold sweat, his own blood smeared across most of his clothes and the floor of the trailer. He took in shaky breaths.

His hand—the one missing a thumb—was wrapped in some of Brecht's shirt.

"What's going on?" Brecht asked.

"Get out of the way." I motioned for him to exit the vehicle. "I have idiots to deal with."

Brecht didn't question me. He hauled Quern to his feet and dragged the other man out of the truck. Together, they stopped a few feet from my location, and then turned around to watch. I climbed into the trailer, went straight to the JUDGE-X0 exoskeleton, and climbed inside. Once the neural connectors snapped into the port on the back of my neck, I embraced the tingle of the static shock that rippled through my body.

Nothing tasted as sweet as raw power.

As the JUDGE-X0 armor fitted around me, tucking me safely into the depths of its cold steel, I tried to imagine the look on Bishop's face when we finally rescued him. What would he say? Would he happily say my name? Make a quip? I wanted him here with me. Building this underground facility, and new world, and empire, seemed pointless if I couldn't keep the people I valued close to me at all times.

"Welcome, Kita Yamasaki," the computer inside the power armor said, the sweet feminine voice dragging me back to the present.

"Hello," I whispered. Then I thought about climbing out of the back of the truck, and the suit flared to life, complying with all my inner demands.

"Would you like to take the tutorial now?" the feminine computer asked.

"Is it quick?"

"This state-of-the-art power armor is intuitive to use and requires little training to master."

With a smile, I nodded. "All right, give me the tutorial."

"Please, move forward."

I stepped out of the vehicle and stood, at least eleven feet tall, maybe more, and hardened myself to the reality.

I was going to kill so many members of this rail gang, it would almost be considered a tragedy.

Then I walked forward, the stomp of my power armor alerting the gangsters to my presence. Several of them popped out of rusted vehicles, or leapt out of shattered windows around the medical complex. They all had rifles or handguns, but each one of them glanced down at their firearm and seemed to make some sort of silent calculation that it wouldn't do them any good in this situation.

They were probably right.

I slammed my steel alloy foot onto the parking lot and headed straight for the buildings. The general practitioner's office was the largest, and it had the most people swarming out of it, like a beehive that had just been smashed on the ground.

The early morning light glinted menacingly off the metal plates of my exoskeleton, and I imagined I looked like something that had stepped right off an old-world propaganda poster. *Join now! Get your own JUDGE-X0 armor!*

One of the rail gangers, more audacious than the rest, fired a single shot. The bullet bounced harmlessly off my armor with a metallic *plink*, then embedded itself into the asphalt.

It was some older man in the window of the doctor's office. He held his rifle with two shaky hands. "Fire!" he shouted. "*Fire!*"

"Your exoskeleton armor is reinforced and more defensive than your average USA tank," the computer said in a cheery tone. "Most mounted anti-tank rifles do not have the power necessary to pierce your outside fortifications."

"Thank you," I muttered. "I'll keep it in mind."

Then I ran. I went straight for the doctor's office and *smashed* through the already busted wall. When I collided with the shooter, I was pretty sure he died upon impact.

"What the fuck is going on?" someone screamed. "Bring it down! *Bring it down!*"

I stepped out of the rubble and cloud of debris, my helmet giving me a readout of the area, even if I couldn't physically see. There were thirty people here. I never would've guessed that. How large were these rail gangs? How were they feeding all their members? Or were they just stealing everything from every small town along the tracks?

Someone, a younger man, leapt out into the parking lot and hefted an RPG—a rocket-propelled grenade—onto his shoulder. He loaded the RPG and then aimed it straight at me.

I wasn't fast enough to dodge. Perhaps the power armor was, but I wasn't used to piloting such a large piece of equipment. The unguided grenade shot straight at me and then exploded, the resulting *bang* muffled by the suit's protective systems.

"As you can see, your power armor is still fully operational," the computer said.

The connectors in the back of my neck kept me integrated with the power armor's programs that suppressed fear and replaced it all with rage. The readout across the inner portion of my helmet told me little damage had been done—confirming the little computer voice's statement—so while the man was reloading his RPG, I lunged.

With one brutal jump, I basically landed on the man, crushing him, and his weapon, in one fatal blow. His insides splattered across the broken asphalt, and the *plink* of bullets rained across me as I turned to face the medical complex a second time.

The remaining members of this ambitious rail gang had set up defensive positions on the roofs of the nearby buildings. They sprayed me with bullets while others gathered up mounts for larger—and heavier—weaponry.

"Would you like a refresher on how the neural connecters on the back of your neck interface with the power armor?" the computer asked.

"Nope. I'm having too much fun."

My enemies didn't run for the train. It probably would've taken too long to fire up, and then even longer for it to gain speed. If they all piled on, it would just mean they would die faster—and all together.

With every step, the weight of the JUDGE-X0 pressed deep into the concrete. The smaller gangsters panicked, some running, others dropping their rifles and raising their hands in surrender. But not all were so quick to bow out. A few daring souls shot out from a nearby building, each of them riding an eclectic dirt bike. They were painted red and yellow, and had Xs across the side.

They revved their engines and circled me, no doubt attempting to find an opening or weakness.

They had speed on their side now, which wasn't a bad start. Then two of them withdrew nets from their packs, and I knew what they wanted to attempt.

The *shock nets* were A-tech designed to take down electric vehicles, and used before the Forever Winter by police during high-speed chases. The nets were thrown over something metallic, and the surge of electricity typically shut down the engine for a short period of time, at least according to all the educational vids I had watched.

These gangsters wanted to throw their nets on me and see if they would stop the power armor from functioning.

"Will a short blast of electricity harm the suit?" I asked the computer.

"No," the feminine voice sweetly replied. "The Mark VI onboard electronics are insolated from external electrical discharges."

The two bikers circled close, and since I wasn't the most agile, I just allowed them to throw their nets across the legs of my suit. A flash of power filled the parking lot as their devices exploded with pent-up electricity.

CHAPTER TWENTY-THREE

Nothing happened to me.

I kicked out a leg, caught one of the bikes, and caused it to flip over in dramatic fashion, sending the rider into the asphalt. His buddies sped into his ruined bike, and his body, and spun out of control. When one tried to drive off, I sprinted in his direction, caught up—much to my own surprise—and tore through the metal frame of his tiny vehicle.

The man's body didn't stand a chance.

If I hadn't been in the power armor, I probably would've felt revulsion or a twisting sense of guilt, but the suit stopped all that. All I saw were enemies.

"Heart rate increasing," the suit said. "Would you like music?"

"No," I replied in a heavy breath.

I just had to end this. We needed a train. As soon as I secured the area, I could step out of the power armor and become myself again.

Someone threw a smoke grenade. Normally, that would be a major problem. Most of these bastards filled the grenades not only with smoke, but with caustic chemicals that burned a person's throat and lungs, sometimes to a fatal degree.

But most models of the JUDGE-X0 exoskeletons had vents and air filters. Even as a blossom of smoke filled the medical complex, I had nothing to fear. If anything, the rail gang were hurting themselves. My helmet highlighted multiple people who took off running in all directions once the smoke wafted over them.

I grabbed onto the roof of a nearby building and pulled myself out of the dark haze of smoke. With all my attention on my enemies, I leapt from the doctor's office over to the dentist's. With a terrible *crash*, and another wave of debris mixing into the caustic chemical smoke, I slammed through the roof and fell into a room with torture-device chairs and rusted tools that were decades old.

Anyone I hit with my power armor didn't stand a chance. They fired their rifles, and tried to run, but I swung my hand out and hit a man so hard, I took a chunk of flesh from his back.

"Run! *Run!*"

The screaming was intense, but I didn't care. The power armor kept me focused.

I killed three more before crawling out of the dentist's lobby, the Mark VI covered in a fresh coat of crimson paint.

Now I looked like a poster from the enemy nation—a propaganda photo about the horrors of war.

I had never felt so powerful before. No matter what they tried, the thugs couldn't do anything to me. All they could do to save their lives was flee. And they did so in dramatic fashion. Some hopped on bikes, others went running. A few of them leapt into sewer tunnels and made their way underground.

I let them go.

Their deaths weren't necessary. I just needed their train.

So, once the readout on my helmet said there weren't any more people in the nearby area, I strode over to the tracks. They weren't far from the medical center, and had once been part of a commercial hub for moving people from a larger city to a smaller shopping area.

The train engine, along with the passenger car, and the boxcar, were just waiting for me. I smiled to myself inside the suit, but I realized I missed the loud music playing while I went through my dance of destruction.

"Next time," I said.

While I still had my suit on, I walked back over to the truck. Brecht, Gascoigne, and Quern all stared up at me, each of them with mixed levels of shock. Quern seemed like he was on the edge of fainting, but I didn't care as much about him. Instead, I grabbed the supplies we had stolen from the Iron-Blooded, and threw them onto my shoulder.

The power armor made transporting heavy objects, like steel crates filled with guns and ammunition, an effortless task. I walked from the truck to the train and back to the truck half a dozen times, and I never felt tired or even stressed. While my body went through the motions of walking—all the way across the parking lot, and the medical complex, and then to the train—I wasn't carrying any weight. The suit did all the real work for me.

On the last trip, we abandoned the truck and headed as a group to the strange train.

Gascoigne went to the conductor's room while Brecht hauled Quern into the passengers' seating area.

I, alone, went to the boxcar. The Mark VI fit into the back, and despite its heavy nature, the train didn't crumble under me. Once I managed to squeeze myself inside, I thought about leaving the power armor, and everything *hissed* as it opened up to allow me out.

For some reason, once the connectors on the back of my neck detached, I grew paranoid.

I walked around to the back of the armor and unplugged the battery cells. Without these, the suit couldn't function. I stuffed them into my cargo pants and then left the suit where it was.

My muscles ached from earlier skirmishes, even if the exoskeleton had carried most of my burdens. I rotated my arms and allowed the fog over my mind to clear as I headed to the engine. Gascoigne was there, poking away at the computer controls, her face twisted in irritation.

"Everything okay?" I asked as I entered the narrow control room. It was meant for a single person, and only had two computer screens to monitor the engine.

"This is a piece of shit," Gascoigne muttered.

"Do you know how to, uh, operate it?" I hadn't considered this part of the plan.

"Of course," she said, curt. "Ex Cathedra runs these types of trains to the border all the time. Supplies, supplies, supplies. I must've been part of the run a dozen times."

"So what's wrong?"

She shot me a glare. "You think these rail gang lackwits take care of their toys? Of course not. Give me a second. I'll get it started, and then we're out of here before those assholes come back to steal it from us."

Could someone steal what was originally theirs?

I didn't voice the comment. Instead, I jumped out of the train, walked over to the passenger car, and then stepped up the stairs and into the seating area.

Quern's blood had dripped across the floor all the way to where he was seated with Brecht. When I approached, both men glanced up.

"Are we ready?" Brecht asked.

I nodded once and then sat down across the aisle from the two men. What would Bishop say here? Something snarky and funny. I didn't have the energy to emulate him. Instead, I turned my attention to the land-scape—and the ever-growing morning that attempted to pierce through the clouds.

The glass across all the passenger car windows was surprisingly clean. Well, for the windows that still had glass. The places where they had shat-tered had been boarded up.

Our trek began with a jolt as the train *clonked* and *sputtered*. Then we rolled backward, only settling into a rhythmic cadence of wheels clacking on metal tracks after several minutes. Every clank and groan of the A-tech machinery reminded me that this had been built during better times, before the world had succumbed to chaos.

If I made a new civilization, I would need to focus on constructing transportation.

I couldn't wait for someone else to do it.

It had to be me.

Outside, the vast desert expanses, once golden, were now a muted gray, speckled here and there with shadows of their past life. The sagebrush, a symbol of the relentless spirit of this desert, still clung to life. Nothing would kill that plant, not even an apocalypse.

"Are you all right, Kita?" Brecht asked. He kept his rifle in his lap, but he didn't have it pressed against Quern's head anymore.

I slowly turned my head, my neck aching. Although I wanted to see Bishop, I longed for rest.

"I'm just admiring the landscape." Then it occurred to me—this was all new to Brecht. "How do you like being here? On the surface, I mean?"

Brecht chanced a glance out the window, and then averted his gaze. He scratched his chest as he replied, "It's beautiful, but far different than I expected. Well, except for the mountains."

"The mountains?"

"They're timeless sentinels. From old photos, to how they are now. They never change, even in the face of utter destruction. It fills me with hope whenever I think about them like that." Brecht exhaled. Then he met my gaze. "And we're heading to your mate now?"

My face heated. "Why do you really need to keep using that word? *Mate?* Did humans in your underground facility really do that?"

"Like I told Justin, that's how all the Teth referred to it." Brecht shrugged. "They found human intimacy to be strange and hilarious, both. Teth take on groups of mates, based on their caste. And everyone is intimate with the architect, or at least nearby the architect."

I was aware. But I didn't stop Brecht from explaining. He seemed like he needed to talk. Loneliness killed people more than bullets sometimes.

"Does Vega like to be around humans?" I asked, curious about the warrior Teth.

Brecht nodded. "Yes. Vega has been a protector for years, and enjoys the role. It was bred into the warriors, or so Vega tells me."

"Do you think it's possible for the Teth to live in human cities? Or will we need to create separate, but equal, districts?"

I didn't want the latter situation, but perhaps Brecht could provide me with some insight into the aliens. I had never lived with them like he had.

"We all lived together in Facility Twenty-Six," he said. "It was peaceful. We never had to separate, even if it became odd at points. The fact the Teth can't see does make things a struggle, but we managed."

"And you enjoyed living side by side with them?" I asked.

Brecht nodded once. "The Teth have a unique view on the world. They're cooperative. I trained to fight the CCP alongside the Teth, but we never considered ourselves different. We were American first, and humans or aliens second."

American?

That was the term those in the United States of America used for themselves. My grandfather loved being American. He said it was the cure for division—all being one people. The Teth liked that. Of course they did— they were a hive species.

I wished my grandfather were still alive. He would've known the best way to integrate humans and Teth.

"Did you have, uh, a mate?" It felt so awkward asking it that way.

Brecht shook his head. "No."

The door at the far end of the passenger car opened. Gascoigne slipped through and into the sitting area before shutting the door behind her. With a long exhale, she sauntered over to us, her expression aggressively neutral.

"What're you doing?" Brecht asked, panic in his voice. "Who's driving the train?"

"The onboard computer," Gascoigne snapped. Then she snorted out a laugh. "Did you think a person has to be there watching it the whole time? Did you think I was yanking levers and pulling on the whistle the whole time?"

Brecht's cheeks flushed a slight pink. He ran a hand down his face, clearing dirt and sweat, and hiding some of his embarrassed expression. "I'm unfamiliar with trains."

"Obviously."

Gascoigne approached him, and then stood a little too close. Brecht glanced up, his head about level with her hips, considering he was sitting and she was standing.

With a smirk, she asked, "You want me to show you how to operate this big, powerful piece of machinery?"

"I . . ." Brecht swallowed some air and then gestured to Quern. "I would love to—but I need to watch our guest of honor."

"Throw him out the train. We don't need him."

She was right. If Bishop was at the quarry, I no longer needed any information from Quern. We could separate ourselves from him, and in brutal fashion. Besides, if the roles were reversed, Quern would've had no problem killing or enslaving us all.

"*Can you speak English?*" I asked in Tethlite.

Quern glanced over, his face dripping with a feverish sweat. His hands were still secured behind his back, and his left hand dripped blood onto his seat at a slow, but steady, rate.

"*Of course I can*," he muttered.

Well.

This was awkward.

Brecht's expression shifted to something disturbed. Clearly, like me, he thought that Quern didn't understand what we were saying whenever we were speaking English in his presence. But this man—an enemy soldier— had just been listening.

And while that could be a problem in some instances, this wasn't one of them. We hadn't really discussed much that we wouldn't want our enemies knowing. If anything, we probably came off as unhinged and lacking overall structure to our plans. But still, it was unsettling. Quern had kept that bit of knowledge to himself, and if I hadn't thought to ask, he'd still be listening in.

"Why are you two so quiet?" Gascoigne snapped. "Can we just throw the man out of the train or not? He's already leaking blood like a broken sink. At this rate, he'll be dead by morning."

CHAPTER TWENTY-FOUR

I stood from my seat. "I don't think we should throw Quern off."

"You just don't want to kill someone," Gascoigne muttered. With a roll of her eyes that almost looked painful, she threw herself onto the seat next to Brecht. Then she kicked up one leg and rested it on the seat cushion of another chair. "It's why you didn't kill me when you had the chance. You get this soft look in your eyes."

I scratched at my scalp and then smoothed my short hair. After a long moment, I sighed. "Well, even if that's the case, I don't want to do it."

Brecht patted his rifle. "Then don't. I'll watch him."

"He's *bleeding to death*," Gascoigne repeated, her tone all sarcasm. "I swear, it's like you're pretending I'm not here spouting facts."

All the Iron-Blooded had nanites in their system. That was how they got their clunky name, after all. Yet Quern still bled, despite the tiny machines in his blood stream and their sole purpose of patching him up whenever his body sustained too much damage.

Which meant he needed medical attention before the nanites could complete their thankless duties.

I glanced around. The train car rumbled and shook as we went over the old tracks, but it wasn't so bad that I couldn't walk around. "This train might have a first aid kit." No one else said anything. They didn't want to get up and look—so I would have to do it.

I strode up and down the passenger car, and then decided to glance under every seat. The coppery tang of blood filled my nostrils. A crimson pool had formed beneath Quern's seat, and I stepped around it as I searched.

It was difficult to imagine this train car used to carry actual people. Everything seemed eerie now. When I glanced up into the luggage compartments, I actually found a few small bags and handful of children's toys. People had used this train car decades ago, but now they were nothing more than ghosts, and their old belongings haunted the corners of this space.

The cushioned seats bore the signs of hasty departures. Tears. Stains. A few crumpled-up papers.

But no first aid kit.

"You can check the engine car," Gascoigne stated.

I sighed as I headed for the door. When I opened it, hot wind blew into the train. I shielded my eyes, walked the unprotected walkway to the engine car, and then shut the door behind me.

The conductor's room was small, but there was a small waiting area outside of it, complete with a little table, a chair, and a place to hang a schedule.

"Come on, come on," I muttered to myself.

Why did I want to save Quern's life? Again, I thought about Bishop. If I couldn't save people, what was the point? I wanted to make a better life, and I couldn't be stopped by simple problems. I had to overcome.

Also, Quern's blood loss was straight up my fault. Guilt ate at me. Perhaps I just wanted to torture him for hurting Bishop—and I didn't like that dark side of myself.

This train really was in shambles, though.

Broken glass and mold filled the corners of the room.

Desperation threatened to overwhelm me, but I fought it back. Taking a deep breath, I entered the conductor's room and glanced at the computer screens. Gascoigne had entered our destination, and the A-tech had taken over everything else. It even had an estimate for our arrival: three hours.

That wasn't so bad, but it seemed we would need to take several tracks. Thankfully, the A-tech railway could switch the tracks itself, but eventually we would arrive at a train station close to the Valley of Fire.

For a moment, I almost wanted to thank those rail gangs . . . almost.

Then I spotted it.

There, mounted on the wall by the door, was a white box with a red cross on it. A surge of relief washed over me. I grabbed the box and accidentally ripped it open, scattering its contents across the conductor-room floor. Bandages, saline liquid, scissors, and an emergency flare all bounced around the dirty environment. I grimaced as I knelt and gathered everything into my arms.

It was all old, and some of the bandages were stiff, but that didn't matter. I needed all of this.

My thoughts briefly went to my satchel . . . and to Justin and our buggy. He was still waiting for us. We probably wouldn't be back for a day or two. Perhaps he would drive back to Richfield, but if he didn't, he would be upset.

Thankfully, the buggy had plenty of food and water.

Justin would be fine.

Once I had all the medicinal supplies in my arms, I headed back to the passenger car. I walked in, allowing the hot air to rush by me, and then closed the door before heading over to Quern.

"*What kind of fucked-up game are you playing?*" he asked in Tethlite. "*You tore up my hand and now you want to bandage it?*"

I sat on the chair next to him. "Would you rather get thrown out of the train?" I asked in English, no mirth in my tone. This was a serious question. If he wanted to die, that would be a lot easier on us. And Gascoigne was itching to chuck him straight out the nearest window.

Quern didn't answer me.

That was fine. I set all the contents of the first aid kit on another chair, and then cut the wires holding his wrists. Brecht stood from his seat and held his rifle at the ready. Gascoigne watched from her seat, content not to move. This probably amused her.

Quern held out his injured hand, and I unwrapped the gore-soaked cloth around his gash where his thumb used to be. Blood wept from his wound, and Quern took in ragged breaths.

"I know a doctor," I said as I used a cleaning liquid to pat down the injury. Did saline solution expire? I didn't know. I hoped not.

Thankfully, Quern had no exposed bone. That would make his recovery faster, at least. I cleaned the injury as best as possible, and then rewrapped the injury using medical tape, gauze, and Cellucotton. From what I could remember of my first aid training, missing toes and fingers could heal gradually, and required careful attention.

"We'll wash it again in a few hours," I said. "If there's any sign of dying flesh, we'll need to cut it off."

Quern said nothing. His paling skin and sweat told me he might be going into shock, but he still seemed rather sharp.

"Do you mind if I ask you a question?" I asked in Tethlite.

He eyed me and then shook his head.

"Why serve the Teth? Why not fight for humanity? Or at least, work along-side the Teth as equals? You don't need to answer to an architect."

"Humanity is the reason the world is like this," Quern said, his words so quick, and so practiced, it seemed as though he may have repeated them hundreds of times before. *"Humanity fucked up this world, so we clearly shouldn't be in charge of it again."*

I shook my head as I packed away the rest of the medical supplies. Part of me wished I had our antibiotics. *"It wasn't humanity. It was the aliens. The Teth and the Vay had issues long before they came to Earth—and they brought all their problems with them."*

"That's just lies they tell you. Forty-nine years ago, human soldiers in Caracas launched a firestorm warhead aimed for coordinates twenty-five point seven north, eighty point two west. Before the warhead even touched down, three were fired in response, and then the cascade happened. If not for the United States and its alliance, versus the CCP and its alliance, we wouldn't be in this mess."

But he was wrong.

"That's not true," I stated. *"That firestorm technology was leaked to the Vay—from one of the Teth. The war we fought was because of their architects. They helped make the alliances. They wanted us in conflict. The Vay wanted to eradicate the Teth. They already got rid of the third faction of aliens."*

"Third faction?"

I lifted an eyebrow. *"The Frest."* When he said nothing in response—he just stared blankly—I held back a chuckle. *"For someone who knows a whole bunch about the war, I'm surprised you didn't know about the Vay wiping out the Frest. Maybe you should speak to Architect Riven and get all the facts."*

Quern hesitated for a moment. *"The history books I was shown told of humanity's many great wars. I was taught it was in our nature to destroy."*

I was surprised Quern said everything with such conviction. No won-der the Iron-Blooded generally detested other humans. They were all told the same lies.

"I really hope you learn the truth one day," I whispered in English as I met his gaze. "Maybe humanity has gone to war, but we've also built great things. And it wasn't *us* who developed those warheads. They're A-tech through and through."

"I can't believe you," Gascoigne muttered.

I glanced over. "What?"

"Stop talking to him. Just tie him back up and get some rest."

Although I wanted to keep talking, Gascoigne was right. Fatigue ate at me. I retied the wires around Quern's wrists, but I kept his hands in front of him.

"Keep your injury elevated," I said.

And while Quern didn't reply to me, he did as I asked.

I shoved the medical supplies into my cargo pants. Then I sat back down and rested in my chair, the stink of blood and sweat still lingering. With a long sigh, I relaxed.

Quern watched me the entire time. I didn't know what to say to him, so I turned away and closed my eyes. We'd deal with him again once we got back to Richfield.

When we arrived at the southernmost train station, it was deserted. I had been afraid of fighting more members of a rail gang, but apparently, they had been warned of us—and our power armor. No one was here, despite the many fortifications and still-warm campfires.

Hope stayed with me as I spotted the vast rocky wastes beyond the station. This was once a natural park. Now it was a graveyard of sand.

Not too far off from our location was the stone quarry. It was nestled deep in a raw wound in the Earth's crust—some sort of crag that had been torn wide open to better facilitate a digging operation. Nothing of interest was around it, just cracked roads and small lots with trucks that resembled the Iron-Blooded vehicles we had seen at the labs.

The quarry itself was a mix of new-world tech and old-world A-tech. A gigantic machine that ran several conveyor belts was working in overtime, hauling white and gray rocks up from the bottom of the quarry to the top.

Men and women, their backs hunched and hands calloused, toiled under the watchful eyes of Iron-Blooded soldiers, each with a rifle. The captives blasted out rocks from the depths of the Earth, and then smashed the larger ones into something smaller, so the chunks would fit onto the belts.

The constant *bang-bang-bang* of hammers, mixed with the occasional controlled explosion, filled the air around us with the music of backbreaking labor.

What were they mining? Marble? Granite? Limestone? I wasn't entirely certain, but I knew they needed a lot of it. Clearly, the Iron-Blooded wanted to start building, and they couldn't do that without the raw materials.

Forcing random rail gangers to do their literal dirty work seemed like a brilliant, if insidious, idea. I could understand why Architect Riven ordered his followers to carry it out. No one would care if the rail gangs disappeared. And few would care to hear they were worked to death in a quarry—the rail gangs were not popular within any corner of civilization.

I stepped out of the train, and Gascoigne followed me.

"You stay here," I said to Brecht. "And keep Quern with you."

Brecht nodded, though his sights were set on the distant quarry. A cloud of rock dust wafted into the sky, mingling with the thick clouds.

"Let me pilot the Mark VI," Gascoigne said, staring down at me with excitement.

"All right. You can be the one to handle our enemy."

CHAPTER TWENTY-FIVE

While Gascoigne mounted up in the JUDGE-X0 Mark VI, I waited at the edge of the train station. I had only slept for a few hours, and my mind felt bogged down with a delirious sense of urgency. My exhaustion took a toll on my ability to rationally evaluate things.

I needed to find Bishop.

It felt like years since I had seen him last. I knew it had only been a few days, but the fog in my thoughts made everything difficult to grasp properly. All I cared about was rescuing Bishop. Nothing else mattered at the moment. Nothing.

Gascoigne exited the boxcar of our stolen train and stomped across the station. The Mark VI wasn't new and glittering like before. The crusted blood from the rail gang thugs gave the power armor a new, darker hue. When Gascoigne stomped by, I took a second to admire my own handiwork.

But right now, I didn't want to kill anyone. While Gascoigne led the charge, I would find Bishop and extract him from this hellhole.

The entrance to the rock quarry was marked with two makeshift wooden towers. Iron-Blooded guards sat on top of each, their rifles at the ready. Trucks drove into the quarry, loaded up on rocks, and then drove off. It seemed like they were in a hurry—I suspected all the Iron-Blooded were aware of the stolen power armor and our presence in their ranks.

Gascoigne marched forward with a determined stride, the Mark VI enhancing her movements, each step a soft quake. The thuds of her footfalls caught the attention of the Iron-Blooded in the guard towers. They took aim, but that was just Gascoigne's signal to speed up.

She ran.

And she moved like she was born to pilot an exoskeleton. With a leap mid-run, she collided with one of the towers, toppling it over in a dramatic *smash* that echoed down into the quarry and then back out. There were screams and shouts, and even a few people firing rifles.

It was difficult to see when a wave of dust and debris rose into the air. I coughed back a mouthful of rock residue and waved my hand in front of my face.

Someone fired a small shoulder-mounted rocket launcher at Gascoigne. The roar and explosion afterward were close enough that I felt the heat, so I quickly hurried in the opposite direction. While Gascoigne had everyone's attention, I darted into the cloud of destruction and headed into the quarry.

Plumes of smoke and fire rose from the guard towers. Gascoigne smashed her way through the second one, her suit practically unstoppable when compared to the makeshift wood structure.

Through the wreckage, I saw the matte black skin of a warrior Teth. It stood nearly ten feet, and rushed for Gascoigne, but she whirled around her plasma blade and cut through its multi-armed body in a single slice. After setting fire to the wood of the tower, using the hot plasma as the starter, she tucked the blade away.

Turning it on and off constantly would drain the battery cells quickly. I hoped she knew what she was doing.

I also thought I heard her unhinged laughter, but I shook my head and I couldn't detect it any longer.

Gascoigne was having way too much fun.

Using the chaos as cover, I stuck to the shadows and dodged between the giant machinery and piles of shattered rocks. The Iron-Blooded soldiers ran by, each of them gathering the heaviest firearms they could. Some of them had RPGs, while others gathered grenades. I ignored them, and continued to a ladder that led down into the quarry's main pit.

I had a vague memory of Bishop mentioning that he would never comply with anyone's demands if he were held captive. I suspected that, if he was here, he'd be in some sort of special holding pen for defiant prisoners.

As I descended the ladder, I spotted something near the heart of the quarry—a fenced-off area guarded by a trio of soldiers. A couple people were held inside the pen, but none of them were moving. Each was on the ground, lying on their back or side, all wearing clothing dirtied from the rocks of the quarry. The guards kept their attention up on the wreckage and action, and none of them gave me a second glance.

I was still wearing an Iron-Blooded uniform, and the harsh shadows cast from the tall walls of the quarry were the perfect accessory to my disguise.

Once at the bottom of the ladder, I made my way toward the holding pen.

My first rule to lying—tell them what they already believe first, then everything that comes after would seem more plausible.

"*We're under attack!*" I shouted in Tethlite, using volume to give myself a masculine edge, even if it was only slight. "*Grab your ammo and head to the trucks!*"

The three men didn't question me. There was no time for questions, really. They took off toward one of the foremen buildings tucked away in the corner of the quarry.

All around me, there was more shouting. The quarry workers, all rail gang members, started bolting from their positions along the rock walls. They hurried toward the ladders—of which there were only three—and started hauling themselves up to the surface. A couple of them were shot down by the Iron-Blooded, but I ignored the sounds of their pained groans and the snap of their bones as they hit the quarry floor.

Instead, I ripped open the wooden pen and hurried inside.

Several half-broken individuals just lay on the ground, barely acknowledging my presence with a sideways shift of their eyes.

I stepped over a man, and then a woman, and went straight for the person in the very back—the one with tally mark scars along his arms.

Bishop.

It was him. Lying on his back.

I almost burst into a show of strong emotion—although, I wasn't sure which emotion—but I kept it all tamped down as I rushed to his side. He was pale from a lack of blood, and his eyes seemed sunken into his skull. Bishop didn't have any visible wounds, though. His clothes were spotted with blood and reeked of desperate sweat.

I knelt and shook his shoulder. "Bishop!"

His eyes fluttered open, and he turned his head to stare up at me.

"Kita?" He furrowed his brow. "Damn . . . I'm hallucinating good . . ."

"No! It's me. It's me." I grabbed his hand and pressed his palm against my cheek, hoping he would understand this wasn't a dream or delusion. "Bishop, you need to get to your feet. C'mon. I can't carry you. But we need to leave."

"What're you . . . doing here?"

His rusted voice, and the agonized way he spoke his words, tore at my soul. I wished I had the Mark VI, just so I could rip apart every Iron-Blooded here.

"I'm saving you," I said, feeling the weight of my exhaustion. But I didn't have time to waste here. The sounds of a frantic battle grew louder. All the Iron-Blooded were after Gascoigne. I just hoped she could hold her ground. The numbers against her were staggering, and her battery cells would only last so long.

I hoisted Bishop up, throwing his arm onto my shoulder for leverage. He was taller than me, and his body was heavy and unresponsive, but I was fueled by pure adrenaline. I could not let him die here. Not after everything we had been through.

"Kita," he said with a groan. Then he managed to hold some of his weight with one of his legs. Bishop chuckled. "You're insane."

I laughed once, unable to stop myself. And then I smiled. "Don't die on me. We need to go on that date, remember?"

"Oh, trust me . . . it's all I've been thinking about."

The staccato burst of gunfire filled the quarry. The looming shadows of Iron-Blooded soldiers raced toward the remains of the entrance, looking for survivors. Their focus was still mostly on Gascoigne, but that wouldn't last.

Half carrying Bishop along, I made for a rock tunnel that led deeper into the quarry. The lone third ladder had less people around it, and Bishop needed leeway to get up.

Once inside, the relative quiet was unnerving. The tunnel was dimly lit by flickering bulbs strung along the ceiling, their power sources wheezing and sputtering. The walls dripped with moisture, the air cooler than outside.

Bishop slumped against the damp rock wall, his breathing labored.

An explosion shook the quarry and a set of rocks crashed down to the bottom of the pit.

"You shouldn't be here," Bishop muttered.

"I would never leave you behind."

That must've resonated with him, because Bishop stared at me for a prolonged second, his gaze more serious than I had ever seen before. Then he half smiled as he whispered, "I love you, too, Kit-Kat."

Before I could respond, the distant sounds of shouting approached, reverberating through the tunnel, stealing my focus.

I grabbed Bishop. *"Hurry!"* I yanked his arm and we went through right before part of tunnel collapsed behind us. The explosions from the top of the quarry were wrecking everything, and we needed to get up higher if we were going to survive.

"The conveyor belts . . ."

The idea had entered my thoughts in a flash second, but I knew it was the best course of action. I half hauled Bishop as I ran for the nearest rock-covered belt. It moved at a leisurely pace, but I didn't care. I pushed Bishop until he was able to roll himself on, and then I climbed up after him.

One good idea always created copycats.

Dozens of the rail gangers spotted us and hurried for the belts. They, too, leapt onto them and then weaved their way up the line, avoiding the shattered rocks and boulders.

I rode the belt with Bishop, hating how slow we went. Once Bishop caught his breath, I helped him back to his feet and hurried him along the line. Bullets *plinked* into the rocks around us, and I ducked as I jogged forward. Were the Iron-Blooded shooting at us? Or were those stray shots from the carnage happening all around Gascoigne?

I didn't know. And I wasn't about to stop to find out.

Bishop and I reached the top long after the other captives had run off. We leapt off the belt before hitting a pile of boulders, and I helped Bishop get his footing before I turned my attention to the entrance of the quarry.

Gascoigne, in the Mark VI, was a fiery angel of vengeance. She leapt through an explosion of fire and crushed the remaining Iron-Blooded soldiers who were stupid enough to face her. The power armor was scratched, but at least cleared of dried blood. The fires around the quarry made sure to cleanse everything, after all.

Then she stomped over to us, each footfall a minor quake.

"Gascoigne," I said, breathless.

She reached out and grabbed Bishop's shoulder with the power armor. Then she helped him walk as she headed straight back for our stolen train.

"Quickly," she said, her voice distorted and robotic through the suit's speakers. "I'm done with this place."

I nodded once and followed close to her, my heart pounding as I glanced over my shoulders more than once. More and more of the rail gang thugs were climbing out of the damaged quarry.

Part of me wished . . .

That I could steal all the raw materials here. Obviously, they would be useful in building a bigger and better city, one that eclipsed Richfield. But our tiny train wasn't large enough to carry everything. I'd need to come back, or perhaps find my own quarry.

"Take him," Gascoigne said as she handed over Bishop. "I'll put the Mark VI away, and then start the train. Don't lollygag. Those Iron-Blooded freaks will send reinforcements."

"They always do," I muttered.

Brecht jumped out of the train as we approached, his eyes on Bishop. He smiled, as though relief was all he could feel as well.

"You found him," he breathed.

"Stay with Quern," I said as I walked over, Bishop on my shoulder. "Don't let him go. Under any circumstance."

"All right, but do you need help or—"

"Just watch him. I have Bishop. *Let's go.*"

CHAPTER TWENTY-SIX

The Town of Richfield, thankfully, was close to the railroad tracks. The gangs had attempted to rob it in the past, due to its close proximity, but now I figured that wouldn't be a problem. We had a suit of power armor, after all—and one of their valuable trains.

The wheels *click-clacked* all the way to the station nearest our city. I sat with Bishop the entire time, but for the most part, we both slept through the trek, our exhaustion levels high. His body was warm, even if he had lost a lot of blood, and I stayed tucked under his arm the entire time.

Bishop never let me go.

When the train stopped, I recognized the scrubland all around us. In the distance, I noticed a crater and three trucks shoved together to form a makeshift home.

Soon, I would be able to rest in my own bed. But my fatigue weighed heavily on me. I allowed Gascoigne to lead us from the train, onto the main road, all the way to the gate of Richfield. Old Man Tim was there at the wall, and he spoke to us. I was too tired to really answer—too tired to comprehend.

We entered Richfield, and my body must've known we were someplace safe, because I swore most of it stopped working. A deep-seated weariness washed over me. The townsfolk went about their usual business. I wanted to close my eyes and sleep in the middle of the road.

As I sluggishly made my way through town with Bishop, Gascoigne maneuvered the Mark VI out of the train, causing a few curious glances and gasps from the people of Richfield. They had seen power armor before, but never in peaceful situations, since no one here had the capability of piloting one. But today, it was a symbol of protection—at least, I hoped they understood that.

I had never seen someone drunk on so little power, but Gascoigne marched through town, showing off the JUDGE-X0 armor as though it gave her the keys to the city. Everyone had to move out of her way or get crushed.

And while we all unloaded the train, Brecht had one job. To watch Quern. He took our captive into town. Thankfully, we had a "jail," though it was definitely in big fat quotes. Richfield used their jail more for disagreeable turkeys than they did people.

Bishop gave a grateful smile, though his pale face made it evident he was still weak.

"Almost home," I whispered.

He nodded, his eyelids heavy, but there was a hint of relief in his eyes. "I thought I was as good as dead."

"You didn't think I would come for you?"

"I didn't think you'd be able to find me in time. Those punks were trying to drain me dry, I swear. The moment they found out I had the machines in my blood. It was only a matter of time."

The nanites couldn't be transferred once infused. Why would the Iron-Blooded want to drain Bishop dry? I shook the thoughts from my head. I didn't have the mental capacity to deal with it at the moment.

We made our way through the town square, passing by a wall that partially hid the bubbling hot springs that Richfield was known for. The geothermal pools were famous for their therapeutic properties, and even now, some of the townsfolk were soaking in them, seeking solace from their daily aches and pains. The rising steam from the springs drifted up above the wall, giving it a mystical look.

I couldn't help but think how wonderful it would be to just sink into those warm waters, letting them heal my physical and emotional wounds. But that was a luxury we would have to postpone. Right now, our priority was to get Bishop some rest.

Well, and myself.

As we passed the hot springs, a gentle gust of wind brought with it the earthy scent of the mineral-rich waters and sulfur.

"We need to take a dip in those," Bishop said to me, echoing my thoughts.

"We will," I replied.

It wasn't long before we reached our home, nestled at the edge of town, almost against the barricade that protected Richfield from the rail gangs. While most of the town was built of brick and stone, our home was wooden and one of the few newer constructions made after the Forever Winter. Sure, some of the walls were patchwork, and one was tilted, which drove me insane whenever I thought about it, but this place was still *home*.

Technically, this was Bishop's home. He had given me half of it after we returned from the Hoover Dam, and I'd turned my room into a sleeping area and workshop. For a few months after the explosion, I had rested and built tiny figurines for the children of Richfield.

Now, I just wanted my bed.

I opened the door, and Bishop got off my shoulder and leaned his weight against the wall.

It was a simple house, with wooden floors and beams, but it was cozy and familiar. The front room was situated around a fireplace. Our couch and table faced it, and a radio sat on the mantle. Bishop collapsed onto the couch, his body finally giving in to the exhaustion.

"Don't set an alarm," he mumbled into the cushions.

He always managed to make me laugh.

It was dark. That was fine. It was better for sleeping.

After a moment of groggily searching for a blanket, I returned to Bishop's side, only to see he had already fallen asleep. I threw the blanket over his body, watching as his chest slowly rose and fell. There was so much to think about, so much to plan for the future. But for now, we were safe, and that was all that mattered.

I shuffled into my bedroom and workshop, changed into a clean T-shirt—probably Bishop's—and slid under my soft blankets. The events of the last few days weighed heavily on my mind, but sleep was inevitable. The chaotic, but pleasant, sounds of the town, the distant murmur of the hot springs, and the peace of being home lulled me into a blissful slumber . . .

Someone slid their hand across my back, and I tensed.

Was I under attack? Was it Quern? Or Commander Dannik? One of the Teth? My heart beat hard, icy adrenaline dumping into my veins as I whirled around, the darkness of my bedroom both confusing and frightening. I had a handgun under the mattress, and I could—

"It's me, Kita."

I exhaled, my body still tense but my thoughts calming.

Bishop eased himself onto my bed. I couldn't see, but I felt him just fine. He was so much larger than me, and my bed was designed for a single person. In order for us both to rest here, we had to snuggle close.

I lifted the blankets, and Bishop slipped under them. He was gloriously warm. I loved it. But he was also naked, which . . . surprised me. After I gave it a moment of thought, I realized I didn't mind. I had seen him naked before, on more than one occasion, even if we never consummated our relationship.

It was too dark to see him, but that didn't mean I couldn't picture everything in my mind's eye.

I rolled onto my side, and ran my hands over his scarred chest. Each tally mark, although morbid to think about, soothed me. This was Bishop. No one else felt like him.

He slid one of his hands over my leg, and then across the curve of my hip, and up my skin, under the T-shirt. His touch left a trail of goose bumps, despite his comforting warmth. I shivered when his hand stopped its journey on my ribs.

I couldn't speak. I didn't know what to say. If I were being honest, I would've told him to continue—to have his way with my body, so that we could finally traverse the last step of intimacy. On the other hand, I was afraid, mostly because I feared losing him, and being alone. What if, after getting this, I lost it?

Bishop's hot breath washed over my lips. We kissed, gently—and this wasn't the first for that, either. But it felt different this time.

When he pulled away, he exhaled.

"No one has ever gone out of their way to save me as many times as you have, Kita," he whispered. "You know I'm not that important, right?" Bishop spoke the last question with a playful chuckle, but I hated it.

"You're important to me," I said.

"You don't need me."

I touched his lips with the tips of my fingers. "I'm going to build a new life for all of Richfield. That includes us. And when I make this new life—I want everyone to know how much I need you."

That was . . . awkward. It was such a bizarre way to say I needed him by my side, but my heart beat so hard I heard it in my ears, and I just spoke whatever words came to me.

Bishop seemed to understand, though.

He always understood.

That was his magical power—the one thing he had over everyone else. He spoke Kita-ese.

"Well, until my body becomes grass, it's yours," Bishop said. I felt his smile through my fingertips.

Then he wrapped his arms around me and snuggled me close. I was still exhausted, so I closed my eyes and just allowed his embrace to soothe my tired body. With him nearby, I didn't feel as desperate and as lost. He had been the one to save me from the radiation, and the one to help me all the way to the Meteorological Plexus . . .

I loved him, of that much I was certain.

CHAPTER TWENTY-SEVEN

When I woke again, it was to the smell of bacon. It wasn't until that moment that I realized I was famished. With more energy than I'd had in days, I shoved off my blankets and sat up.

Bishop was gone, but the crackle of sizzling pig fat told me exactly where he was.

I yawned and stretched. It was the afternoon, and after everything that had happened, I wouldn't be surprised if I had slept for three days.

The room wasn't the largest in our modest wooden home, but every inch of it was infused with my personality. An eclectic array of wire figurines sat displayed on wooden shelves that lined the wall near the window. The figures ranged from humanoid shapes to grand buildings I had found in history books I had scavenged from the wasteland. Each of my figurines was made from various types of wire, some shiny and silvery while others had a dark patina, hinting at their age or the metal's origin.

My workshop sat against the next wall over. A sturdy, well-worn wooden table dominated this corner, bearing the many scars of countless hours of labor. I had blueprints and books on architecture, and I made a mental note to review everything. If the people of Richfield gathered up the greenhouse parts from the factory, I wanted to learn more about their construction.

A desk lamp with an adjustable neck was positioned next to my bed. Sometimes, because I was a weirdo, I liked to think it was positioned in such a way to watch my room while I slept. A bizarre and childish musing, but sometimes I enjoyed the simple thoughts.

On my other nightstand, I had a few books about warfare, their spines worn from frequent reading. My clothes were piled under the nightstands, mostly because they were the least important things in my room.

I kept my T-shirt—a conscious choice—and walked out of my bedroom and into the living room. The kitchen wasn't far, and I followed the smells of a fresh morning breakfast until I arrived at our tiny aluminum kitchen table, complete with two plastic lawn chairs.

Bishop, dressed in jeans and nothing else, stood by the stove, one that had been scavenged then refurbished. He had one pan with bacon, and another pan with eggs, all the cooking utensils at least fifty years old. All the food came from Miss Timo, who loved raising the livestock. Her sons all made the various dairy products from Richfield's few cows.

Humming a little tune, Bishop threw a fistful of Timo's cheese onto the eggs. And then another.

"You think that might be too much?" I playfully asked as I sat down.

Bishop didn't even turn around to face me. He snorted back a chuckle. "I've made plenty of mistakes in my life, but adding more cheese than what the recipe calls for has not been one of them."

I smirked, propping my chin up with one hand. "You look amazing this morning. That rest did wonders for you."

Bishop winked over his shoulder, flipping the eggs with finesse. "Oh, absolutely. It'll take a lot more than explosions, backbreaking labor, and forced blood extraction to take me down."

I laughed once, and it bounced around a tiny kitchen. We had an icebox and a counter and that was about the extent of everything. When I made our new city, I'd make sure to do better. Everything would be bigger—sturdier.

"You live through everything," I said.

Bishop lifted an eyebrow. "Only when I'm trying to impress a certain wire artist who happens to live with me."

"Very charming."

He scooped some eggs and bacon onto two plates and then carried them over to our table. He took a seat across from me and slid one of the plates over. The silverware was included. "For you, I'd take on all kinds of dangers. Now, eat up. You'll need your energy."

I picked up a fork and poked at the eggs. "Promise you'll always make me breakfast like this?"

"Tsk. As long as there's bacon in the world, and cheese to be melted, you shall never go hungry in the mornings. You have my word."

I couldn't help but laugh. Bishop always made me laugh. "But what if we run out of bacon?" That was a stupid question, obviously. I didn't know what I was doing, I was just trying to flirt with him. Asking questions was flirtatious, wasn't it?

Bishop shot me a mischievous look, his gaze hungry. "Then I'll just have to find other ways to make your morning delightful."

My face grew hot, and my throat tight. Although I was hungry, I could barely eat my food. All I wanted to do was continue this one moment for hours. We had just been in several life-and-death situations, and I still had yet to shower—the stink of blood and desperation lingered—but despite all of that, Bishop made this morning wonderful.

He scooted his chair closer to mine, the squeak of the plastic almost making me laugh. But then Bishop gave me the once-over, his eyes lingering on my bare legs. When he leaned over to me, and brought his lips to mine, I swallowed all my unchewed food just so I could savor the moment of intimacy with him.

He tasted like breakfast.

Which was a stupid thought. I couldn't help it.

Bishop was never uncertain in these moments, though. He brought his hand to the back of my neck, and pulled me close, his lips pressed hard against mine, until his tongue guided itself into my mouth. I had never felt so taken by a singular moment. I closed my eyes, and focused on the way his lust ignited my own.

Bishop nibbled my lower lip and only pulled away for a quick breath before pushing back against me. He was rougher this time, more urgent and needy. His fingers laced themselves into my small hand, and when he broke away from our second kiss, his breathing was husky.

"Kita," he whispered.

I opened my eyes and met his gaze. He seemed so serious.

"I don't want to wait any longer," he said.

Words failed me. I wasn't sure how to respond.

Perhaps he knew that about me, because Bishop continued. "I think you should go."

Before I could say anything, Bishop ran his other hand up my bare leg, and only paused when his fingers slid under the hem of the T-shirt.

"If you stay, I don't think I'm gonna be able to stop myself." Bishop gripped my upper leg and smiled, a mix of predatory and playful. "So, while you still can, I think you should take your breakfast and get changed in your room."

I counted my heart beats for a few seconds, weighing my options. Then I pushed the plates on the table to the side, since I didn't think we would need them. And then, with all the courage I could muster, and without any words, I stood.

Bishop watched me, never blinking.

I straddled him and slowly sat down on his lap, his hands sliding all the way up my legs until they rested on my hips. My face felt hot, and I still couldn't speak, but through my actions I thought I had made myself rather clear.

I wasn't going anywhere.

Bishop and I sat in the bubbling waters of a Richfield hot spring. Nothing quite compared to the heat emitted from natural sources. Sure, the air smelled a bit of sulfur, which was akin to a rotten egg, but I still enjoyed the otherwise relaxing experience.

All the hot springs were natural, with rock pools that were rough to sit on, but some of the stones had been worn smooth from use. I sat next to Bishop, allowing the rejuvenating properties of the environment to help me. After all the combat, and uncertainty, over the last couple days, I was mentally in need of a break.

Also, after this morning, I was a little sore, and the waters did me good.

Bishop rested his head all the way back on the rocks, his gaze up toward the sky. "You okay?"

"Yes," I replied.

"Good, good." He rubbed my shoulder with a tender graze of his fingertips. "What're you thinking about?"

"How to best organize the townspeople to haul materials over long distances." I bit on my pointer finger as I dwelled on the problem. "I think, from what I gathered from the factory near the air force base, that a nearby greenhouse is still a day or two away by vehicle. Too long for walking."

Bishop chuckled. He didn't move, or even avert his gaze from the sky. "We could take the train."

"That depends." I exhaled. "I haven't seen the underground facility. Without knowledge of what's around it, I can't suggest we take the trains.

It's so far away, I'm not familiar with the territory, or who runs it. I haven't even really discussed my biggest concern yet."

"What's that?"

"That someone else has claimed the underground facility for themselves."

After meeting Brecht, my imagination had run wild. What if people were already living in this underground greenhouse area? What would I do then? Would we kick them out? Absorb them? What if they were more like the rail gang thugs? What if they were Iron-Blooded? Or what if they had their power armor, and they weren't willing to share their underground resources?

There were too many problems to deal with in the abstract.

I would need to go there, scout the area, and determine our best course of action. That was the only thing left to do before I organized Richfield into a moving operation.

"Well, look what we have here."

Gascoigne's voice broke me out of my musing. I glanced up, and then immediately regretted my decision.

She was naked, and I quickly glanced away, my brain jarred straight out of its analytical state. Female nudity didn't bother me too much, but Gascoigne was scarred and stood with her feet apart, for some awkwardly aggressive reason. It was disconcerting, at least to me.

Bishop tilted his head back into the upright position. He gave Gascoigne the once-over and smirked.

"Well, would you look at that." He chuckled. "Your body reflects your personality—as fun as a box of scorpions."

"Shut up," Gascoigne snapped as she stepped into our pool of hot water.

"What a burn. I'll never recover from that."

That got her to smile. "You never stop, do you? Just rambling. Saying anything that pops in your damn head."

"Whatever, Scorpion. At least I don't look poisonous."

It was a large hot spring, capable of accommodating at least twenty people, no problem. Despite that, I had wanted to spend the entire afternoon with Bishop. And just Bishop. But perhaps having Gascoigne close wasn't a bad thing. She had stayed with me through the entire rescue operation for Bishop. She had proven herself loyal time and time again.

Gascoigne slid into the water, practically melting as she sat at the deepest point, the springs coming up to her chin.

"Everyone in town is waiting to hear what's going on," Gascoigne muttered. She closed her eyes. "They want to know why you radioed them to gather equipment from the factory, and why we brought home a shit ton of grenades and ammo."

"We needed ammo," I quickly stated.

"We brought home a lot."

Bishop snorted. "Who is complaining about more ammo? No one."

"They're just suspicious," Gascoigne stated. "I would be, too. Especially since we also brought along a prisoner. The damn Iron-Blooded pilot won't speak to anyone."

"Well, none of my plans are concrete yet." The water in the spring was opaque, and concealed everything beneath the surface—for which I was grateful. "I was thinking of traveling north. To do some scouting. Only once I have my answers will I address everyone of Richfield."

Gascoigne snorted, causing ripples in the bubbling waters. "When are we going to pick up Justin?"

Her question caused my heart to stop.

I had completely forgotten about Justin. The poor teenager was just left out in the wilderness with our traveling supplies and buggy. That was it.

"Justin *Riddle*?" Bishop asked. He laughed again. "That kid go chasing more booty? Or did something happen?"

"I-It's a long story," I said. Then I eyed Gascoigne. "Would you mind going with me to get him? It shouldn't take long. Just four or five hours of travel."

She exhaled. "That punk gets on my nerves, but I've been meaning to drive around the area ever since we got back. I have a bad feeling that the Iron-Blooded are going to mount an attack against us. After everything we've done to them lately? You bet your ass they're going to consider us a real threat."

"I'm going as well," Bishop said. "I don't care how banged up I am. We're not separating."

Gascoigne spun a finger through the air. "Sure. The whole damn town will go. Why not? Iron-Blooded need to be discovered. The more eyes, the merrier."

She was right. I had dealt with the Iron-Blooded and their Teth for too long. After everything that happened at the Hoover Dam, I suspected they had wanted to go their own way and put that whole chapter behind them—including the memory of me and the Meteorological Plexus.

But now that I had been resurfacing, and stealing things from them, it was only a matter of time before Architect Riven would want to end me. I was too much of a hassle, too much of a pain. However, they probably didn't know every attack on their locations was me.

Well, they would eventually know—as soon as we released Quern. Which was why we couldn't send him on his way yet. He knew too much, and would lead the Iron-Blooded straight to us. So, for now, he was our prisoner.

But we still needed to move locations, before anyone could do anything to us.

And quickly.

That afternoon, we headed for Justin. Gascoigne drove our truck. I sat in the middle and Bishop sat near the door. I leaned on him the whole time and he kept his arm around me.

"What do you think of that Brecht?" Gascoigne asked to no one in particular.

Bishop chuckled. "I've known him less than two hours, but he seems nice. Also, a little unstable. So, overall, just like the rest of us."

"You have no other thoughts than that?"

"I've given you all the insight I'm legally allowed to provide."

I held up a hand, interrupting their sarcastic banter. "Brecht is an ally. You don't need to worry about him."

"That's not what I was asking." Gascoigne tightened her grip on the steering wheel. "He's a man who lived with the Teth. In an underground facility. You don't think he might run off?"

I shook my head. "Where would he go?"

Gascoigne huffed a laugh. "Good point." Then she hardened her expression, her gaze on the harsh roads ahead. "I like him, but I get the feeling he's holding back."

Holding back? I didn't really know what she meant by that. Bishop didn't seem to understand, either, because he didn't respond. Instead, he tightened his grip around me. I snuggled against him. I found it difficult to trust people—I always had—but Brecht seemed innocent. He didn't know what was going on. That was why I trusted him.

"Oh, look," Gascoigne said with a chuckle. "It's our little boy."

Our truck rumbled over to a large set of scrub bushes with a buggy sticking out of the back. Justin Riddle stood next to the vehicle, his arm filled with boxes. He dumped everything into the buggy just as Gascoigne pulled up next to him.

Justin immediately whipped out the gun I had given him. "B-Back off, Gangers! This is my loot, fair and square."

Gascoigne casually threw open the driver-side door and stepped onto the cracked pavement. She gave Justin a look of disappointment and the man straightened his posture.

"Oh. It's you." Justin lowered his weapon.

"Why didn't you drive the buggy back to town, ya sandwich?" Gascoigne barked.

"Because I can be useful, too." Justin motioned to the vehicle. "Look! I found things. I'm a real junk hunter now." He motioned to some ammo, medical supplies, and hardware tools. "A real manly man."

Gascoigne nodded once. "Sure, kid."

Justin had found a decent pile of supplies for one or two people, but it wouldn't help all of Richfield.

Still. It was nice that Justin attempted to help. I knew both he and Gascoigne were being sarcastic, but he did seem more manly now.

Bishop opened his door and leaned out of the truck. "Hurry up. We need to get back to town. We're going to become tally marks if we have to drive through the darkness."

CHAPTER TWENTY-EIGHT

That evening, while the sky wept, and the roads became glazed in foul water, I checked on the heart of Richfield. There was a fission battery that powered everything in town, and would continue to do so for centuries. It was a powerful device—one I had given them—and it was capable of providing power for the battery cells used in JUDGE-X0 suits.

Thankfully, the heart of the town had several power converter ports. It wasn't difficult to plug-n-play with different types of rechargeable batteries, including those that used lithium. Once all our battery cells were charged—all six we had stolen from the Iron-Blooded—I decided to take them.

In my mind, there were only two options. Leave the JUDGE-X0 armor here, for the town's defense, or take it with us, and use it if we ran across trouble.

If we left the suit, to defend against any potential Iron-Blooded assault, I would need to stay behind, or I'd have to leave Gascoigne, as we were the only two capable of piloting the armor. I didn't like those choices, since Gascoigne had already proved herself, time and time again, a capable soldier out in the wastelands.

Additionally, Richfield had defended itself from many attacks in the past, and now they had more weaponry than ever before.

Plus, I suspected the Iron-Blooded wanted me, specifically, and assaulting a highly defended position only to come up empty-handed wouldn't be a prudent course of action. And while the Iron-Blooded probably held a grudge, and hurting the city would harm my mental health, the Teth were more pragmatic than that. Architect Riven wouldn't want to deplete his own resources for a revenge shot. That wasn't how the Teth operated. They were about expansion and building, and would go out of their way to delete threats, but never in their history had they extended war over past injustices or petty personal reasons.

At least, that was how I remembered everything I'd learned about them. Since Richfield had everything covered, I felt secure leaving.

"Perhaps I should even let the Iron-Blooded know I'm leaving," I whispered to myself as I exited the powerhouse and headed for the medical clinic.

The rain sprinkled over me, coating my clothing and messing up my short hair. I didn't care, but I did shield my eyes. It was best not to let the water splash into my vision.

Upon reaching the clinic, I found it relatively silent. A few people waited in the small lobby, each of them reading an old-world book, one of which was titled *Still Stripping After 25 Years*, with a picture of an old woman and a quilt. She had an odd tool in her hand, so I suspected *stripping* had something to do with making quilts, but that was an area outside my specialty.

DC entered the room, tall and beautiful, and a beacon for anxious souls. Everyone glanced up and smiled. Even I did.

"DC," I said, water dripping from my clothing onto the clinic's tiled floor.

She approached, her brow furrowing at the sight of my drenched form. "Kita. Are you well? You shouldn't be out when it's raining like this."

"I'm sorry, but I just came to tell you I'm leaving. With Bishop and—"

The door opened again, and the whole lobby went still and quiet. I turned around, my body tense. In the doorway stood Vega, the hulking Teth with muscles the size of bowling balls. Its eyeless head tilted to the side as it squeezed itself into the room. Using its tiny crafting arms, it closed the door once inside.

"*Kita,*" the alien said in Tethlite. "*I've been searching for you.*"

I glanced around. "Is something wrong?" I asked in English, my default.

"No," the alien replied. Vega also switched to English, probably not to be rude to everyone else in the room. "But I wish to accompany you. Brecht and Gascoigne told me of your plans to head out and secure a route."

"You're leaving again?" DC frowned. "So soon?"

After a deep inhale, I sighed. How many people were going to accompany me? We couldn't take a buggy this time. We'd need to take one of Richfield's trucks.

"All right," I said to Vega. "You can come."

The alien nodded once. "Thank you." Its slurpy voice sent a chill down my spine, but I tried to ignore the feeling.

DC locked her gaze onto mine. "I'll ensure this city remains safe. The people here are my family, and I won't let them come to any real harm."

Her statement had everyone in the lobby smiling. I nodded once, happy to have a Winter Survivor on my side. DC had the best bedside manner. Even if she couldn't defend the town, I suspected she said so to put on a good show—to give everyone hope.

"I never doubted you for a second," I said. "Just . . . promise me you'll be careful."

"Always am. Besides, if I recall correctly, you're the one who tends to jump headfirst into danger. Well, you and Bishop both. Take care of him."

I glanced around, hoping I would've seen Chelsy. She lived in the clinic, after all. Not because she was dying, but because she was frequently sick. She had been born mute, and with that came a few other medical problems, likely due to fallout that still lingered from the firestorm bombs. DC had been helping her recover over time, and things had gotten better, but only with constant care. The nanites in Chelsy's system gave her a fighting chance of reversing minor imperfections, since the machines never knew when to quit.

Where was Chelsy? I hadn't seen her since I returned.

"Your daughter went to your home," DC said, practically reading my thoughts. "I think she's been waiting for you there most of the day."

"Thank you."

I turned, almost jumped when I realized Vega was looming over me, and then carefully scooted around it. Once out the door, I headed through the wind and rain to the lone house near the wall. Everyone else was already gathering up our materials, and Gascoigne was counting all the ammo and supplies Justin had gathered.

When I entered my house, Chelsy was, in fact, waiting for me. And while she wasn't my biological daughter, she reminded me a lot of my sister, and it was easy to pretend, especially in moments like this, when her whole face lit up upon seeing me.

Chelsy held up a small piece of paper. It read: *Welcome home!*

I hurried to her, and we embraced. She squeezed me tight, and I did the same in return. Then Chelsy broke away, frowned, and pulled another piece of paper out of her pocket. She had already written on it. The note said: *Why is there bacon and eggs all over the floor?*

I turned around and stared at the kitchen. Two plates were on the floor, food everywhere, and the aluminum table was pushed up against the wall in a bizarre fashion.

My face was red, and I wasn't sure how to respond. Instead, I turned back around to Chelsy and nervously chuckled. "It was an accident. I'll clean it later."

Chelsy quickly pulled out her notepad and pen. Her dark hair and clear eyes reminded me of her father, Dallas. When she was done writing, she frowned and showed me the note. It read: *Are you leaving again?*

"Yes," I said with a sigh. "I'm sorry. It'll just be for a bit. Once everything is done, I'll be home more often. I promise."

She scribbled again, showing a message with a pouty face drawn next to it: *Who's going to save me from Old Man Tim's awful kidney bean casserole when you're gone?*

I chuckled. "I told you that you don't need to eat it. Even a post-apocalyptic world can't justify how bad that stew is."

Chelsy grinned, her eyes sparkling with mischief as she jotted down another message and held it up for me to see: *Why did the coffee file a police report? It got mugged!*

She did that sometimes—just told me jokes to get me to smile. It made me wonder if I was too somber. I needed to remember that Chelsy looked up to me. I had to put on a brave face.

I patted her head and smiled wide. "Crouton, I'm going to leave this house in your care while I'm gone. W-Well, after I clean up breakfast."

That seemed to make her happier than ever. *Crouton* was her favorite nickname—the one Bishop had given her. She wrote: *Really? I can watch the house?*

"Of course." I squeezed her arm. "And I'll be back before you know it."

Chelsy wrote one last message, her handwriting quick and shaky: *Just stay safe. Please.*

"I promise."

She gave me a tight hug, which I returned, soaking her a bit with my wet clothes. As we pulled apart, she scribbled one more thing, showing it with a smirk: *Now I need to change.*

CHAPTER TWENTY-NINE

The next morning, we left the Town of Richfield.

Our truck was much roomier than the Iron-Blooded vehicle we had previously driven. This was the type of truck with a cab capable of seating four people—as long as the two people in the back didn't mind being squished.

Bishop drove. He refused to let anyone else drive.

I sat behind him, just to remain close. I loved his presence, and I couldn't stand the thought of letting him out of my sights. No one would take him from me.

Gascoigne sat shotgun, because she really was a scorpion. The mere thought of sitting in the back drove her to all sorts of irritation.

Brecht sat next to me in the back. He fidgeted a lot, and continually glanced out the windows, watching the landscape pass us by. I suspected he was worried about Vega, who was in the very back of the truck, away from us all. It was dark back there, since there were no lights, but that didn't matter to one of the Teth, who had no eyes. They actually preferred darker places, so perhaps this was for the best.

I glanced out the window and stared at the wasteland as Bishop picked up speed. We were heading north. Everything I had read from the factory, and all the information I had in Richfield, said our underground facility was north of us.

The barren wastelands and scrubby vegetation blurred past us, blending into an endless montage of dusty browns and grays. Abandoned towns, dilapidated buildings, and an omnipresent red hue painted the horizon, and I wondered if we should stop to search out some of the distant locations.

Junk hunters went through the skeleton of civilization all the time, searching for hidden caches of valuable A-tech. There was always something to be found, but currently, we didn't have time for that.

"I fuckin' hate travelin'," Gascoigne muttered, leaning against the window. "Last time I did this, I got stuck in Boulder and then got abducted by aliens. I have a bad feeling about this trip."

Bishop clicked his tongue in disapproval. "Tsk. You got me this time, Scorpion. I'm a good luck charm."

"You almost died at the hands of the Iron-Blooded. A few days ago. *Kita* is your good luck, asshole. You're a walking disaster."

Bishop didn't argue that. He just laughed. Like always. I loved that about him.

"I'm excited for this trip," Brecht said, chiming in. No one replied. He shifted uncomfortably in his seat and then shrugged. "I thought I knew what I would find when Vega and I started traveling across the wasteland, but nothing is as I imagined it. This is . . . one big adventure."

Gascoigne ran a hand down her face. "Oh my God. You sound like a twelve-year-old."

The moment she mentioned children, it reminded me of something. I glanced over at Brecht, my eyebrows knitted. "Speaking of twelve-year-olds . . . was there a reason you didn't like speaking to my daughter, Chelsy?"

Brecht grimaced as he leaned back in his tiny, cushioned seat. "Sorry. I just . . . We had several kids her age living with us. I . . . wasn't able to get them out. Seeing Chelsy just reminded me."

He didn't elaborate, but his strained voice, and the way his gaze drifted to the distance, told me he had a hard time accepting that he hadn't really saved anyone from Facility Twenty-Six.

"That's fine," I said. "I understand. For a long time, I didn't like picking up guns, because of old memories."

Only Bishop really knew my history with that, and he kept it to himself. I appreciated that, because I really didn't want to talk about my sister again.

Silence stretched between us. No one wanted to talk about dark moments in their past.

Bishop clicked on the radio.

"—and those are our stories for this hour," DJ Slam said, his voice so cheery, it actually elevated my spirits. "Which means it's time for me to go home, folks." I thought he was going to leave, which was disappointing, but then the DJ just laughed. "*Just kidding!* I don't have a home to go to. This radio station is where I live, and the water cooler is where I relieve my bladder whenever it gets too full."

Gascoigne slowly turned to face Bishop, her eyes narrowed in disgust and mild disbelief.

"Now time for some more tunes," DJ Slam said, as though nothing he had admitted even transpired.

An upbeat song started up, and Gascoigne returned her attention to the window.

Hours went by. The sky remained overcast—it would be like that forever. The radio played song after song, and DJ Slam just allowed it to continue without adding in his ever-increasingly strange commentary.

But as our truck crested a broken road, and entered the graveyard of yet another abandoned city, Bishop snorted back a laugh.

"Did you know Chelsy has started telling more jokes?" he asked me.

I nodded. "She told me something about a coffee pot."

"Okay, okay. But . . . why did the scarecrow win an award?"

"Why?" I asked.

Gascoigne groaned, as though she already knew the punch line and hated every syllable of it.

"Because he was . . . *outstanding in his field.*" Bishop smiled wide.

Everyone in the truck groaned—even me. I wasn't really a fan of puns.

The ruined cityscape disappeared faster than normal. We drove by a collection of motels with signs so faded, I almost couldn't see the lettering. Then the surrounding desert gave way to rugged hills. Our shattered road led us up, and then down, and I worried we had ventured too far east, toward the mountains—and toward Ex Cathedra.

We couldn't afford to go there. If we came across one of their judges, we'd be torn apart. Well, everyone outside of the Mark VI would be.

But we passed a green sign that read CASINO FORT, and under that it said IDAHO 152 MILES.

While I wasn't extremely familiar with the layout of the United States, I knew that Idaho was north of us, and was the location for the greenhouses. We were heading in the correct direction. That knowledge relaxed me.

The truck shook.

I gripped the back of Bishop's seat. "What's going on?"

He motioned to the window with a jerk of his head. I glanced out, squinting to see beyond the dark shadows cast by the terrible weather.

There were signs of a conflict. The roads were scarred and burned, remnants of barricades toppled over, and blackened patches of earth that hinted at recent fires.

"What happened here?" Brecht asked. "Some sort of war zone?"

The barricades were patchwork, and the fires made of broken buildings. This was a war that happened after the Forever Winter, not before. If I had to guess, I would've said some sort of gang was responsible, but I wasn't sure.

The grim evidence was everywhere. Discarded weapons littered the ground, and burned-out vehicles stood like rusting monuments to the chaos. At first, it was a small affair, but then I spotted the bodies.

So many bodies. Charred corpses scattered across the road and the fields beyond, some clad in ragtag civilian attire, while others were so burned, they no longer had any clothes at all. This wasn't a war zone—it was a massacre.

At least two hundred bodies were here. At least. More than all of Richfield put together.

Silence settled in the truck. Even Gascoigne, always quick with some morbid comment, remained silent, her face ashen.

Brecht was the first to speak. "We need to keep moving. Whoever did this might still be around."

Bishop nodded, steering the truck around the worst of the gore. Each bump in the road felt amplified, a stark reminder of the death surrounding us. No one spoke for a long time, not until we had driven beyond the field with the bodies.

Then the back of the truck shook.

"What's happening?" I asked, clutching Bishop's seat.

Bishop frowned. "I don't know. I think it's coming from the trailer." He stopped the vehicle in the middle of the road and then placed it in park.

All four of leapt out. The smell of cooked meat, smoke, and chemicals lingered on the air, even if we couldn't see the bodies. Bishop walked around to the trailer door and threw it open. Vega stepped out of the truck, its dark skin practically glistening. Was the Teth sweating? Did they sweat when hot? I wasn't entirely sure.

"Do you smell it?" Vega asked, lifting its head high.

"What?" Brecht asked in Tethlite. *"All I smell is gore."*

"It's not of this world."

Vega stood at its full height, practically towering over the trailer of the truck. Everyone watched and waited while the alien sniffed the winds.

"Is our dog catching the greenhouse's scent?" Gascoigne quipped.

"You're a comedian now?" Bishop crossed his arms and watched Vega inhale a wisp of smoke.

"Better than your damn scarecrow joke."

With a laugh, Bishop snapped his fingers. "Chelsy told me another one. Listen to this. Why did the bicycle fall over?"

If looks could kill, Gascoigne would've murdered us all. And while Brecht was more concerned about Vega, I decided to humor Bishop.

"Why did the bicycle fall over?" I asked.

"It was two-tired." Bishop snorted and then shook his hand around, jazz style.

Gascoigne pinched the bridge of her nose. "Jesus Christ."

Vega tensed. When the Teth became agitated, their muscles hardened and became more prominent. I watched as Vega lowered its head and flashed its teeth. The sharp canines were impressive, but not as much as the way Vega spoke English this time.

"It's the Vay," Vega stated. "They're here."

CHAPTER THIRTY

The Vay?" I asked.

Bishop, who seemed not to care about this news at all, merely shrugged. "We stopped the truck for *that*?"

"The Vay are here. Somewhere." Vega growled, its whole chest rumbling with displeasure. "At least one. Perhaps more. They've infested this area."

The Teth had a sense of smell far more powerful than anything a human could take credit for. If Vega said the Vay were here, I had to believe the information was accurate. The aliens always used a sense of smell—as well as their own scents—to properly communicate.

But from everything I had read, the Vay were on a different continent. Their architect had arrived to Earth and landed in Xinyang, within the Henan province of China. All information about the Vay, and their whereabouts, suggested they had never left Asia.

How were they here? In North America? Had they traveled here during, or after, the Forever Winter? And why?

"We should go," I whispered.

The others didn't argue.

Vega's head continued to move in a slow, predatory manner, each sweep of its nostrils taking in more of the air, trying to pinpoint the direction of the elusive scent. The wind whispered through the bare trees, carrying away the cloying scent of decay from the massacre site.

I shivered, disgusted with our surroundings. Even if I didn't know the Vay were here, it was obvious death stalked these shadows.

Bishop took a moment to look at the skies. The horizon was painted in deep purples and blacks, dominated by heavy clouds. The winds picked up, hinting at an oncoming storm. I hated the rain.

"Does anyone know anything about the Vay?" Gascoigne asked.

Brecht shot her a disbelieving glare. "Are you serious?" When she didn't reply, he continued, "I was taught all about the Vay. They're allies of the CCP, and mentioned in all the reports we were given. They're war hungry, and violent. Unlike the Teth, they're venomous, and hostile toward most life. Think of it like . . . the difference between *bumblebees* and *genetically-altered-to-be-even-deadlier killer bees*."

"And which are the Teth?" Bishop asked.

"The bumblebees."

Bishop made a sarcastic *whew* noise, and then wiped away imaginary sweat. I knew he did it as a joke, but right now I wasn't feeling any mirth.

The Vay were *here*? Damn.

Brecht, ever the practical one, motioned to the truck. "Time's wasting, and if there's any truth to what Vega says, we're not safe here."

The atmosphere around us had shifted. While previously there was an undercurrent of unease due to the chilling sight of the massacre, now there was palpable tension. This new, unseen threat, lurking just beyond our senses, was even more terrifying than the thought that the Iron-Blooded were stalking me.

Vega took a final deep breath, then nodded at us. "North," it said simply.

Which was unfortunate. Because that was the direction we needed to head.

I hoped beyond hope the Vay weren't anywhere near our underground facility.

With that singular directive, Bishop took the wheel once more. The electric engine of our old truck growled to life, a comforting sound amid the uncertainty. Everyone else piled in, including Vega into the back.

We continued down the road, the truck's tires crunching over the gravel. As we traveled, the landscape shifted, with sparse trees giving way to denser forests. The forests of Idaho, I mused. We were on the right track, but every shadow now held a possible threat, every unexpected noise made me think twice.

Night settled over us, offering more shadows in which to hide. I wished the others would've started a conversation, but no one bothered.

And the radio signal for DJ Slam had died, because we were too far away from his tower, leaving us with nothing. I missed the bizarre host, and his strange musings. Even if he started reading erotica, I would've taken it over dead silence.

"Reports said warrior Vay could cloak themselves," Brecht said, breaking the silence, "becoming one with their surroundings. Like chameleons. I would suggest we stick close to Vega at all times. The Teth can smell the Vay through their pigment shifts."

Gascoigne leaned back in her seat. "Fuck me. And we're supposed to navigate through this area, with the possibility of those monsters lurking around?"

Bishop's hands tightened on the steering wheel, but he said nothing. I sensed his determination, the fierce drive to protect, to keep moving forward. I admired him for it.

The hours wore on.

Periodically, the truck would shake, and Bishop would stop again to allow Vega to disembark. Our Teth companion sniffed the air, trying to track the elusive scent of the Vay. Each time, we would wait with bated breath, hoping that it wouldn't detect them too close.

It was also our time to use whatever was nearby for a bathroom break, or to eat a snack. The travel was tense, and I hated every second of it.

For some reason, it was getting colder.

I walked around a patch of dead grass as Vega sniffed the air, staring close to the truck. It was night, and every small noise, including from giant crickets, put me on edge.

"It's them," Vega intoned as it moved closer to the truck. "We are not alone." Its English was gravelly, and I hated the sound.

Vega seemed frightened.

The weight of that realization was like a physical blow. Gascoigne hefted her rifle, checking it over. Brecht pulled out his handgun. A cold pit of fear settled in my stomach.

"Get back in the truck," Bishop ordered. "We're not far from where Kita said we should find our greenhouse. Once we're there, we'll be safe."

He didn't know that. Why even say it? Was it to give us a sense of hope? I almost wanted to correct him, but I kept that to myself. Perhaps we would be safe. I hoped so.

With slow and careful movements, everyone got back into the truck. Bishop started it up, and we continued on, but the feeling of being watched, of being hunted, grew with each passing mile. Several times, shadowy figures darted between trees in the distant woodlands.

It could've been animals, but my imagination wasn't that kind.

Hours seemed like days.

Finally, my stress eased enough for me to close my eyes. If I rested for just a moment, everything would be okay when I awoke.

But what felt like a second later, Brecht was shaking my shoulder. "Kita," he said. "*Kita.* We're here."

My eyes snapped open, and I stared out the front windshield into the encroaching darkness. Ahead, the headlights of the truck illuminated a thick grove of trees, and there, hidden among the foliage, was the outline of a large sign.

Bishop turned the truck and parked it in a long-forgotten parking lot. Pine needles and leaves covered almost every inch, hiding the asphalt from the world. Thankfully, the metal posts outlining the lot still stood.

For some reason, Bishop took the time to park in an obvious spot for trucks. It was odd, but I didn't mention it. Instead, I slipped out of the vehicle, took in a cold gulp of air, and made my way over to the sign.

It seemed to have been forged from sturdy iron, though time had laid its claim on it. Rust crept along the edges, like red ivy. The sign declared in large, slightly faded letters: *US Sanctuary Housing #4*

That was the name of the facility we needed. This was it. I brushed my hand over the sign, clearing away some dirt.

Surrounding the title, several intricate designs were etched into the metal. They seemed to depict mountains and rivers, interspersed with patterns that might've represented human settlements or perhaps the various tribes and families that had come together over the years.

As the cold wind blew, causing the trees to rustle in hushed tones, I took in the sight, wondering if I could somehow use it for my ultimate city.

What would I name my city?

Sanctuary?

"Is this it?" Bishop asked as he crunched his way across the parking lot.

"Yes," I called back. "This is it. The underground facility should be here. It's supposed to have a greenhouse."

Bishop held his rifle with white-knuckled intensity, as if expecting a Vay ambush at any moment.

Brecht crept along behind Bishop, his eyes scanning the area, weapon in hand. Vega unfolded its tall frame from the back of the truck, sniffing the air as it went. Gascoigne followed, her fingers dancing nervously on the barrel of her rifle.

Bishop walked to my side, and then forced a smile. I pointed to the walkway beyond the metal sign. He nodded once and then went forward. With my heart pounding in my chest, I followed him. The weight of my anxiety hovered around like an unseen fog.

"Be careful," Brecht whispered as he hurried to my side. "This place could be infested with the Vay, or worse. Vega, can you smell anything?"

Vega tilted its head back, inhaling deeply. "I smell soil and plants. Life. But also . . . decay. Old and new."

Gascoigne brought up the rear, the only one in our whole group who seemed interested in the shadows. "So, we're going in or not? If the Vay are close, I'd rather not meet them aboveground."

A tall building, standing in the middle of what seemed to be a park, was all that greeted us at the end of the walkway. The signs around the front door were more faded than the sign. There were no windows—a sign this place was made by the US government. They'd done this to all their special facilities after the Teth arrived.

Bishop approached the front door. An old computer screen flared to life, and then blinked several times. "Welp, it's locked." He flashed me a genuine smile. "You think you can crack this?"

That was my specialty. I could break into most of the old-world computer systems. No one was updating those operating systems to patch out system vulnerabilities, after all.

Vega growled low in its throat. "Hurry. The smell is changing. There is something else in the air."

I hurried over and tapped at the computer screen. The old code was still present, even in this computer, and I navigated my way past the password input. This all gave me hope. First off, the facility had its own power, or else this computer wouldn't have worked. Secondly, according to the logs, no one else had entered in over forty years.

The Vay weren't inside. At least . . . probably not.

I switched the door from *locked* to *unlocked*.

With a great heave, the door shuddered and creaked open. Musty air greeted us, carrying a scent that was partly chemical, partly organic.

Gascoigne coughed and choked back a wheeze. "Perfect. I'm sure we'll catch some disease that no one has ever heard of."

"We have enough real problems as it is," Brecht muttered. "Do you have to make up fake ones, too?"

The two of them eyed each other. Then Gascoigne snorted back a laugh. "You know what I forgot to ask before we rolled around the other night? Whether you have any STDs."

Brecht's whole face went red. I would've laughed if I weren't feeling so tense. Instead, I awkwardly glanced between them and then motioned for Bishop to go inside.

Before I followed, I pointed to Vega. Obviously, the alien couldn't see, so I cleared my throat and said, "Vega, please watch the truck. Our power armor is there, and I'd rather no one stole it."

"*As you wish,*" Vega said in Tethlite. The alien turned its hulking body and continued to sniff the air around our vehicle.

One by one, the rest of us filed into the dark front room. I pulled out my trusty flashlight and swept it. The walls were damp. Leaking pipes drained onto the old drywall, creating mold and causing cracks. The front room led to a corridor, which, in turn, led to stairs downward, deeper into the belly of the facility.

I coughed back the thick smell of mold as I stood at the top of the stairs.

It wasn't safe to breathe the air of old, dilapidated buildings. That was Junk Hunting 101. Then again, if we managed to get into the heart of the facility, I could likely activate air filters.

"Don't breathe too deeply," I said as I headed down the stairs. I pulled the collar of my shirt up over my mouth.

CHAPTER THIRTY-ONE

At the bottom of the stairs, we arrived at another door, this one less fortified but equally old. Bishop pushed it open, and ancient lights flared to life, flickering as they turned on, row by row, illuminating a gigantic underground warehouse.

It was . . . massive.

Too massive.

It took me several minutes to take it all in.

The place was empty, but it contained several pieces of equipment, as though someone had stopped mid-construction. There were fish tanks, for massive fish farms, barrels of soil, hundreds of light bulbs stacked in boxes, trellises, nets, and even pots for moving plants. The tech built into the walls, including hands and sprinklers, were all of Teth design. This was the most advanced facility the US could've offered before its eventual collapse to the bombs.

The warehouse was vast. Someone had big plans, but clearly, they had never finished.

And according to the computer on the front door, this was just one of five warehouses. If they were all this large, and filled with machines and supplies, perhaps moving the people of Richfield could begin immediately.

I stepped forward, giddiness replacing all my anxiety from before.

Gascoigne eyed the warehouse, her gaze lingering on the machines, and then on the farming supplies. "Ex Cathedra would kill for something like this."

"According to the air force base, these underground facilities were mostly built on the West Coast," I said, my voice barely above a whisper as I hurried over to the fish farming tank. "Apparently, the natural cave systems in the region were perfect for the initial construction. So . . . Ex Cathedra doesn't have this."

"But United California does?"

I shrugged. "Yes. I suppose. But if no one has found them yet, they're just wasting away."

And the only reason I'd found this one was because of my knowledge of Tethlite, and my curiosity for digging through old-world computer databases. From my experience, that wasn't common among people from the wasteland or U-Cali.

"Let's look at the other warehouses," I said, trying to keep my elation to a minimum. "We need to take stock."

"I'm so glad the people before the Forever Winter loved us so much," Bishop quipped. "What a bunch of nice tally marks."

Brecht gave him a confused sideways glance, but said nothing.

Together, as a group of four, we made our way to one of the doors built into the side of the warehouse. It was in pristine condition, and I marveled at how white and clean everything was. This was more than a dream come true. I practically wanted to make out with the metal rivets of the door hinges.

Too awkward a thought, though. I kept all that to myself.

The door was locked, similar to the front door, and I had to search for the computer controls for a moment before finding the screen recessed into the wall. I poked at the screen, bypassed the passwords, and then opened the door.

It *hissed* open, automatic and functional, but what I saw on the other side stole my breath.

Unlike the first warehouse, the *second* warehouse was filled.

Shelves lined the walls, each one filled with row upon row of plants stretching as far as the eye could see. Verdant vines crawled up trellises, and a sea of leaves shimmered like emerald under the soft, artificial sunlight.

Vegetables and fruits of all kinds hung from the plants: tomatoes, beans, apples, berries. Here was life, a thriving oasis hidden beneath a scarred and dying world.

It smelled delightful. Better than anything I had inhaled ever before.

Gascoigne shoved me aside and then hurried into the second warehouse, her mouth hanging open. It took a full thirty seconds for her to find her words. "Well, damn. It's like the Garden of Eden down here."

Brecht stepped into the warehouse and immediately went to one of the plants near the door. He plucked a leaf off the stem and twirled it around. "It's real." He spoke the words as though even he couldn't believe it.

But the marvel of the moment was shattered when an ear-piercing scream filled the warehouse. Bishop, Gascoigne, and Brecht all lifted their weapons, their instincts were to shoot first and ask questions later, obviously.

I held up a hand, my eyes rapidly panning over the area.

A lone man stood between two potted apple trees. He wore a pair of brown sweatpants, a white shirt, and a pair of gardening gloves. That was it.

His brown and gray beard fell from his chin down to his waistband, and the hair on his head was held back in a tight ponytail. The faint lines near his eyes spoke to his age, but in my heart, I knew this man was like DC—a Winter Survivor. They all had the same plump look to their features, and the same haunted tint to their eyes.

They had lived a little too long, in human terms. Much longer than people were ever supposed to live.

And this man, with his long beard, seemed wiry and muscled—something was off about his physique.

Bishop held up his rifle. "Who are you?"

The man blubbered out another high-pitched scream. Then he ran a hand down his face, his eyes wide, his gaze searching. He looked like he would faint at any moment.

"W-What are you doing here?" the man said, his voice entirely too nasal and rusted. How long had it been since he last spoke to someone? "Get out! *Get out!*" The high-pitched screaming made him seem . . . unstable.

"My name is Kita Yamasaki," I said, stepping forward. "Do you have a name? We'd like to talk."

"*Get out!* Get out, you're not welcome here! You're not! You're not welcome!"

His screaming grew so loud, my throat hurt with empathetic pain. I glanced back at the others, hoping they would have a better idea on how to interact with the man.

"I've known bricks with a better grasp on reality," Gascoigne quietly quipped.

The man's eyes darted back and forth between each of us. He reached for something behind one of the apple trees and produced a hoe a moment later, one with sharp metal and a well-worn handle. His fingers twitched as they wrapped tightly around the gardening tool.

"What did you do to my plants?" His voice was now a whisper, but there was a tinge of wildness in it. His eyes settled on Brecht, who still held the leaf in his hand.

"I did nothing," Brecht said. "I was just determining if they were alive."

But the man's reaction was swift and intense.

He ran forward and then lunged at Brecht, swinging the hoe with abandon.

Brecht dodged the man's assault, backing up a few feet, his handgun at the ready. Gascoigne fired a shot into the air, the sound echoing loudly, including the *plink* as the bullet slammed into the ceiling.

"*Don't!*" I hissed. "You could damage something."

Gascoigne rolled her eyes. "You're all so soft."

"You've killed them! They're all I have!" Tears streamed from the man's eyes as he swung his hoe again, trying to strike Brecht in the head.

Fortunately, it wasn't like this wild man was a trained combatant. The entire "combat" was more sad and more pathetic than dire.

Bishop darted forward, reaching for the old man's wrist in an attempt to disarm him. But the man was surprisingly strong for his age and physique. The struggle sent both of them tumbling to the warehouse floor.

"What the fuck?" Bishop shouted as the man tried to bite him. "I'll fucking shoot you, ya lunatic! *Don't test me!*"

Gascoigne grabbed the man by the shoulders and hauled him off. I helped Bishop to his feet.

Brecht and Gascoigne, together, threw the man to the floor a second time, and piled on top of him. The man screamed and kicked and flailed for what felt like five solid minutes, until he clearly tuckered himself out.

The man breathed heavy, spittle leaking from the corners of his mouth, his eyes wild.

Gascoigne actually laughed. "Man, I wish all our enemies were this stupid."

"I think he might've been here—all alone—for decades." Brecht rubbed one of his eyes. "And I think he spit on me."

Bishop stared down at the trembling figure. "He's lost it, truly lost it."

After another two minutes, where we just watched as the man exhausted himself in a feeble attempt to struggle, he finally stopped thrashing about. I stepped close, knelt, and tried to make eye contact, but it was difficult. The man made me nervous.

"My name is Kita Yamasaki," I said again. "What's your name?"

"J-Jack," he managed to rasp. "Jack Matthews . . ."

"What're you doing here?"

"*I live here!*" he screeched. "This is my home! *Mine!* You can't have it!"

The last statement got me tense. I glanced up at Bishop, and then Gascoigne and Brecht. They all regarded me with shrugs. Then Gascoigne chuckled.

"Let's just shoot the guy," she said, her tone filled with exhaustion. "C'mon. You let everyone go. This piece of shit has lived way too long. And he's clearly insane. Putting a bullet in his head would be a mercy."

"*Leave me!*" Jack Matthews screamed. His voice was becoming so horse, his spittle became pink with blood. "This is my home! *You're in my home!*"

Nothing made me feel more like a villain than the idea of shooting an old man in the head to take his house. What was wrong with Gascoigne? Couldn't she see he was clearly in distress? And this place was so large, everyone from Richfield could live here along with Jack. We just had to convince him.

I turned to Bishop, hoping he would say something to contradict her.

He lifted an eyebrow. "What? I agree with Scorpion. You should definitely kill this one. I've never seen a better tally mark."

That was when I turned to Brecht. He kept rubbing his eye.

"I don't think you should kill him," Brecht said, much to my relief. "But I do think we should remove him from this warehouse. You saw how upset he became when I took a simple leaf. He's not stable."

The others regarded me with cold stares. They wanted *me* to make a decision. Well, Gascoigne would make it if I took too long, I saw that in her expression, but that wouldn't come to pass.

I knew what I wanted, I just wasn't sure how I was going to handle it. Clearly, this Jack fellow was deranged, and a hazard to everyone around him. On the other hand, he seemed perfectly content taking care of his plants before we arrived, which meant the source of his hostility was clearly—and without question—us.

We were the bad guys.

However, I had a town of people to care for, and a city to build. Would I stop any of that for a single, unhinged man?

"This is my home," Jack said, his voice garbled with saliva. "*You have no right to take it!* No right!"

CHAPTER THIRTY-TWO

Although I wanted to solve this, my words caught in my throat. How was I supposed to convince him? And what if I failed? I didn't want to shoot him.

Part of me thought of this like a test run for when I had to convince all of Richfield. What would I say to move people like Old Man Tim? He loved Richfield. Would he really travel several days north, though the wilderness of the dark roads, to live in an underground facility? What could I possibly say to him to convince him?

Jack's eyes darted to mine, filled with both rage and fear. His life had been thrown into chaos by our intrusion. But I couldn't walk away now. I just had to think.

Think.

Bishop placed a hand on my shoulder. He smiled—easygoing, never rushed—and then he helped me stand. I stared at him for a long while. Before I could say anything, Bishop knelt next to the man.

"Jack," Bishop said, his tone strangely kind, "I understand that this is your home. And that these plants, they mean everything to you."

Jack's wild eyes darted from Bishop to his beloved plants and back.

"I don't want to uproot you, Jack."

Brecht snorted at that comment, but then swallowed all his reactions. I shot him a glare. He half shrugged in an attempted apology.

Bishop continued. "None of us want to uproot you. No more than one would uproot a tree that has spent its life nourishing the soil it's planted in." Bishop gently touched Jack. "Think of us as gardeners, coming to tend to a plant that has overgrown. We want to help it flourish."

"*I'm sorry,*" Brecht said in Tethlite, probably so that only he and I would understand. "*Does he have to keep using plant analogies? Please, I'm going to laugh if he doesn't stop. No one can take this seriously.*"

I hoped Jack didn't understand the language. Given that the man's eyes were still wild, and he made no indication that he understood Brecht, I assumed we were in the clear.

"*Don't laugh,*" I commanded in Tethlite.

"You've been alone for a very long time," Bishop said, ignoring all our Tethlite. "That loneliness has wrapped around you like ivy, squeezing the light out of you. But we're here now. Here to help."

Brecht's lip twitched at the mere mention of ivy. What was wrong with that man? It wasn't even that funny.

"We can coexist, can't we? You can guide us in caring for these plants, teaching us how they should be treated."

Jack relaxed a bit, his once wild eyes now taking on a look of cautious curiosity. "Coexist?"

I knelt next to Bishop, my thoughts turning hopeful. "Yes. With more people. More, uh, gardeners. We're here to help. Grow more things."

Bishop nodded in agreement. "The plants need a caretaker, someone who knows them. And you, Jack, you might just need us as much as we need you."

Jack looked from face to face, no doubt searching for signs of deceit. If it weren't for Brecht on the verge of laughter, I would've said we all looked quite serious.

"I . . . I don't know," Jack muttered, a pool of saliva forming under his cheek.

"Think of it this way . . ." Bishop patted his shoulder. "These plants, they've thrived under your care, but they can do so much more with the help of others. Instead of a single gardener, imagine an entire team, working together to make this underground garden even more . . . What's the word? *Bountiful.*"

Gascoigne rolled her eyes but remained silent. Everything about this seemed to hurt her in her soul. Her violent side really knew little bounds.

"Let me go," Jack said.

I motioned for Gascoigne and Brecht to release the man. We all stood, and then moved away. Jack slowly got to his feet. He picked up his hoe and stared at it for a long moment, his face set in deep thought. I was about to tell him about Richfield, when the man swung his gardening tool in a wide arc, clearly aiming for my face.

I ducked, and the hoe swung by. Bishop leaned away, and the tool struck Gascoigne in the shoulder, the corner of the metal hoe slashing the sleeve of her shirt and cutting deep into her flesh, enough to draw blood.

"*What the fuck?*" she snapped. Gascoigne whipped her rifle butt around and clocked Jack so hard in the temple his grandkids felt that hit.

Jack crumpled to the warehouse floor, a new pool of blood mixing with his drool from before.

Silence.

We all just stared at the man. His chest lifted and fell in rhythmic patterns. He wasn't dead, but he clearly wasn't conscious, either.

Gascoigne applied pressure to her injury. She turned her attention to me, glowering hard. "Are you serious? Next time we fuckin' kill whoever has what we want, all right? Just once?"

I motioned to the body and then to the far door. "Let's just take him and tie him up in the truck. Maybe DC can speak to him. If he's a Winter Survivor, perhaps they'll have things to talk about."

Bishop grabbed Jack and hefted him over his shoulder. The man was limp, and didn't struggle, thankfully. I hated taking Jack against his will, but I wasn't about to let him attack us.

"Let's go," I said.

The trip to the truck was silent, save for the sound of our footsteps echoing throughout the warehouse and Gascoigne's occasional grimace of pain. When we entered the empty warehouse, I pointed to the computer screen by the door. Before we left, I tapped away at the screen.

I searched for information. I silently cursed myself for not doing this earlier . . .

Jack Matthews wasn't difficult to find. Sure enough, the computer had him down as ninety years old, which was quite the impressive number for a man who attacked us all.

No other names were listed, however, which meant this whole underground facility—and all the wondrous plants—had been a pristine paradise for exactly one person. Jack had lived here for more than forty-eight years, tending to plants, free from the pain of bombs, gangs, and disease.

No wonder he was insane.

I switched off the computer screen and gestured for Bishop to exit the warehouse. All of us headed for the entrance. I needed time to think of what we were going to do. Perhaps I could leave Vega, and it could tend to the facility's needs while we went back to Richfield to gather a few dozen people.

This place needed to be maintained, after all. Now that we had unlocked it, and taken its sole resident, I couldn't leave it alone for too long. It would fall apart, even if the automated A-tech here could handle almost 80 percent of everything on its own.

We headed up the stairs and through the thick haze of mold to the lobby. I coughed and wheezed my entire way until we made it to the parking lot. Then a cold shiver ran down my spine. The outside was quiet—and I didn't see Vega by the truck.

My hand instinctively reached for my side, hoping to find a handgun, but I hadn't carried one on me. Was anyone here? Or was my mind playing tricks on me?

The truck lay ahead, half-hidden in the shadows. Bishop, who continued forward with Jack slung over his shoulder, paused, his body tense.

From the silence, a low growl rose from the darkness between the trees.

"They're here," Brecht whispered.

Three *beasts* burst out of the foliage of the nearby forest, each with blackish matte skin, similar to the Teth. But these creatures were bonier and their skulls flatter. They reminded me of the dinosaurs I had read about when I was younger, and still in school, but these monsters had no eyes, just gaping maws filled with fangs, and claws the length of a standard pencil.

Their skin held a shimmery shade of green that matched the nearby trees, and I realized then that they were Vay drones.

They lunged for us like rabid dogs, but they were each the size of a motorcycle.

Gascoigne and Brecht opened fire, their rifles filling the parking lot with the din of war. The *bang-bang-bang* of their shots hurt my ears, but the bullets managed to take chunks from the Vay drones. The aliens still made it to us, though—they didn't die that easily.

One swiped at Gascoigne, obviously drawn to her because of the blood. She stumbled backward and fell, but she never stopped firing.

"Get to the truck!" Brecht shouted. "Now!"

The drone attacking Gascoigne died on top of her, and I had to stop to help her to her feet. She was covered in a blackish, vile blood, and her hands shook as I half dragged her to our vehicle. Bishop had a difficult time, the weight of Jack's unconscious form slowing him down. He fired at one of the drones, bringing it down next to the tires of our vehicle.

From the shadows, Vay warriors emerged. Their slender, black forms glinted eerily once Bishop got into the truck and turned on the headlights. Unlike Teth warriors, which were bulky and tall, these creatures reminded me of panthers—if they stood on two feet. Sleek, agile.

They had spines on their elbows, knees, and shoulders, though. And their fangs were so large, the canines didn't fit into their large mouths.

Bishop, showing remarkable strength, hurled Jack's body into the back of the cab before hitting the gas. The rest of us piled in, practically shoving our way into the vehicle as the panther-like Vay leapt for the side of the truck.

I needed to get to the power armor. If I could get inside, and get it all started, I could fight these aliens . . . But without it, we were going to get swarmed.

One of the Vay shouted something, but I didn't understand its garbled language.

Bishop reversed the truck, hit one of the warriors, and then punched it into high gear. Our vehicle didn't have great acceleration, and every half second it took us to gain speed took years off my life from stress.

Beside me in the cab, Gascoigne, even with her injury, was managing to fend off a couple of Vay warriors with sharp, precise shots out the window.

"Take that, fuck face," she shouted.

Sometimes, I thought she enjoyed moments like this a little too much.

We were vastly outnumbered, but Bishop's quick driving allowed us to exit the parking lot without getting swarmed.

Bullets slammed into the side of our truck, and I realized then that some of the Vay warriors were armed with their own rifles. They were trying to shoot out our tires. Bishop hit the gas—the pedal all the way to the floor—and the electric engine struggled to gain the speed he wanted.

The truck surged forward, tires screeching. More shots echoed behind us, the haunting hum of the Vay giving pursuit.

"Stay inside the vehicle," Bishop shouted.

Gascoigne leaned in right as a branch smashed against the side of the truck. Leaves spilled into the cab from the blow, and the wind afterward swirled them all around. I took deep breaths, my thoughts only on the Mark VI.

I needed it.

Gascoigne, clutching her injury, shot Bishop a glare. "Next time, *I'm driving.*"

"If you don't die first," Bishop said with a laugh.

More bullets. They hit the trunks of nearby trees.

"We can't leave Vega," Brecht shouted. "We have to go back. We have to!"

CHAPTER THIRTY-THREE

"Where's Vega?" I asked.

Brecht shook his head. "Vega wouldn't leave us . . ."

As we drove faster, and farther away from the Vay, there was an eerie silence that greeted us in the wood. The Vay weren't just mindless animals. They had a strategy. A plan. And that unnerved me more than anything. I glanced at the side mirrors, wishing I could see where they were.

The forest's shadows masked our pursuers. Every now and then, a pair of gleaming eyes would flash, and a Vay drone would leap forward, only to be lost again in the foliage. They moved like water, their skin shifting colors to blend with the environment. They were fast, too.

And quiet.

"They're chasing us," Bishop muttered, his eyes on the same glints in the forest. "What the fuck? I've never seen drones this fast."

Brecht gripped his rifle. "They're deadlier than the Teth. Everyone knows it."

"I need my armor," I whispered, turning my attention to the trailer of our truck.

As long as I could get the batteries into the spine, and myself settled into the pilot's seat, I could get it operational fast. But with the Vay on our tail, every second counted. Gascoigne smiled. Her sadistic glee at the thought of killing helped instill some confidence in me.

"Just wait until Bishop can slow down, then hop into the back," she said. "The door is still open."

Bishop turned onto a cracked road, and then shot out of the wooded area. The drones slowed when they reached the tree line, clearly favoring the element of surprise. Once they hesitated, Bishop slammed on the breaks to allow me out.

"Go," he shouted.

Brecht and Gascoigne leaned out opposite sides of the truck and opened fire, creating a momentary shield as I clambered into the back, making my way to the Mark VI. With shaky hands, I went straight to the battery ports on the spine and plugged in the battery cells. As soon as they flared to life, I rushed into the pilot's seat.

The connecters attached to the back of my neck and sent a flare of static electricity through my body. I closed my eyes as the whole suit closed around me, encasing me in power.

Nothing felt as great as having all my fears forcibly shoved away.

The truck started again, picking up speed as the Vay drones slammed their bodies into the side of the trailer. My suit activated, and the computer whispered greetings, but I ignored all of it.

I had to act.

Fast.

Using the enhanced strength and agility of the suit, I leapt out of the truck, crashed into the road, and then stood in one fluid motion. The Vay drones, probably just as mindless as the Teth variants, leapt for me.

I activated the plasma sword, the hot blade flaring to life with the bluish-white edge. Then I took aim at the Vay. I sliced through one, burning and searing its bone and flesh, cutting its head in half, its skull offering little resistance. It shrieked as it died, and three more leapt for me, biting and tearing with claws.

But they couldn't claw through my power armor.

I sliced my plasma blade, knowing full well my battery cells were at maximum before this started. I had plenty of power to cull this whole forest. Several of the Vay fell, but more kept coming. They were relentless, moving with a purpose and intent I hadn't seen in them before.

"I need to find Vega," I whispered as I cut yet another drone.

Bishop drove the truck from my location, but I didn't care. As long as I had the Mark VI, I would be safe. They needed to get as far from here as possible.

Taking a deep breath, I cut down the remaining two Vay drones, and ran into the forest. At first, I hit a tree branch, and I thought I would be knocked down, but I clearly didn't understand the full power this suit brought. I smashed through the tree limb, and it barely hindered my stride.

When another Vay drone came for me, I cut through it in one swipe, but I also slashed through a tree, and the felled log crashed into another tree, creating a cacophony of wreckage. My hot plasma also set one of the trees on fire, and the flames slowly crept up the trunk.

I didn't care.

I pushed forward, running back along the road Bishop had taken until I arrived at the parking lot. There were Vay warriors near the door of the sanctuary facility. That bothered me.

I leapt for them.

With brutal power, I cut through one, slicing away its panther-like torso and splattering its half-cooked flesh across the dirty parking lot. The other Vay screamed something, but I didn't understand. They didn't speak Tethlite.

The Mark VI kept my mind focused. I didn't feel pity or regret or fear—I just felt the need to continue. I cut down the other Vay warrior and then turned to search the forest.

It was dark, but the power armor gave me a thermal readout of the surroundings, and provided night vision unlike any other. It wasn't difficult to spot the other warriors—the ones with guns—waiting in the woods.

I also spotted Vega. It was hulking and different than the rest, and hiding in the woods beyond the parking lot. Had it sensed the Vay's approach and taken cover? Or had they dragged it away?

It didn't matter. I stomped across the parking lot and headed for my enemies.

The Vay would die.

I shot forward. Every Vay warrior, every twitching leaf, every hint of movement became a target for my plasma blade. I slashed as I went, culling the forest and wrecking Vay.

When I reached Vega's location, I realized it was fighting three other warriors. The Teth was larger, but the Vay were faster. Despite that, I leapt to his side, slicing off the head of a Vay warrior as I entered the combat.

In an instant, I was amid them, plasma sword swinging with a deadly grace. The Vay with guns fired, but my suit protected me from the worst of their attacks. With every stroke of the plasma blade, another Vay fell. They tried to surround me, tried to overwhelm, but the Mark VI made me an unstoppable force.

They all died. Even the ones that came as backup.

I stopped counting after five, my mind filled with the power-hungry fever of the suit's onboard computer. It refused to let me feel anything over than delight.

When it was all over, and my heart was hammering with anticipation, I was almost sad there was nothing else for me to cut down. Almost.

Vega, bleeding from massive rents across its flesh, swayed on its feet. Its massive form cast a shadow over the clearing.

"*We need to go*," it growled in Tethlite.

I nodded. My HUD indicated that the truck was on its way back, and I silently thanked all the good graces of the universe that Bishop always had my back.

As we made our way back to the sanctuary facility, I grew concerned about Vega. The Teth walked slowly, and its blood soaked the forest floor.

When we reached the parking lot of the sanctuary facility, I stomped out a small fire. Although the facility wouldn't be destroyed from a forest fire, I also didn't want to call attention to the area. Why were the Vay here? Were they looking for the underground greenhouse? Or was this a coincidence?

Bishop drove our truck into the lot, and I thought it would fall apart at any second. Thankfully, it held together as he parked near me.

Bishop jumped out of the vehicle and hurried over, smiling wide. "Kita!" Then he turned to Vega and chuckled. "We thought we had lost you, big guy."

Vega grunted. "You almost did." The Teth used three of its four arms to hold an injury closed.

The silence of the still forest surrounded us. Well, except for the crash of another tree that had been teetering on the verge of falling after I sliced through half its trunk.

The Vay had either retreated or were dead.

"We should gather some of the bodies," I said, my voice echoing out of my suit, mechanical and odd. "We should investigate their physiology as best we can."

I wished we had proper labs.

But maybe . . . there were labs in the sanctuary facility.

"It's going to be a long journey back," Bishop said, glancing up at the tree canopy and shivering when the cold wind rushed by. "We need to be careful . . . there might still be others hiding."

Brecht leapt out of the truck and hurried over to Vega. Using his scarf, Brecht wrapped the cloth around the Teth's injuries, trying to help stop the bleeding. "We need to allow Vega to rest. And we should get it back to Richfield as soon as possible."

"*Don't worry, kin of different blood,*" Vega said in Tethlite. "*The worst has passed. The scent of the Vay is thick, but waning. The drones were following the orders of the warriors, and they were a scouting unit.*"

"*You're certain?*" Brecht asked.

"*I am.*"

Brecht shook his head. "That doesn't change the fact you're hurt." He motioned to the truck. "Come on. You should sit. Please. For me."

Vega used its free hand to touch Brecht's head and face. Only then did they move to the back of the truck, when it seemed Vega was satisfied with its appraisal of Brecht's emotions.

I stepped closer to the vehicle, my power armor damaging more of the parking lot. "Let me put the Mark VI back there, we'll take one of the Vay drones, and then we'll set up Vega in a comfortable position. Don't worry. Everything will be fine."

I said the words because I needed to, though I didn't know if the others believed it. I hoped Vega's assessment of the situation was accurate. However, if this *was* a scouting group, that meant there were more—and they were searching for something.

If we left Sanctuary undefended for too long, someone would take it from me.

We had to get people here as quickly as possible. We had to claim it.

And defend it.

With Vega and the Vay body stowed, we headed back to Richfield. The quiet of the night was punctuated by the low hum of the electric engine, the distant calls of night creatures. And, also, Gascoigne's snores.

Brecht had opted to stay in the trailer with Vega. I didn't blame him. Brecht seemed more than worried about his Teth companion, and I understood. Vega was the last living thing Brecht had from Facility Twenty-Six.

I sat behind Bishop in the truck cab, running my fingers through his hair. He stayed awake, even though I knew it was difficult. We hadn't slept at all.

At one point, I knew Jack had woken up, only because we heard crashing and screaming from the trailer. A moment later, it all ended. Either

Jack was knocked right out, or he was dead. In this instant, it was hard for me to care. Exhaustion once again took its toll.

Hours seemed to stretch endlessly before the dawn came. The long stretch of travel was mind-numbing, but I kept my attention on the road, and with Bishop.

I knew we were in familiar territory when the radio blasted again with DJ Slam.

"—and her hair was silken and soft, a haze of inky black, her eyes just as dark." The cheery voice helped to reinvigorate me. DJ Slam, reading his stories, was somehow oddly comforting after everything we had just gone through. "She unhinged her breast-binders and revealed two firm, upthrust white globes tipped with dots of pink flame. They were high and close together, as though no gravity worked on them, and the valley between them was six inches deep. Wait, maybe *eight* inches."

I . . . almost couldn't believe what I was hearing. Not because of the obvious—but because eight inches of globe unaffected by gravity was just preposterous. Even for erotica, that was bad.

Bishop must've thought the same thing, because he flipped the radio off. Gascoigne snored in response.

"I prefer them smaller," Bishop said as he glanced over his shoulder at me.

My cheeks heated as I twirled my fingers through his hair. "T-Thanks."

"Kita, you can get some sleep if you want. I'll stay awake. We'll make it back to Richfield just fine."

His voice soothed me. I leaned my head onto the back of his chair and closed my eyes. "All right. But please . . . wake me if anything happens."

"I will."

CHAPTER THIRTY-FOUR

The rhythmic hum of the vehicle's engine and Gascoigne's loud breathing combined into a lullaby, pulling me into a dreamless sleep. I was aware of Bishop occasionally adjusting the radio controls or murmuring to himself, but it all felt distant, like I was underwater, listening to sounds from above.

A gentle hand on my shoulder roused me from my slumber, and I blinked, trying to clear the fog in my mind. Outside, I spotted familiar sights, but I was slow to remember what I was doing. Then it came to me. We were near Richfield. It was dusk, and another night was almost upon us. We had been traveling for nearly a full day. I wondered if Bishop had taken a longer route to avoid something, or if he just took it slow since he was fatigued.

"We're nearly there," Bishop murmured, his eyes still fixed on the road. "Wanted to keep my promise and wake you."

I sat up, stretching my stiff limbs and neck. "You haven't slept?"

"Scorpion wouldn't let me."

Gascoigne, who was now awake, glared at Bishop with all the iciness of glacier. "Asshole—I told you I wanted to drive. This piece of shit stayed awake *specifically* to deny me access to the steering wheel."

"I've got this," Bishop said. "Relax. Take a deep breath. Enjoy the scenery."

"Fuck you."

With a laugh, Bishop brought the truck to the front gate of the town. Old Man Tim—it was always Old Man Tim—opened it for us. The truck squeaked a bit as Bishop took it toward the garage. I suspected the vehicle looked like it had been blown around in a tornado. Most people in Richfield gave us odd glances as we drove by.

"Bishop," I said. "Drop me, Brecht, and Vega off at the medical clinic."

He narrowed his eyes and stared at me through the rearview mirror. "Why you?"

"I need to speak to DC about organizing people into groups. We need to secure that sanctuary facility before more Vay show up—or anyone else discovers it."

Bishop, clearly on the same page as me, nodded once. "All right, Kit-Kat. But remember you need to rest, too."

"I will. Thank you, Bishop."

The Town of Richfield didn't have a lot of *experts*. That was a major problem.

I wanted specific people to help me secure the sanctuary facility—although, at some point, I just started telling people it was the city of Sanctuary, which stuck. That was our new home. Sanctuary.

But experts would've made this transition smoother. If we had defensive experts, or botanists, or people who understood A-tech, I could take them first, to help secure the underground facility. Unfortunately, we didn't have that. We had standard farmers, militia, and people who could fix a car, but didn't understand Tethlite.

So, I would need to make a new plan . . . one where I could use everyone's skills to their fullest.

If I moved only twenty people to the underground greenhouse facility, who should be the first to go? People who understood plants? Or people to hold down the fort and keep it safe from the Vay?

Ultimately, I had to make a decision.

I sat in the clinic, in the one area for patients, and stared down at the list I was writing on DC's desk. Who to take?

The first thing I considered was food. Without sustenance, every other plan would fall apart. We needed the farmers. They had the knowledge to cultivate the crops we had and adapt to new conditions. And if the underground facility had any unfamiliar plant species, their skills would be invaluable.

So, five seats were immediately reserved for farmers. Anyone would do, but I specifically listed the younger ones, as the trek would be difficult.

Next was defense.

While the Vay threat loomed large, we didn't just need brute force . . . we needed strategy and vigilance. I needed people who could patrol, keep watch, and understand when to fight and when to retreat. The militia had trained for these scenarios.

I earmarked seven seats for the militia, including the man in charge of training everyone, Aaron Smith. With him on board, I felt reassured that Sanctuary would remain secure so long as we also had the Mark VI.

Health was another critical consideration.

DC had trained exactly two nurses. Of these two, Lila Ollen was my must-have. Her extensive knowledge on natural remedies and her ability to handle emergencies made her indispensable. Along with Lila, I chose two individuals who had assisted her in the past and had a basic understanding of medical care. They weren't nurses, but it wasn't like we were taking a ton of people immediately.

That left five more seats.

Mechanical skills were important.

I wrote down Scrapyard Pete's name. He had a talent for improvisation and might not understand Tethlite, but he could fix almost anything if it broke down. His skills would keep our essential equipment running.

For communication and record-keeping, I chose Emily Meyers. Though primarily a teacher, she had a knack for documenting events and maintaining records. In a new world, preserving our history and knowledge was vital.

I wanted . . . someone to keep track of everything in Sanctuary. I hoped this wasn't my hubris speaking, but I felt it was important.

Maybe I was just being pessimistic. The better records we kept, the more likely someone could come to run the town if something happened to me. Whatever the reason, I wanted her with us.

The last three seats were the toughest to decide. There were so many people who would be a valuable asset.

But considering our situation, I chose Himiko Akia and her two children. Himiko was one of the few people with a green thumb, and while her kids, Alex and Hiro, were only eight and nine, she had taught them much about caring for her personal garden. It would be useful to have all three tending to the many strange plants we'd spotted in Jack's warehouse. Someone had to do it, after all, or Jack may lose the last few brain cells he had left.

As I listed out the names, I dreaded the many other convoys after this.

Hopefully, the next few would be easier, but I somehow doubted it. As long as this one was successful, we could probably convince everyone the trek was safe.

If we had problems on this trek, I knew it might become impossible to move everyone.

I glanced up from my list and found DC standing next to the desk. She stared down at me, a slight frown on her face. I pushed the list over.

"You want to take only these people?" she asked.

I nodded once. "That's all the trucks will hold, unfortunately."

"Is that your plan? Only twenty at a time? Set them up and move more?"

I half shrugged. "My real plan is to get more vehicles. We also should probably find one more JUDGE-X0 suit, so that Gascoigne can wear it. The more we have in defenses, the better off we'll be."

DC sighed. She took the paper and slipped it into her coat. "I'll tell everyone personally. They'll accept it more if it comes from me." Then she tapped the desk. "You know, Justin Riddle asked to go with you. I didn't see his name on the list."

"He's sixteen." I furrowed my brow. "And not the greatest at following instructions. And while I appreciate him gathering supplies while he was waiting for us, I don't think it's indicative of his overall skill."

"He admires you."

I held back a laugh. Then again, if he wanted to help, I shouldn't treat him like a child. We should embrace him. "All right. I'll exchange one of the militia men for him."

"And what about Chelsy?"

I had given a lot of thought to her. "She needs to stay near you," I whispered. "Wherever you go, she goes. That's the end of the story."

That seemed to be enough for DC. She offered me a smile and then headed for the door. She said nothing as she left, and I wondered if she hated the idea of leaving Richfield. Hopefully not—she didn't mention it if she did.

After another deep sigh, I decided to head home. Tomorrow, we would also need to discuss how we were going to move supplies.

And right now, I needed plenty of rest.

In my mind, moving the people from Richfield to Sanctuary was as simple as putting people on a truck and driving them from point A to point B. Obviously, I didn't understand human beings like I thought I did.

Every single person I had put on my list needed to bring *things*. Not just clothing or food or ammunition, but personal belongings, good luck charms, or an entire shed's worth of family mementos.

In the cold of an early morning, I stood next to our two trucks, with Gascoigne and Bishop loading everything we would need. The trailer with the Mark VI was already pushing the weight capacity, so the space around the power armor was reserved for some of the smaller people.

Lila, however, wanted to bring a cart full of books. And while I loved knowledge from the old world, and most of hers were on the practice of medicine, nothing weighed as much as *books*. They were clunky, and also somehow delicate.

"I think they're important," she said to Gascoigne.

"We're not taking them." Gascoigne motioned the cart away. "We only have so much space."

"What about a few? Just a handful. These ones." Lila plucked out a handful of books on survival, and one of snakes and snake bites. I was unfamiliar with the wildlife of the area around Sanctuary. It seemed like a good idea to have these.

I walked around the other truck, trying to be a *presence* or a *leader*, but in reality, the others were handling everything just fine. I supposed that was for the better. My mind kept slipping back to the fact that I hadn't searched the underground facility at all. I had barely done *any* investigation; I had just been so gung ho to get everyone there.

We could take Jack with us, and see what he had to say, but when I turned to face Richfield's "jail" I knew I didn't want to go anywhere near there. The brick building was one of the oldest structures in the whole town, made of bricks that were probably laid down over eighty years ago, with bars over every small window, and a steel door on the front.

Quern and Jack were still there—our permanent prisoners until I came up with a solution. Jack had gotten fairly roughed up during the trek home, since Vega and Brecht were allowed to keep him subdued, but all the Winter Survivors were durable thanks to the special medical implants they carried in their bodies. He would be fine. I hoped.

"We can't leave without this!" someone shouted.

I returned my attention to the trucks.

Aaron, the man who trained most of our militia, was a tall man. I suspected he stood nearly six and a half feet, with shoulders that looked like they could rival that only in width. He wore practical clothing, and was one of the few citizens of Richfield who'd come here just a few short years ago. Apparently, the man had been a junk hunter, much like Bishop, before he managed to convince the citizens of Richfield he was useful, and wouldn't betray them just to steal their belongings.

"This is too much," Bishop stated. "We have these kinds of supplies at Sanctuary."

"You told me you didn't know."

I walked over, only to find them arguing about a cart full of blankets, pillows, rations, and cot frames. Clearly, Aaron was afraid of us not being able to sleep.

"We have two children coming along," Aaron stated. "We *need* this. Trust me."

"Justin is a fully grown man," Bishop said. "And he did gather some supplies when he was on his own."

"Not *Justin,* you dunce. Himiko's kids. They're young."

Bishop waved away the comment. "Trust me. They'll have a place to sleep. We can't take any of this. Move it away from the trucks. After everyone is settled, I'll do a supply run myself, but we can't take it now."

The more times we drove in and out of Richfield carrying supplies, the more likely it was someone would raid us. It happened all the time with smaller towns that needed to relocate due to natural disaster or worse. Anytime any of the nearby gangs thought they could get away with something, they would. That was what made the wasteland so much more dangerous than living in the war-torn Ex Cathedra or U-Cali. No authority to stop that kind of behavior. You had to be your own protection at all times.

The rest of the loading process was tedious. I watched as each person grappled with what to leave behind and what to take. At least some of the items seemed a little more irreplaceable. Himiko, for instance, wanted to take a set of wooden instruments and a set of educational pamphlets she had been using to teach her children how to read and write.

After hours of organizing, we finally had everything and everyone in place. This was later than I wanted to leave. In the middle of the afternoon was never a good time for any of this, and it meant we would arrive at Sanctuary in the morning of the next day, maybe later depending.

Gascoigne walked over to me, her expression serious.

"When we moved troops across Ex Cathedra, we always needed sup-plies for the vehicles, too," she said to me, keeping her voice low. "In case a tire goes flat or worse. We currently have none of that."

I stepped close to her, thankful she raised this concern. "Ask Scrapyard Pete if we can bring anything. Maybe we can . . . strap some things to the top of the other trailer."

She nodded once and left me to my thoughts.

Taking into consideration everything that could go wrong was just as stressful as imagining what to do if everything went correctly.

I just had to . . . stay focused.

This was ultimately for the better.

As long as everyone survived the trek to the facility.

CHAPTER THIRTY-FIVE

I already hated this drive.

Gascoigne and Brecht were in the first truck carrying the Mark VI and most of the supplies. I sat next to Bishop in the second truck with the most people in the back trailer. We had radios for the two vehicles, just in case we needed to communicate—or if we got separated.

Bishop rubbed his arm. "I made a couple more tally marks . . . but I think I'm going to start running out of room."

"Hopefully it won't become an issue once we move," I said.

"Tsk. I think you might have an unrealistic view of the future, Kit-Kat." He gave me a sideways glance. "If this place is as amazing as you think it is, there's no way someone isn't going to come looking to take it from us."

I tried not to think about that, but I knew . . .

He was right.

While its location had been hidden to all those who didn't know Tethlite, or how to break into the old-world computer systems, now that I had uncovered it, *anyone* could come take it. And that meant a lot of people would try.

I stared out the window. The scenery wasn't the best. I tried to commit it all to memory, though. What if I needed to make this trek on foot? It would take more than a week, I knew it in my heart, but there was always a possibility I would have to do it.

An occasional dilapidated building or rusted vehicle would break the monotony of the desert wasteland. The soil was a deep orange hue, and the strange rocks that dominated the horizon reminded me of jagged puzzle pieces.

Sparse, resilient vegetation peppered the landscape: cacti with their prickly exteriors and hardy desert shrubs that had adapted to the harsh environment, defiantly announcing their presence. Here and there, skeletal trees dotted the area, their leafless branches reaching out to the overcast skies.

The problem with this trek, and probably why not many made their way north, was the complete lack of *anything*.

Down near the Hoover Dam, and Boulder, there was life, and cities, and people . . . But here it felt like dead scrubland and flat valleys of salt. Even if I wanted to make Sanctuary the greatest city of all time, the one civilization to bring humanity out from the settled dust of disaster, we wouldn't be expanding southward, that was certain.

I closed my eyes and thought of the maps I had seen of this continent. If I wanted to make a civilization worth a damn, I would need to secure routes west, to the ocean. That would put us into conflict with U-Cali . . .

"You drifting off?" Bishop asked.

I snapped my eyes open and shook my head. "I'm here."

"Why didn't you bring the Teth eggs with us?"

I glanced over, surprised he would be concerned with those. "I'm not familiar with Sanctuary yet. I need to have a thorough layout of the interior, and a place to raise the Teth babies."

"When will they hatch?"

"They're, um, in a type of stasis. Architect Riven had them in A-tech containers that preserved them without killing them. Like a type of cryostasis. Once I open them, they'll *thaw*, for lack of a better word, and then hatch."

Bishop mulled that over, bobbing his head as he did so. "Are you going to raise them yourself?"

"I was hoping the whole community would raise them," I said. "And now that we have Vega on our side, perhaps he would as well."

"What about the Vay? You going to kidnap some of their children?"

I hadn't thought of that. I hadn't given the Vay much thought at all, actually. Up until a few nights ago, I hadn't thought they even lived anywhere on this continent.

"I doubt it," I muttered.

There was an eerie silence, punctuated only by the hum of the trucks' engines and the occasional jostle from the rocks on the shattered old-world road. Bishop didn't seem to have any more questions.

Although awkward, I slowly reached over and took hold of his free hand. He offered a smile and squeezed my knuckles.

"Hey, no need to worry. I was just curious." When he chuckled, it set me at ease. "I know I'm not the *planner* of our group, but I still wanted to stay informed. Don't worry about anything. We have a new home to set up. This should be exciting."

I nodded once. "Right." Then I returned my attention to the scenery. "Right."

As the hours rolled on and the trucks ate up the miles, night fell. The temperature dropped and I leaned back in my seat, my heart beating evenly. I wished I was back in the power armor, if only for the feeling of being secure—no fear whatsoever.

I closed my eyes, and allowed some sleep to take away my anxiety.

I woke up to the first truck exploding.

It was so instant, and so brutal, I thought, at first, I had to be dreaming. The flames from the road had erupted from underneath the cracked asphalt, and it almost seemed surreal. But then it struck me—there had been an A-tech mine or something equivalent set on the road.

The truck didn't topple over. The sides of the trailer burst, all the glass shattered, and the tires caught fire.

Bishop swerved our truck straight off the road and into an old fence. We smashed through the aluminum barrier and drove across dirt, only stopping once we were a few dozen feet away from the explosion.

Where were we?

We were somewhere near the edge of the desert, with trees speckling the distance, and rocky terrain all around us. The road had desert on one side, and tall rocks on the other. Old-world signs warning about landslides were posted everywhere, some of which had graffiti on them with smiley faces.

It was almost dawn, and the roil of the clouds overhead told me it was going to rain.

Bishop leapt out of the cab, clearly intent on helping Brecht and Gascoigne, but he stopped once he rounded the engine.

"Oh, fuck me," he said, his eyes wide.

I turned and stared at the window. Standing atop one of the rock formations was one of the Teth aliens—warrior caste—wearing its own version of judge armor. The JUDGE-Z12, designed for the aliens and much larger than anything humans wore.

The monster's power armor was spray-painted black, with white Teth skulls holding human skulls within. It was the Iron-Blooded, and they had brought along one of their alien buddies.

And it wasn't *just* the alien. It held a railgun over its bulky armored shoulder, a chain of bullets already strapped in and ready for firing. It was one of the many "accessories" someone in power armor could lift and wield like a normal gun, even though it must've weighed a few hundred pounds.

Six of the Iron-Blooded were around on the rocks, each with their own rifles.

They had come here for me. They had known we would take this road—and now they wanted to reclaim everything we had stolen from them.

The alien judge leveled the railgun and took aim for my truck. I held my breath, my heart beating so fast, I didn't know if I'd be able to take a proper breath.

Our truck had most of the people from Richfield in the back.

Rifle fire lit up the street at the same instant the alien judge pulled the trigger for his heavy assault weapon. Powerful bullets from the railgun— each capable of tearing a man in half—slammed through my truck.

Brecht and two militia men from Richfield were on the street, firing their rifles, aiming for the Iron-Blooded. Vega, with its hulking form, effortlessly leapt up the rocks and slammed into the first enemy it came across, its claws tearing through the man's flesh in a matter of mere seconds.

I leapt from the truck and threw my arms over my head as I hit the ground. Bishop did the same thing. There was no fighting a barrage of railgun bullets.

Thankfully, the alien judge stopped. The whir of its heavy firearm paused as it released the trigger and turned its attention to the conflict in the streets.

The first truck's back door exploded outward as Gascoigne, wearing the Mark VI, lunged out of the vehicle. The fire reflected off her suit as she stood at her full height, once again laughing so loud that the power armor broadcasted it to the surrounding area.

The alien judge turned its railgun toward her.

Without hesitation, Gascoigne charged. Her armor allowed her to close the distance rapidly, and she was strong enough to haul her whole form up the rocks until she was at the top with our enemies. Bullets pinged off her as she moved, as some of the Iron-Blooded had turned their rifles against her.

The alien judge's railgun let out a ferocious roar as it released a barrage of shots at Gascoigne. The power of the weapon was enough to knock Gascoigne down. She tumbled off the rocks and hit the road, cracking the already ruined asphalt and sending a burst of debris into the air. The alien deftly slid down the rocks, stopping its fire as it gave chase.

Gascoigne quickly got to her feet.

Bishop, seizing the distraction, ran to the back of our truck. He threw open the door and waved everyone out.

"Go, go!" he shouted.

There had been thirteen people riding with us, but only ten darted out of the vehicle. All of them wore clothes stained with crimson, and I knew the enemy's railgun had done more harm than I ever wanted.

Then Bishop leapt into the truck, and came out with some of the militia's weaponry. Specifically, a compact grenade launcher. He loaded a shot, barely took aim at the clustered Iron-Blooded soldiers on the rocks, and fired. The resulting explosion not only scattered three of the six soldiers, but it damaged the rocks, causing some to crash onto the road, and plumes of dust exploded into the sky.

Vega fell as well, shrapnel cutting into its dark skin. It didn't seem to faze Vega that much. Once the alien hit the road, it lunged for the nearest Iron-Blooded and took the man apart.

I ran to the truck and searched inside, hoping to find something of use. We hadn't brought much, and I feared throwing grenades, since even Bishop's one hurt our own team.

I grabbed a handgun and ran close to Bishop. When one of the Iron-Blooded attempted to leave the road, I took aim and fired, striking the man's neck. He collapsed to the ground, but the firefight all around us prevented me from hearing anything specific.

Gascoigne and the alien judge clashed. Their power armor struck each other, sparks and a rumble dominating the area. The enemy judge tried to fire more rounds from its railgun, but in close combat, it was next to impossible to aim it and pull the trigger. Gascoigne activated her superior weaponry—the plasma blade—and then slammed it straight into the railgun, twisting metal with the superheated blade.

The strength of the alien was evident. The judge grabbed Gascoigne's arm, and even with the power armor amplifying her strength, the alien was able to remove the blade from the gun. Gascoigne slammed a leg into the side of the alien judge, and the resulting quake shook everything.

The firefight on the roads died down.

The Iron-Blooded who had accompanied the judge were dead, but so were at least five citizens from Richfield, perhaps more.

Brecht and the others focused their fire on the alien, trying to overwhelm it. Gascoigne had gouged out a rent in the armor, and the bullets that managed to hit that area caused damage. Smoke poured from the alien judge's suit.

"*Cascading system failure,*" the judge's suit said in Tethlite, the creepy mechanical tone dying partway through the last word.

But I knew what that meant. Most of the old-world machinery had fail-safes to prevent their technology from being used by the enemy, and having the power armor destroy itself if ever there were a system failure was one of them.

CHAPTER THIRTY-SIX

The alien judge slammed into Gascoigne and held on with its larger arms. The beast screamed, and its voice was broadcast over the whole area. A pulse of energy, invisible but palpable, cascaded from its power armor. The shockwave was immense; people were flung to the ground, and even the massive form of Vega was pushed back several feet.

Gascoigne bore the brunt of the force. The Mark VI seemed to handle the surge of power from the enemy suit, though. Even though it was obvious the alien judge's whole exoskeleton was about to self-destruct, Gascoigne's maintained.

Bishop grabbed me and flung me behind the truck. *"Move!"*

I barely had time to comprehend what was going on.

The explosion that followed was deafening. My ears rang for minutes afterward, and my vision was blurred. What had happened?

Obviously, the alien judge had taken its own life. My head throbbed as I attempted to stand, but Bishop kept an arm over me. He held me tight, and I pressed against him. Minutes dragged on, and my heart pounded hard against my ribs.

What were we doing?

I had to get up.

I stood, my legs shaky, and Bishop pushed himself to his feet to stand with me. We stared at each other for a bit.

As the smoke cleared, I realized the landscape had changed. The rocky outcrop was shattered, and where the alien judge had stood was now a charred crater.

From the edges of the road and from over the rocky outcrops, several other Iron-Blooded soldiers emerged, their dark armor perfect for lurking in the shadows. There were at least a dozen more, and I wondered if they had just been waiting for us to fail.

Gascoigne's armor was battered, scorched, and emitting a faint whirring sound, suggesting some internal damage. Yet, she managed to rise. She turned and faced the first few Iron-Blooded who approached, and they clearly hadn't been expecting that.

The instant she turned the exoskeleton to face them, the men retreated. They screamed something in Tethlite, but I couldn't understand what they had said. However, it was evident to me that they wanted the Mark VI. That was probably why they came here—to ensure my death and take back their advanced piece of tech.

Once the Iron-Blooded were gone, the world became much quieter.

The citizens of Richfield picked themselves up, faces smeared with ash and dust. Vega lumbered to its feet, shaking off debris. Brecht was with it, his face half-burned from the truck's earlier explosion. He held an arm close to his body, and blood dripped onto the road from his pants.

"Is everyone okay?" Gascoigne asked, her voice hoarse even when coming from her power armor.

Bishop, breathing heavily, nodded. "More or less. I'm not a tally mark yet, at least."

I ran a shaky hand down my face, my gaze on the dirt. Were the Iron-Blooded waiting nearby? I glanced around, my vision blurred. Did we have time to look?

"Bishop," I said.

He turned to me, his expression cold. "Kita?"

"We need to go." I pointed, my arm unsteady. "Please. Gather up . . . the people. And the bodies."

"All right." He stepped closer to me. "Are *you* okay? You don't look right."

"I just need to sit down."

He pointed to the truck. "Don't worry about this. I'll handle it. Go. Rest."

"I'll do that . . . Thank you."

The Iron-Blooded and I had a long history. Which was rather unfortunate, because I didn't want to deal with those lunatics at all. But it seemed I would need to take drastic measures.

We lost one truck, and five people, to the Iron-Blooded ambush. Thankfully, we were still able to make it back to Sanctuary. Gascoigne's suggestion to bring spare parts made the difference. During the fighting, there had been so much damage that the other truck needed repairs before we could set off again.

I didn't want to think about the five people we had lost. Bishop assured me he would handle it, so I allowed him to deal with all the details.

When we arrived at the parking lot in the woods, the one before the Sanctuary sign, I was exhausted, but determined.

I hopped out of the truck, and headed for the facility. Beyond the mold-scented lobby, and down the stairs, I reached the first warehouse, filled with farming tools. And while Gascoigne, Brecht, and Vega gathered everyone to lead them into the underground facility, I decided I would continue to look around.

I needed to know about everything here.

The second warehouse, the one filled with plants, smelled wonderful. I walked through it and went straight for the third warehouse, though. There was little time to dillydally.

The entrance to the next section of the facility was secured with a heavy metal door, rusted at the corners but still holding strong. Like the front door, it was electronically locked. The computer system was already familiar to me, and when I poked in all the security codes, the door groaned as it slowly opened.

The third warehouse was larger than the other two combined.

The dim lighting from the ceiling emitted an eerie glow, revealing the warehouse's contents. Massive shelving units reached to the ceiling, and there were rows upon rows of medical supplies. Everything from bandages and surgical tools to preserved blood packs and antibiotics.

I walked by the shelves, taking note of the dates on several of the containers. Things here were almost fifty years old . . .

I stopped when I noticed a canister of nanites. It was a small thing, but I recognized it right away. I snatched it up and then shoved it into my pocket, my hands shaky.

"Don't be silly, Kita," I said to myself. "You already have them."

But other people didn't, and the more we had, the better we would be as a people. The nanites helped make everything better, not just immediate injuries.

Along the far wall, there was a whole section dedicated to nonperishable food supplies. Canned goods, dehydrated meals, grains, and bottled water were stacked up by the dozen. Adjacent to those was a small section with seeds—likely from an old-world seed bank—to ensure that farming would be possible when the time came to settle and grow food.

Who had made this place?

I remembered reading the pamphlet for the BC Oasis, and how it was a resort for the rich and wealthy to live underground, away from the bleak realities of alien conflict. Were all the underground facilities some sort of resort? It was starting to feel that way.

It made me wonder why Jack was the only person here, though.

There was so much in this one warehouse, I suspected a few thousand people could live comfortably for a few years before they would need to start panicking and looking for a way out.

Farther into the warehouse, I found an area filled with A-tech equipment. Radios, satellite phones, batteries, generators, and solar panels were all organized meticulously.

"Kita!" someone shouted, their voice echoing throughout the warehouse.

"Yes?" I yelled back.

"What're you doing?"

It was Gascoigne; her harsh edge was recognizable anywhere.

"I'm taking stock of our inventory," I replied. "Give me a little bit."

She scoffed and huffed loud enough for me to hear on the other side of this massive room. "What do you want me to do with all the civilians? Just tell them to do whatever they want?"

"Just . . . get them unpacking all their equipment and set it up in the first warehouse. I'll be there in a little bit. And make sure to guard the entrance! The Iron-Blooded know we're here."

Gascoigne didn't reply to that. She just let me do what I had already been doing: investigating.

Satisfied with everything I had here, I went to the next door, heading to the fourth warehouse. The area here was so clean and pristine, it made me wonder if parts of the facility were falling apart, and that was why the last door had rusted slightly.

I would need to make repairs.

The fourth warehouse door had a piece of tape over the computer screen. I had to remove it to even gain access to open the thing. Once I did, the door opened with an almost inaudible hiss. The room was colder, with the faint hum of what seemed to be once-functional life-support systems.

The chill bit into my skin as I walked in, and the peculiar aroma of sterile lab spaces combined with the unmistakable scent of decay hit me all at once.

I wanted to gag.

On either side of the vast warehouse were glass enclosures, not unlike those of old-world zoos or research labs. Each held a different environment, from desert to rainforest. Clearly, this place had once been used for holding and studying a diverse range of animals.

But now, every enclosure held the grim sight of lifeless corpses. Animal carcasses lay strewn about, some reduced to mere skeletons, while others were in various stages of decay. Many looked as if they had tried to escape their confines, clawing at the glass or walls, long scratches down every inch of their cage they could scratch.

"What the fuck?" I whispered to myself.

Wasn't Jack living here? Had he just not wanted to care for the animals? Or had something else happened?

Near the entrance was a control panel with monitors overhead. As I approached, some of the screens flickered to life, showcasing feeds from security cameras. These screens showed various parts of the warehouse. When I tapped on the database functions, I realized the computer had been recording much of the last few decades, but stopped when it ran out of space for the many, many videos.

The last few recordings held the tragic details of the animals' final moments. Their panic, confusion, and futile attempts to find an exit or food.

No one came into this room. Not Jack. No one.

One larger central enclosure caught my eye. It seemed to have been a place for aquatic creatures. Large tanks, many cracked or shattered, filled with murky water. The remains of what looked like exotic fish and even larger marine animals floated lifelessly, their bodies becoming a type of mush that bled into the water.

I tried to piece together the puzzle, but something had obviously gone wrong here. Maybe the life-support or feeding systems failed, or perhaps there just hadn't been enough oversight after the cataclysm above ground. I didn't know.

Now, this warehouse was a mausoleum.

Pushing away my melancholy thoughts, I decided to look for any data or logs that could give more information about the place. I found a few, though they were scattered. It seemed that, in order to save more videos, some of the research logs had been deleted.

A few read:

Date: January 14th, 2031
Researcher: Dr. Emilia Larson
We've begun the first stage of what's been dubbed "Project Helix."
The goal is simple on paper, yet incredibly complex in execution: devise a pathogen that specifically targets the extraterrestrials known as the Vay, while unable to harm those referred to as the Teth. The first challenge? Their biology is so vastly different from ours, but preliminary studies indicate some similarities with certain Earth species. Our hypothesis is that some animals might have diseases that could be effective against them.

Date: February 6th, 2031
Researcher: Dr. Jack Matthews
Our initial trials on amphibians show promise. Salamanders, in particular, possess a microbe that has a peculiar effect on some of the Vay samples. It seems to interfere with their respiratory function, albeit mildly. It's a start.

Date: March 23rd, 2031
Researcher: Teth Miri'Cova
We've managed to isolate the specific strain of bacteria from the salamanders. Naming it *Bacillus xenophobus* for now. Preliminary tests indicate that when modified, B. xenophobus produces a toxin that affects the Vay's cellular function. More tests needed.

Date: May 12th, 2031
Researcher: Dr. Emilia Larson
We've experienced setbacks. The modified Bacillus xenophobus had a catastrophic impact on the local fauna when accidentally released into a controlled environment. It wiped out the entire population of test amphibians. We need to be careful; this could be as dangerous for Earth's ecosystem as it could be for the Vay.

I stopped reading at that log, and it suddenly hit me.

This was a resort. For researchers under the employ of the US government and the Teth architect. My grandfather had told me about this—that the Teth were researchers and engineers. Jack Matthews's name was here, but so was *Miri'Cova*, a Teth.

I had heard Miri'Cova's name before . . . in old research logs . . .

I decided to read further.

Date: July 1st, 2031
Researcher: Dr. Jack Matthews
We've found that certain arachnids, specifically a rare species of spider, have venom that affects the nervous system of the alien samples. While the venom isn't lethal, it causes temporary paralysis. We're working on isolating and synthesizing the compound.

Date: September 18th, 2031
Researcher: Teth Miri'Cova
The synthesized spider venom, combined with a modified version of Bacillus xenophobus, seems to be our best bet. The venom weakens them, and the bacteria inhibit their respiratory functions. However, there's still the considerable risk of how this combination might affect Earth's own ecosystems.

Date: December 9th, 2031
Researcher: Dr. Emilia Larson
Project Helix has been temporarily halted. The combined pathogens have proven too volatile and unpredictable. We've had more casualties within the facility due to unintended exposure. The general will decide if we should proceed or find another avenue of defense against the Vay.

Date: January 5th, 2032
Researcher: Dr. Jack Matthews
It's been decided. We are to halt all experiments involving live animals and synthesized pathogens. Tension between nations has grown too high, and the facility is to focus its efforts on flora that may yield compounds capable of counteracting Vay venoms. Our team is being moved, and all our findings are being archived.

My findings didn't surprise me. The Teth and the Vay were out to get each other long before they arrived on Earth. This just confirmed everything I knew, though it surprised me the Teth got so close to biological warfare. It made me wonder if they couldn't do something like this on their home planet because the fauna was too similar to their own physiology.

But on Earth . . .

I stepped away from the computer and decided to investigate the last warehouse before heading to the center of this grand facility.

CHAPTER THIRTY-SEVEN

I approached the entrance to the fifth warehouse, expecting another rusted door, perhaps something smaller than the rest. Everything else had been huge at this point, at least the size of a football field, perhaps larger. This door, however, was completely different: multiple electronic locks and a timed release.

It was a vault door, thick and unforgiving, covered with a layer of dust that hadn't been disturbed in years.

I grazed my fingers over it. "What is this?"

Everything about this place was different than how I had imagined. Obviously, it was a military facility. I should've known when I found details about it in an air force base . . . but I hadn't imagined something like this.

I tapped at the computer screen and went straight to the BIOS. All the flaws in their security made me happy. I would've hated to have been locked out of this facility.

Once I managed to bypass the passwords, the timed release on the main lock began. Apparently, I would need to wait thirty minutes before it fully unlatched. I wondered why.

But that was fine. I took this opportunity to wander back through the other warehouse areas, searching out the details, and hoping I could gather a few materials to give to the others to help with the setup of our city.

Thirty minutes flew by fast, though.

When I returned to the massive door, it had unlocked, and I yanked it open. The door creaked open agonizingly slowly, revealing an enormous space bathed in dim light that flickered to life as I entered.

Rows upon rows of metal racks stretched as far as I could see. Each was securely anchored to the floor and laden with boxes, crates, and canisters of varying sizes and shapes.

"Hello?" I asked.

My voice echoed off the cold steel.

The atmosphere was heavy, and the air felt thick, as if the weight of what this place held pressed down upon me.

My eyes widened as I saw what was neatly stored on some of these shelves . . .

Old-world firestorm warheads.

Some were smaller tactical types; others were larger, clearly intended for maximum destruction. All were carefully sealed and labeled with warning signs and hazmat symbols, leaving no doubt about their deadly purpose.

Next to each warhead was a touch screen tablet, securely mounted, and from a quick scan, I realized they were digital manuals. Yield, blast radius, effective range, and a counter for the time it would take to arm them. Some of the devices were sophisticated enough to have bio-neural interface options, suggesting a level of A-tech that would allow for remote deployment.

On another set of shelves, I found rows of suits designed for handling hazardous material, complete with full-face respirators and thick gloves.

My heart pounded in my chest.

There were fifteen warheads here. Were they ready for deployment? I tapped on one of the screens, wondering if we were sitting on a massive explosion waiting to go off.

Thankfully, it seemed these warheads couldn't trigger until they were properly armed. But still . . . they were here. What was I going to do with them? It wasn't like we had a missile launcher here. This was clearly some sort of storage.

Footfalls echoed throughout the warehouse, and I almost jumped out of my skin.

"Kita?"

It was Bishop. I breathed a sigh of relief as I hurried away from the warheads and went straight for the door. My vision tunneled as I went, and I hoped beyond hope that I wouldn't need to use this area ever again.

When I spotted Bishop, he stood in the doorframe, his face pale.

"I know," I whispered. "I can't believe it."

"There are so many dead animals." Bishop huffed. "That place reeks. If anyone sees it, they're going to get second thoughts about this place."

I blinked once, realizing he wasn't disturbed by *this* warehouse. It was the animals, not the warheads, that had given him a second thought about everything.

With a shaky hand, I motioned to the shelves behind me. "Do you recognize any of these things?"

Bishop looked over the contents of the cold warehouse, his eyes shifting over the shelves with barely a flicker of recognition. He eventually shrugged. "Weapons? They look like bombs, I suppose. What are they?"

"N-Nothing. Never mind. They're just bombs." I motioned to the door. "Look, we should focus on setting up in the first area. I need to find the power source for this facility. Can you please help Gascoigne and the others?"

Bishop nodded once. "All right. Whatever you need."

"Thank you."

The first full day in Sanctuary, and the people of Richfield set up a small workshop. Thankfully, there were trees nearby, because Scrapyard Pete wanted lumber to build various *things* we might need.

While they were busy, I continued my investigation.

So far, we had a warehouse of unused equipment. Another one with various types of flora—trees, vegetables, shrubs. And another warehouse filled with supplies, obviously meant to keep someone alive for a while. The fourth and fifth warehouses were dread-filled wastelands, as far as I was concerned.

Dead animals. Firestorm warheads.

I wasn't sure what to do with them.

So when I found the heart of the facility, I pushed everything out from my mind. I just needed to know what powered this place.

The corridor leading to the central power room was narrow, lined with exposed piping and industrial lights that emitted a warm yet clinical glow. I was alone as I wandered forward, my footsteps terrible company.

Eventually, I found a heavy blast door with the word "CORE" stenciled across it in large, caution-yellow letters.

"Well, thankfully they weren't subtle," I quipped.

The same type of computer system was used to keep this door secure, and at this point, I almost felt like a burglar who had stolen the keys to a house before robbing it.

When I bypassed all the security, the heavy door opened with a *whoosh* and *hiss*.

Taking a deep breath, I cautiously stepped inside. The core was vast and humming with an energy that I could feel vibrating through the soles of my boots. Blue and white lights blinked from consoles scattered around the room, while thick bundles of cables snaked along the walls and floor, congregating around two small rectangular power ports that housed fission batteries.

Unlike traditional power sources, these fission batteries were a marvel of pre-apocalypse engineering, designed to extract energy from atomic nuclei through a controlled process, providing an enormous power output. It was the ultimate A-tech, one of the greatest "discoveries" the Teth gave to humanity.

We had one in Richfield, but having *two* here was unbelievable. If one was powering the facility, what was the other for? They couldn't both be powering this place.

Each battery was housed in a protective transparent casing, revealing a mesmerizing blue glow emanating from within. Their energy output indicators showed they were still operational and undamaged.

Beside each battery was a console, providing real-time data on its operation, energy output, and efficiency. I noticed that one of the batteries was running hotter than the other. Something required a lot of juice.

Something . . .

Along one wall, a massive circuit breaker panel showcased the distribution paths of electricity throughout the facility. Each section was clearly labeled: living quarters, greenhouse, the warehouses, and the outer security doors . . .

I took a moment to absorb the magnitude of what I was witnessing. These two fission batteries had kept the entire facility running for who knows how long. With proper maintenance and some expert know-how, they could continue to power Sanctuary for decades, maybe even centuries.

But for now, my immediate concern was ensuring the batteries remained stable and operational. If we were to have any hope of survival in this underground haven, keeping the lights on was paramount.

"You've got this, Kita," I whispered to myself, both giddy and on the verge of panic.

Two fission batteries?

I took a deep breath as I backed out of the core room.

It was a shame so many of my friends weren't the types to appreciate my discovery. I wanted to shout this at someone, and laugh for hours. Although we were sitting on deadly weapons, and maybe an engineered virus, we also had enough power to last a lifetime!

How was this not an amazing discovery?

I turned and ran down the hall, intent on finding the others.

I had to tell someone, even if they had no idea what I was telling them.

CHAPTER THIRTY-EIGHT

And we have *two* batteries?" Gascoigne asked. "I almost died trying to take back the one from you."

I pointed at her. "Yes! Exactly! You know. They're valuable. So very valuable!"

Gascoigne, Bishop, Brecht, Vega, and I all stood around an industrial kitchen. It was located near the living quarters, and made almost entirely of stainless steel. The appliances, the counters, even the hoods that caught the heat were all the gray, shiny material for clean cooking. Only the walls and floor were made of white tile.

Gascoigne sat on a countertop while Bishop sliced up some tomatoes he had stolen from the plants in the warehouse. He ate a couple slices, smiling the whole time.

"Okay, so what I'm hearing is . . . you like the place?" Bishop glanced over at me. "Right? You seemed to *love* everything here."

"How do you *not* love everything here?" I asked. I motioned to the kitchen. "Look at this place! It's untouched from the war!" I pointed to the seventeen stove burners. "And it's all electric. We have power."

Bishop nodded. He definitely didn't seem . . . impressed.

He was stealing some of my thunder, really. I wanted everyone to be as ecstatic as I was.

Bishop chuckled. "I've gotta admit, I never thought I'd see the day when you'd be so excited about kitchen appliances. But hey, the future's looking bright, right?"

"Brighter than my flashlight during a blackout." Gascoigne smirked. "Which, let's face it, has been often."

I rolled my eyes. "Yes, because when I dreamed of Sanctuary, I definitely imagined Bishop as our resident tomato thief and chef."

Brecht, ever the pragmatic, weighed in with, "If we ration properly and cultivate more food from the farming warehouse, we could be eating good meals every night. Just like when we lived in Facility Twenty-Six."

"*Yes, just like in Facility Twenty-Six,*" Vega muttered in Tethlite. "*We had our food, and people to prepare it.*"

"*We almost have them again,*" I said, answering him in Tethlite.

Bishop raised an eyebrow, slicing another tomato. With a smirk, he said, "Oh? So, Brecht, do you propose we start with caviar nights or lobster feasts? What exactly did you all do in that wacky facility?"

"Anything besides *another canned beans night* will make me happy," Gascoigne muttered.

Which actually got a chuckle from me.

Bishop gulped down the last of his tomato, his smirk turning into a broad grin. "Honestly, with this kitchen, I wouldn't be surprised if we start a post-apocalyptic radio show. *Cooking with the Last of Humanity.* It'll be a hit, trust me. If DJ Slam can get away with *reading hour*, we'll become famous."

"I can already see it," Brecht quipped. "Today's special: Exquisite Ratatouille, brought to you by the last eggplant on Earth."

"If this were Ex Cathedra, the damn cooking show would include the obligatory warning—*Everything was sliced into micro-thin pieces so everyone gets a bite.*"

I didn't know why, but this rabbit hole of jokes made me smile almost as much as the damn discovery we had two batteries. Years ago, I was alone, in a ditch somewhere, with no one. But here . . . it felt different.

Bishop snapped his fingers. "Or how about this? *Top Chef: Apocalypse Edition.* Contestants must use a surprise ingredient from a mystery can with a faded label." He pointed at Vega. "Or maybe—*we have one of the Teth try everything. Which thing is radioactive?*"

But then the kitchen went quiet. People chuckled, sure, but when they turned to me, it was with more serious expressions that betrayed their concern.

"This is going to work," I whispered.

Gascoigne rotated her shoulder and grimaced. "I've almost died several times just hauling equipment here, but if you think this is worth it, we'll stick it out. Besides, we're too deep into this to quit now, I suppose. Every fucker and their fuck-face sister knows we're up to something."

"We just have to gather more resources," I said, my gaze falling to the tile floor. "And then we'll build something the likes of which humanity has never seen."

ABOUT THE AUTHOR

Shami Stovall is an award-winning fantasy and science fiction author. Previously, she taught history and criminal law at the college level and loved every second. When she's not reading fascinating articles and books about ancient China or the Byzantine Empire, Stovall can be found playing way too many video games, especially RPGs and tactics simulators. She loves John, reading, and writing about herself in the third person.

www.ingramcontent.com/pod-product-compliance
Lightning Source LLC
Chambersburg PA
CBHW020654120726
47906CB00001B/263